WHEN THE BEAR HAS BEEN POKED

By

Jomo Sekou Henderson

To request permissions, contact the publisher at
tvpc.agency@gmail.com

ISBN Paperback: 978-6-27754437-9

ISBN Hardcover: 978-6-27754438-6

ISBN E-book: 978-6-27754436-2

First Paperback Edition: November 2021.

Edited by Rita Relle & Jomo Sekou Henderson

Cover art by "psalmyy"

Layout by *Rita Relle, Publishingspot, & Jomo Henderson*

Photographs' by Markay Mason

Website: www.theunderdshadow.earth

Printed in the U.S.A.

TVPC Agency(dba)[Publisher]

703 Bullard Manor

Whiteman AFB, Missouri 65305

DEDICATION

There is a saying from the New Living Translation's book of Luke in the Christian Bible; But someone who does not know, and then does something wrong, will be punished only lightly. When someone has been given much, much will be required in return; and when someone has been entrusted with much, even more will be required. (Luke 12:48).

To enforce laws, that enforcer ought to be lawfully led. In both integrity and compassion over those they serve. For this is their mandate. Not just pursuing or safeguarding their insatiable lust for authority and power over others. – My View.

Here is another saying from the New Living Translation's book of Matthew; And what do you benefit if you gain the whole world but lose your own soul? Is anything worth more than your soul? (Matthew 16:26)

Peer pressure nor group think do not dissipate or disappear on their own. Their impact over one's decision making and behavior is determined by each moment the temptation to consider their empty trinkets of relevance or approval by others presents itself and fought back with vigilance. I would continue further to say due diligence as well. – My View.

My Dedication:

I absolutely must dedicate this book to the immeasurably long list of all those individuals who have lost their life at the hands of unjustified and unnecessary measures taken by members of the entire law enforcement community as a whole. I do not have a choice in this, nor would I want to consider another pathway. Sending my deepest condolences and hopes of whatever peace that can be had to anyone who have been victimized in this way. The same is said and sent to all of the families and friends of all who have lost their lives in this way. Sad as it is, there may be more names added to this list after the time of the publishing of this novel, and that sentiment of condolence extends to the future victims as well. Regardless if those names were mentioned here today. I Also dedicate this book to son, Marcellus Sekou Henderson. I hope these words find you soul, and engages your mind, while embracing your heart.

For the unarmed who were stolen from their loved ones:

Henry Dumas, May 23, 1968; James Earl Green, May 15, 1970; Phillip Lafayette Gibbs, May 15, 1970; Rita Lloyd, January 27, 1973; Barry Gene Evans, February 10, 1976; Randolph Evans, November 25, 1976; Arthur Miller Jr., June 14, 1978; Eula Mae Love, January 3, 1979; Michael Jerome Stewart, September 28, 1983; Eleanor Bumpers, October 29, 1984; Yvonne Smallwood, December 9, 1987; Mary Mitchell, November 3, 1991; Nicholas Heyward Jr., September 27, 1994; Frankie Ann Perkins, March 22, 1997; Dannette "Strawberry" Daniels, June 7, 1997; Tyisha Shenee Miller, December 28, 1998; Amadou Diallo, February 4, 1999; Margaret LaVerne Mitchell, May 21, 1999; LaTanya Haggerty, June 4, 1999; Malcolm Ferguson, March 1, 2000; Prince Carmen Jones Jr., September 1, 2000; Patrick Moses Dorismond, March 16, 2000; Earl Murray, June 12, 2000; Ronald Beasley, June 12, 2000; Timothy DeWayne Thomas Jr., April 7, 2001; Nelson Martinez Mendez, August 8, 2001; Orlando Barlow, February 28, 2003; Kendra Sarie James, May 5, 2003; Alberta Spruill, May 16, 2003; Ousmane Zongo, May 22, 2003;

Timothy Stansbury, Jr., January 24, 2004; Henry "Ace" Glover, September 2, 2005; James B. Brissette Jr., September 4, 2005; Ronald Curtis Madison, September 4, 2005; Kathryn Johnston, November 21, 2006; Sean Bell, November 25, 2006; DeAunta Terrel Farrow, June 22, 2007; Tarika Wilson, January 4, 2008; Oscar Grant III, January 1, 2009; Shem Walker, July 11, 2009; Victor Steen, October 3, 2009; Kiwane Carrington, October 9, 2009; Aaron Campbell, January 29, 2010; Steven Eugene Washington, March 20, 2010; Aiyana Mo'Nay Stanley-Jones, May 16, 2010; Danroy "DJ" Henry Jr., October 17, 2010; Derrick Jones, November 8, 2010; Reginald Doucet, January 14, 2011; Raheim Brown, Jr., January 22, 2011; Derek Williams, July 6, 2011; Alonzo Ashley, July 18, 2011; Kenneth Chamberlain Sr., November 19, 2011; Ramarley Graham, February 2, 2012; Manual Levi Loggins Jr., February 7, 2012; Raymond Luther Allen Jr., February 29, 2012; Dante' Lamar Price, March 1, 2012; Nehemiah Lazar Dillard, March 5, 2012; Wendell James Allen, March 7, 2012; Jersey K. Green, March 12, 2012; Shereese Francis, March 15, 2012; Rekia Boyd, March 21, 2012; Kendrec McDade, March 24, 2012; Ervin Lee Jefferson, III, March 24, 2012; Tamon Robinson, April 18, 2012; Sharmel T. Edwards, April 21, 2012; Shantel Davis, June 14, 2012; Alesia Thomas, July 22, 2012; Chavis Carter, July 28, 2012; Reynaldo Cuevas, September 7, 2012; Noel Palanco, October 4, 2012; Malissa Williams, November 29, 2012; Timothy Russell, November 29, 2012; Darnisha Diana Harris, December 2, 2012; Shelly Marie Frey, December 6, 2012; Johnnie Kamahi Warren, February 13, 2012; Jamaal Moore Sr., December 15, 2012; Kayla Moore, February 13, 2013; Kimani "KiKi" Gray, March 9, 2013; Clinton R. Allen, March 10, 2013; Kyam Livingston, July 21, 2013; Larry Eugene Jackson Jr., July 26, 2013; Carlos Alcis, August 15, 2013; Jonathan Ferrell, September 14, 2013; Barrington

"BJ" Williams, September 17, 2013; Miriam Iris Carey, October 3, 2013; Darnisha Diana Harris, December 2, 2012; Andy Lopez, October 22, 2013; Jordan Baker, January 16, 2014; McKenzie J. Cochran, January 29, 2014; Yvette Smith, February 16, 2014; Gabriella Monique Nevarez, March 2, 2014; Victor White III, March 3, 2014; Dontre Hamilton, April 30, 2014; Eric Garner, July 17, 2014; Tyree Woodson, August 2, 2014; John Crawford III, August 5, 2014; Michael Brown Jr., August 9, 2014; Ezell Ford, August 11, 2014; Dante Parker, August 12, 2014; Tanisha N. Anderson, November 13, 2014; Akai Kareem Gurley, November 20, 2014; Tamir Rice, November 22, 2014; Rumain Brisbon, December 2, 2014; Jerame C. Reid, December 30, 2014; Natasha McKenna, February 8, 2015; Janisha Fonville, February 18 2015; Tony Terrell Robinson, March 6, 2015; Meagan Hockaday, March 28, 2015; Mya Shawatza Hall, March 30, 2015; Phillip Gregory White, March 31, 2015; Eric Courtney Harris, April 2, 2015; Walter Lamar Scott, April 4, 2015; Freddie Carlos Gray Jr., April 19, 2015; Brendon K. Glenn, May 5, 2015; Sandra Bland, July 13, 2015; Samuel Vincent DuBose, July 19, 2015; India Kager, September 5, 2015; Jamar O'Neal Clark, November 16, 2015; Corey Lamar Jones, October 18, 2015; Quintonio LeGrier, December 26, 2015; Bettie "Betty Boo" Jones, December 26, 2015; Alton Sterling, July 5, 2016; Philando Castile, July 6, 2016; Joseph Curtis Mann, July 11, 2016; Korryn Gaines, August 1, 2016; Terrence LeDell Sterling, September 11, 2016; Terence Crutcher, September 16, 2016; Alfred Olango, September 27, 2016; Deborah Danner, October 18, 2016; Chad Robertson, February 15, 2017; Jordan Edwards, April 29, 2017; *Fetus of Charleena Chavon Lyles (14-15 weeks), Charleena Chavon Lyles, June 18, 2017*; Aaron Bailey, June 29, 2017; Bijan Ghaisar, November 27, 2017; Dennis Plowden Jr., December 28, 2017; Stephon Alonzo Clark, March 18, 2018 Saheed

Vassell, April 4, 2018 Antwon Rose Jr., June 19, 2018 Botham Shem Jean, September 6, 2018; Anton Milbert LaRue Black, September 15, 2018; Chinedu Okobi, October 3, 2018; Charles "Chop" Roundtree Jr., October 17, 2018; Emantic "EJ" Fitzgerald Bradford Jr., November 22, 2018; Gregory Lloyd Edwards, December 10, 2018; Sterling Lapree Higgins, March 25, 2019; Javier Ambler, March 28, 2019; Ronald Greene, May 10, 2019; Elijah McClain, August 30, 2019; Atatiana Koquice Jefferson, October 12, 2019; John Elliot Neville, December 4, 2019; William Howard Green, January 27, 2020; Manuel "Mannie" Elijah Ellis, March 3, 2020; Breonna Taylor, March 13, 2020; Daniel T. Prude, March 30, 2020; Michael Brent Charles Ramos, April 24, 2020; Dreasjon "Sean" Reed, May 6, 2020; George Perry Floyd, May 25, 2020; Tony "Tony the TIger" McDade, May 27, 2020; David McAtee, June 1, 2020; Carlos Carson, June 6, 2020; Rayshard Brooks, June 12, 2020; Dijon Durand Kizzee, August 31, 2020; Jonathan Dwayne Price, October 3, 2020; Marcellis Stinnette, October 20, 2020; Sincere Pierce, November 13, 2020; Angelo "AJ" Crooms, November 13, 2020; Casey Christopher Goodson Jr., December 4, 2020; Andre Maurice Hill, December 22, 2020; Angelo Quinto, December 26, 2020 Vincent "Vinny" M. Belmonte, January 5, 2021; Patrick Lynn Warren Sr., January 10, 2021; Marvin David Scott III, March 14, 2021; Daunte Demetrius Wright, April 11, 2021.

The List of Courtesy of https://www.reneeater.com/on-monuments-blog/tag/list+of+unarmed+black+people+killed+by+police

In the truly unfortunate probability that one could read the list of 172 lives listed above that were stolen over a span of 53 years, and wondered in disapproval as to when this list would finally come to an end. Please know there are so very many who also read that list and with a somber, broken heart, and waning frustration unable to breathe properly wondering when will this list cease to grow longer as well. Wondering when a next encounter with law enforcement will not produce the unease or anxiety all of its own trauma. We are waiting for this as well.

For all the truly brave, bold, courageous, and fearless members of the law enforcement community that abhors systematic racism. The many who risk it all blowing the whistle each time the blue wall of silence gains another brick. We see that you do exist. However, these are the times for you to make sure the entire world knows not only that you do exist in larger numbers than the criminals who violate the policies and procedures that you value. Wreaking havoc on many. Far too many indeed. This is your time to stand as tall as you can. Create an atmosphere where such abhorrent and egregious actions are irrefutably unacceptable and untenable. Hold your leaderships and administrative bodies strictly accountable without falter. For this madness and these maddening acts must end. Before some do take that bolder leap into taking matters into their own hands. Possibly with less-than-honorable considerations for collateral damage.

Thank you to my Lord and Savior, Jesus Christ for starting my life where and exactly how he chose to start it and with whom I was given to. Regardless of how I may have been begrudging or uncooperative in my growth throughout my earlier days, you saw fit to stay the course with me. Utilizing more than I can comprehend to forge me in ways I could not have without your hand. Many may and many will balk at these statements. That will be ok. I seek not to offend any kindhearted person. I do seek to set a wall of fire in between myself and anyone who finds my contribution as anything less that contributive to progress and awareness of the need to be real about what is valid and not in regards to the positive exchange of ideas. Just as I have heard many share my voice will be orated. Balance.

Acknowledgments

First and foremost, I need to thank my Lord and Savior. I sin and I work on minimizing my transgressions as a thoroughly flawed human being.

With that being said, I want to acknowledge that the process of starting and finishing this important book occurred as a major change of the guard took place in my life this year. I need to Thank these powerful matriarchs who towered above life, and showered me in their awesome amazingness while doing so:

Mayme Dunbar, Izetta Boone Henderson, Louise Johnson, Madelyn Ward, Dorothy Jackson-Brown, Virginia Moore, Cynthia Bowie-Coleman. I miss each of you dearly. Thank you for continuously giving me the gift of support and motivation to pursue excellence. With the passing of each of you to the last of you, I have been forever changed. A Hall of Fame with a vert short list of names left to follow.

This experience has brought me through many opportunities to persevere. I have made new acquaintances and I have built older ones into stronger ones also. As an empathic person who seeks to pursue positive energy, and powerful experiences, the word gratitude is often the used to describe how I define life for me.

I extend love to anyone who has spent time in my presence and understood for themselves what it is to be in a moment with me. Past, present, and future.

I want to Thank my father, Laverne "Larry" Melvin Henderson. I imagine you reading my works often. Thanks to Rodney Morrison who taught me that "Yes, a Black Man can."

With so very many moving parts to my budding operation of budding operations it is imperative that the extension of appreciation be shared for ALL WHO HAVE PLAYED, CURRENTLY PLAY, AND WILL PLAY any role of fruitful contribution in these endeavors as we press forward.

CONTENTS

Chapter 1

"MEETING OF THE MINDS"

June of 2017, ducked off on the upper level of the hallowed Harlem Library of New York City.

It is June 19th, more affectionately referred to as "Juneteenth" around locations similar to this. There are many celebrations across the nation, just as the nation is ironically finding itself distracted once again.

Eric Castille and Gregory Martin are longtime friends from their early childhood years who have sat at this table in the corner of the upper hall near the librarian's desk for longer than they could either remember. It's here that for about the last eight weeks the two have come on many nights to meet to discuss quite thoroughly the subject matter and intricate details of what they have planned over the last four years.

On many of these gatherings they would also be joined by Eric's cousin Michael. Michael is an attorney from the community who practices law from an office not far from where the library is located. He has been operating his firm for shortly over seven years.

"See, the people I have out there gave me the word on the street. No bullshit. No sauce. Winston Price was just getting off work from the bank. He was supposed to have been going on a date with the newly hired lady he was cozying up to from another department at the bank. He just purchased a new vehicle. He didn't have the car for even a week at that point. That man was living his best life, or so he thought.

"There was about ten to fifteen people at the intersection of American Legion Boulevard, North 4th East Street, and North 6th East Street as Winston pulled up to the light heading eastbound. That's when those two officers pulled out from where the crowd was leaving the TCBY. Many of them reported that when the officers saw Winston in that car, it was instantly obvious what they had planned to do," Eric says.

Gregory interrupts Eric, "To pull his Black ass over because that new car just had to be stolen, right?"

"You already mutherfuckin' know," is Eric's response as he takes a second to bead his eyes back and forth over the floor as completely as he can, getting a quick glance over what is his overall peripheral window.

The smell of paper in various stages of decay fill the room, along with a faint odor of what you would find in a building as old as this library is. Something no renovation could fully mask, but what brandishes a distinctive mark of familiarity at the same time. The weak, almost inaudible, sound of pages being individually turned slowly fill the hall more consistently than any other sound that manages to obtain a decibel level beyond that of an occasional hushed conversation.

"Okay! OKAY!" Gregory exclaims sharply, with slight impatience as he waits for Eric to complete his chain of thought.

His strong utterance earns him a nasty look from the librarians. The librarians are huddled at the desk, sitting in front of their computers. They're eager to maintain order and a low volume soothing atmosphere for those who are reading in peace expected in a library.

"Yeah, so they shot right behind his vehicle fast. For all to see, like they didn't even care how obvious they had been with their crooked tactics. They played with him at the light as they were parked behind his vehicle while the light was still red. Shortly after, the light flipped to green. Not even more than ten seconds of him pulling down Legion did they cut their lights on and pull him over. They must have called into their dispatch for backup because it was like less than a minute after that, a second car came sprinting from off North 7th while a third squad car came up North 4th!"

"Damn," interrupts Gregory, "that's real foul. You sure sound like you used to be in Iowa man. You calling off streets kinda quick like you must of lived there before or something."

"Tell me about it, but its Idaho fam." says Eric quickly as he continues. "Then all the officers got out of their vehicles and approached the first car on the scene. After they all sat there for about eight to ten minutes, finally, two officers began to approach the driver's side of the vehicle Winston had been patiently waiting in. They spoke from what I was told for a few minutes, then two of the others still speaking with the actual officer who pulled Winston over walked over just as the first two returned back, apparently with his license and insurance information. While they were doing whatever they be doing at that time, that's when shit went crazy. The big officer quickly pulled Winston out of his vehicle and threw him on the ground. But his technique wasn't very good, and he ended up falling over on his back after tripping. And somehow in the commotion, Winston fell on top of him."

"What the fuck?!" shouts Gregory.

This time, both librarians remind him simultaneously that he needs to keep his volume down.

"Listen, listen. You already know it was then that all six of them officers started to book over there and they beat the shit out of that dude Winston. Like really bad. They must have called for backup like they be doing before they went over there because as they were stompin' him, a whole different group of unmarked cars and Elmore County Police cars flooded the area. Even the state troopers showed up for this one."

Gregory just sits back and is barely able to keep his whole mouth from opening even wider as he listens to Eric tell him what he was told by someone he knew that was there in Mountain Home, Idaho when it all happened.

"Before you could imagine, my guy was telling me that the local media outlets wasted no time at all. First, it was two media crews reporting as the ambulances was still arriving to the scene. Not too long after they had arrived, along with what he told me had to be law enforcement leadership, was triple the original amount of news media. The area was drowned with reporters and their camera teams."

Mountain Home, Idaho is now the new city to join that list of growing cities that have the national spotlight for police brutality incidents.

"A simple misinterpretation of events and over eager men with authority took a small city with less than one thousand local residents into a media frenzy. By that night, there were more members of the news out there than there were actual people who lived there!"

"That's real wild!" says Gregory, this time applying more awareness to the loudness of his words.

Eric pushes his hand out towards Gregory, quickly flicking him on his wrist with a slight popping sound that is easily heard. "That's not even the end of it."

Gregory repositions himself to lean back in his chair in preparation for more.

"Winston was living on the Air force base," Eric continues. "His older sister was an Intelligence Officer stationed there. He lived there with her as he worked himself through school and built his credit and savings up for the next step of his life. He was only twenty-four years old."

Gregory's eyes are almost frozen as they remain open extra wide. His pupils are near dilation as he sits in that chair too numb from what he is hearing to move in any recognizable way. He becomes angered for that young person as he just sits there, unable to move, unable to respond with anything. His forehead is now beginning to show signs of slight perspiration. Gregory starts to tug at his clothing in a futile attempt at finding an escape from the heat coming from within him over the information shared with him and what it means.

As Eric speaks, he is easily able to identify and emphasize with what Winston was said to have experienced while just moments before he was just living his life and minding his own business.

Once again, groups of other outraged citizens— White, Black, Hispanic, and Asian Americans— gather in major cities across the nation trying to protest their way into some effect or change of this looming epidemic of power abuse. The nation somehow found its way back into a state of civil unrest.

In recent history, during times such as this, the leaders would utilize their most tactful techniques to quell the masses. This is not those times. The painfully burdensome remarks of President Ace during the Mountain Home incident, and after the not guilty verdict had been delivered from the jury to the judge, was widely inconvenient and irksome to many.

Much of the nation had been infuriated with the results of this case. Many of the other politicians affiliated with the president agreed with the African American community that his remarks were disturbing, without merit, and unnecessary as the nation needed to move forward in the direction of finding ways to deal with the factors that led to the gruesome events of that case as well as the case months before him with Ahmad Bell in Jacksonville, Florida. Ahmad Bell was the prior recipient of notoriety for their experience with police brutality in the United States.

This time, the incident was in the state of Idaho. Right outside the gates of a military installation, involving a member of a military family. This was a public relations disaster for the law enforcement community, the city of Mountain Home, the county of Elmore, and the State of Idaho as a whole.

Eric's cousin Michael Crawford is seen by the two men as he ascends the staircase into the upper-level study hall. Without making a scene of his entrance, Michael just nods to both men as he sits in the closest empty chair, gently pulling it to the table they are sitting at without gaining the unwanted attention of the librarians. Eric and Gregory for the most part share much agreeance on all these matters as these incidents too often populate the backgrounds of their transitions from toddler to young adulthood and during their friendship spanning over thirty plus years. Being older than both of them, Eric has more of a dominant leadership role amongst them.

Eric begins speaking again after Michael arrives, "I am at this point just about out of energy."

To which Gregory responds, "Well, you need to get your body reenergized and real quick, Man. What this ongoing bullshit doesn't need is for one of its more promising minds to be asleep on the job or distracted by fatigue."

Michael chimes in in a modest defense to his cousin, "Well, we all have a mind for this subject. Let's not place the full burden on Eric right now. We know he's clutch in the moment. We are all pretty much in a state of shock. Believe me, Brothers, I haven't been right all day. Just couldn't find the rhythm to get back on stride. I think… No. I am *certain* that I have had enough of this pattern."

Both remarks bring Eric to a smirking expression across his face as he recollects his overall facial expressions to reflect that he accepts the challenge delivered to him through the gentle jab from his brother and longtime friend.

"I know. I know. Ain't that some shit? Truly no rest, not even for the weary, huh? You both know I am still processing all of this, and where we have travelled from as a people. Let us not get caught up on who is not saying this or that. Instead, let's take full advantage of the time we have right now before we return to our families and personal lives. Let's discuss what I asked you guys here in advance to our normal weekly meeting of the minds to discuss."

Eric responds with a brief chuckle that can barely be heard, but his demeanor and body language transmit much more. "I have been working on a plan. I have been putting it together secretly for about eight years. It wasn't until the acquittal and the reaction from the country to that acquittal that brought me to realize the overall importance and accountability to more than just myself to bring this plan into fruition."

With that, both Gregory and Michael are interested to hear more. Eric takes a moment to gaze meticulously through the immediate library area that surrounds them. Then he looks fixedly towards the librarian's desk. After making peculiar eye contact with the librarians, the librarian then takes the cue to depart their desks and escorts all others on the upper floor towards the lower level. Once the librarian has completely departed from the area, Eric slowly sips on his bottled water, then leans in closer towards the men across the table and speaks.

"This is a plan that will change everything if done right!"

Gregory quickly speaks, "Well speak on it, Eric! There isn't a need for all of that! Get it out, Man. You got too much going on right now."

Eric folds his fingers with their own distinct purpose from one hand to the other. He disregards the request to get to his point as he looks at them both, taking turns with his focus as he shuffles his hands to a slow but persistent rhythm.

"Gregory. I need you to reach out to your Uncle Ezell. Tell him what I tell you, and get him on board so you can build with him on gathering the gang leaders and community leaders across the map sections I have laid out for you. This will be right up his alley."

Now looking at Michael, Eric says, "I need you to conduct some very specific legal research on a project that will include the inclusion of a few law firms I have been tracking that have been active in civil rights cases nationwide. Also, we need to take a few additional trips before you get started on that. These trips that will involve some strategic elbow rubbing with some elite individuals. To do this, we need to fly out tonight. I already have our tickets."

As Eric gestures his hands with a two-finger point arrangement of his fingers, he speaks again to Gregory. "You need to wait for me or Michael to give you the signal in order for you to know the appropriate time has come for the next phase of the plan. Until then, these in-person communications will not take place. There isn't a need for it, and we will not be in the same place as one another for our own safety and freedom. More thorough contingency plans will be shared with you both at the appropriate time. Stay ready, Brothers. Stay on point. We stepping over the edge and into new territory on this one."

With both men on the end of their seats, focused on his every utterance, Eric states, "Gregory, you're greatly appreciated. Michael is my cousin, and we been linked since Similac, but you and I forged a relationship from youth that has proven formidable through many tests. This is and will be the ultimate test, My Neez. The absolute ultimate one. I have no question of your resolve either."

Michael methodically and smoothly brings his face to a wide smile as he speaks in response to what Eric has just said. "See! Like I told you, Gregory, he was just waiting to collect his thoughts. You just made him focus faster."

As both Gregory and Michael smirk with teemed excitement, they await Eric's next words. The three men continue to speak into the hours of the evening. The librarian has long since departed, escorting all the others out of the building. When the men finish speaking, they depart the building. Gregory departs in his direction, leaving Eric and Michael stepping into a vehicle heading in a direction different from Gregory of their own. The two men shuffle around, reaching in their respective directions to grab ahold of their seat belts, then securing them in place before pulling off from the curb.

While inside the vehicle, as it moves across the roads that lead to highways on their route to the airport, Eric continues to speak, "So, we're about to take a flight to New Orleans, Mike. Once we touch down, I will get you in touch with a private investigator I have in place who has been following the activities of the chief counsel and principal partner of the firm that can potentially play a significant role in our plan overall. Your role at this point is to follow the team in place and use your keen abilities of discernment to ascertain the virility of the information acquired to this point as to whether or not this firm is the firm we need with the personnel that will be efficacious in facilitating our needs. And moving forward, we have several other ideal candidates if you feel the need to scrap their candidacy.

"I am going to take the trip with you. Once we arrive in New Orleans, I will have you set up properly. Literally, several contingencies have been enacted, so, make no mistake, once I am seen standing next to you when we arrive, it will send the message that you are the new point of contact from that moment on. The new leader of that operation. This is because this was what I trained them to understand and respond to all this time as we have fought tirelessly to prepare for the appointed time.

"That time is now. This unit is yours. Lead accordingly, like we know you can."

The vehicle arrives to an intricate set of fences and an even more intimidating steel gate with several armed security staff, trained German Sheppards, and blood hounds. The smell of metal and jet fuel fills the air rather thick despite the brisk wind that is moving in just about every direction around them. Both Michael and Eric continue to converse as the driver communicates with the men at the security gate.

After the driver presents his credentials and a few other documents that had been kept in plastic sheathing that he pulled from within his center console, the gate starts to rise very slowly. The group of armed security begin to move from where they had been standing in various positions around the parked vehicle waiting for it to obtain approval to enter the premises.

Michael is unable to pretend that he never realized that he had never come through this entrance to the airport he's been utilizing his entire life. He pretty much loses focus on what Eric is trying to say to him. Eric doesn't take long to see that Michael is significantly distracted. He takes in more air through both of his nostrils in a slow and exaggerated motion, bringing both of his lips to the bottom of his nose. He begins to look on at Michael as he peers through each window trying to see all that he can as the vehicle makes haste across the path leading to the private hangers.

Eric scoots up slightly and then leans a bit deeper into his seat. When he does this, Michael catches the movement in his peripheral and speaks out to him in a slightly embarrassed tone while still in awe of his first experience unfolding layer by layer before him.

"My bad, Brother," Michael apologizes.

"Don't worry about it, Mike. I didn't even realize. Do you. Soak it up. When this is all said and done, I hope you get used to it all. We may be far from shit like this for quite a minute. Soak it up, Man. That's my bad right there. You're straight."

Michael begins to find himself slightly more anxious as the rate of progress begins to decrease in speed. This must be notification that they have reached their destination. The vehicle pulls up to a rather huge silver metallic structure with a rounded off top. The driver reaches into his pocket, opens an app on his mobile device, plugs into some finger taps, and like a garage door opener, the doors to the metallic hanger begin to slide away from one another.

The way the interior of the hanger is illuminated is beyond spectacular to Michael. Each recessed lighting source feels to be in the perfect place to shed the specific amount of light to make the space bright to a degree he's never seen before.

As the vehicle pulls into the hanger, past the now opened doors, there she is. A seemingly brand-new Gulfstream 550 private jet. The jet is freshly cleaned and detailed. There is a crew of men near its fuel port in the process of refueling it up. There is another group of men walking around the jet with clipboards wearing uniforms that appear to be the pilots. They are accompanied by another individual who seems to be with the airport administrative staff, judging by the clothing she is wearing.

With the vehicle stopped, Eric has his door opened for him by the driver. Used to every step in this process, Eric steps out of the vehicle as the driver closes his door behind him. Before he does so, he has to lean over and grab Michael's arm to prevent him from opening his own door. "Just wait. The driver will open your door after he finishes with mine."

Michael then smiles with slight bashfulness and retreats back into the seated position he had been in before he sprung up towards the door handle. When the driver does arrive at his door, he turns its handle so that it is ready for him to step through and out. Michael does and is even more marveled from doing so.

When the two pilots and airport administrator see Eric, they hurry over to him to brief him about their process of preparation and how long before they would be cleared to hit the runway. One of the women who had been already on board the jet disembarks down its staircase and greets Michael and Eric. Eric gestures with his hands to Mike, waving him politely on to converse with the flight attendants while he finishes dealing with the group he is talking with. Michael follows the direction of those flight attendants and walks towards the staircase and starts to board the plane.

Another attendant goes and retrieves all their luggage from the trunk of their vehicle. He had brought a medium sized metal rolling dolly for luggage. Item by item, the luggage handler loads it all onto their cart and then pulls it to the cargo hold of the area of the plane.

"Stop playing! How many rooms are on this plane?" Michael asks, giggling. "Have I drank that whole bottle already? Wow! Yeah, that's enough for me right now. I think I will take you both up on that massage you both were explaining to me."

Michael is having himself a good time. Eric finally finishes with what he had to address and walks into the cockpit of the plane. When he sees how inebriated Michael is so quickly, he can't help but laugh at first. While Michael is completely distracted with his massage, Eric leans over and whispers into the ear of the second attendant, "How much did he drink?"

"He finished off a fifty milliliter bottle of Hennessey."

"Great…," replies Eric.

Not completely thrilled, while not remotely upset, Eric sits alongside his friend and takes a sip of a small drink. The attendant positions herself behind him as she prepares to give him a neck and shoulder massage. Eric is more aware than Michael is regarding what lies ahead. This may be one of the last moments of uninterrupted enjoyment to be had for them both for quite some time.

They both have a completely enjoyable trip. Eric just made sure that there was enough time before the fun. He ensured that there was time to recover so that when they reach their destination and land, they will be able to handle the business at hand.

As the plane re-connects with the tarmac at the Greater St. Tammany Regional Airport, both Michael and Eric collect themselves and prepare to depart the jet. There was car service provided by Eric that had been on site before their plane lands. Their flight has now concluded.

The departure from the jet is almost symmetrical to how they boarded the jet to begin with. Michael is ushered to his place within the vehicle that had been waiting on them to arrive while Eric lingers back to discuss matters with the pilot first, then airport officials. Once both men are inside the inconspicuous and deeply tinted vehicle, they quickly make their way towards the next destination.

As the SUV makes its way onto the freeway, the sign is barely visible to Michael. All that he is able to read of the sign at the exit they turned onto is signifying that they are heading towards Lewisburg and the Lake Pontchartrain causeway. Their route includes taking the "thirty-six" to the "ten eighty-eight" that leads them eventually to the "fifty-nine highway". Then they eventually find the "ten-eighty-seven" that lead to the causeway that they cross. During which time Eric is explaining the details of the overall campaign and tactics to be utilized in fulfilling their objective.

Eric reinforces to Michael about how he is the main point of contact to their operations in New Orleans. Eric makes things extremely clear what needs to have been successfully accomplished by the appointed time. He explains that the discipline would be fierce in order for him to avoid certain pitfalls and potential setbacks to his goals. By the time the two of them will stand next to one another, many things will have to properly take place.

As they cross over Lake Pontchartrain then into the junction leading them onto the I-10 freeway, they begin to discuss specific subjects pertinent to the successful completion of the campaign in New Orleans with utmost effectiveness. Their SUV has now arrived at the Windsor Court Hotel. Eric and Michael depart the vehicle. The two of them casually stride past the check-in desk and towards the elevators as if they'd been on the verge of clearing week eight of routine activity within the hotel.

They both approach the designated room for the introductions. Once inside, Michael looks over the room and its inhabitants. Immediately what becomes obvious to him is that this is obviously the farthest thing from a small operation by any means. Anyone with money can arrange to fly on a jet, but to have a room full of expensive equipment and people who all look independently capable of handling their own operations is something else altogether.

The room that they have entered into is a suite that has doorways on both sides that lead to adjoining suites. The two step inside and close the solid door behind them that produced a solid thud as it sealed shut. Then from both of the adjoining rooms, left and right, enters several individuals. Each and every person that file into the room is dressed to the "T". A group of individuals who seem more adequately compared to nothing less than elite, professional, and of pristine class.

What Michael could not have known is that this specific room had not been accessed until that precise moment of when Eric was to enter that room. The moment of when Eric was ready to present their operational leader for the next phase of operation. Eric takes a few moments to best acquaint the required connections amongst the group.

"Everyone, listen."

Then there is complete silence across the room full of people.

"As expected, as foretold, here is my cousin Michael. Just as I explained how this was going to go down, here we are. We are on the precipice of taking the hard work and investigative might to a higher level. Michael is the personification of that level and several beyond that point. What you all need to recognize and implement is bringing him up to speed and allowing him the time to access the data for himself.

"He is a brilliant mind, both in strategy, whether that's the psychology of people-to-people interaction, or the strategy of the legal field that will need to be proficiently navigated precisely. This is what this team has been waiting for. Each test that comes my cousin's way, you will see more and more clearly why he was appropriately chosen to lead y'all. Support him on the strength of my word until he demonstrates his excellence to each of you.

"I do not need to explain to y'all what the importance of what we are doing is or means. As previously discussed, I am on to the next leg of this marathon. When we see one another again— if we do— we will know what it is and what the objective will be. I love you all, and I wish to see you on the other side of this. Do what you were brought here to do. Hold my cousin all the way down. Nothing less than ten toes down and two thumbs up. Period!"

To reiterate his expectations to the previous command on the ground of his operation, he discreetly gives his cousin a dap, drawing him in close, and holding him tight as he whispers a brief sentence into his ear.

Eric makes his way from inside suite, back out into the hallway. Inconspicuously, Eric lurks his way to the stairwell and out into the rear of the building. Finally, back into the vehicle that had originally taken them from the airport to the hotel. That vehicle is now waiting for Eric in the rear of the building. His next flight, off to Los Angeles, California. L.A.X. it is.

Eric, a former Marine, is by nature a quick-thinking, fast-maneuvering individual. He is also a focused and determined soldier once he finds himself properly motivated.

With a large part of the initial phase of his plan in place, there is still some related business on the West Coast to see to, which is the purpose of his flight. Eric has a history in the famed City of Angels. A city where he spends much of his flight reflecting on those times. Spending most of that time reminiscing over individuals he had fond, and even some bitter sweet, memories with. One of which is first on his list to visit first: Asshams "AB" Sabbie.

AB has a larger reach into the inner city in and surrounding LA County. As an active member of a gang, and with more than enough history of high-level gang participation, AB is more than just connected to the street. He literally organizes its day-to-day. He and a team of others with similar backgrounds.

Connected to the elite consortium that controls what plays out on the streets, AB has a seat at the table himself. Eric is aware that Gregory's Uncle Ezell also has pull as well. Ezell is tightly connected to some who align with their age respective consortium stemming back to the sixties. Eric sees fit to link with those connected in his sphere of influence first. So by the time Gregory and Ezell make their humble rounds, the table will already be set. AB is the best person to get on board to facilitate such a contingency plan.

Eric and AB meet with the group. Moments later, they return to the curb. The Table is in high favor of Eric's plan of action. In fact, The Table is quite exhilarated to hear such a robust plan had been put together. To the effect that such bold risks are being taken for the sake of the Black community, against the bight of the ongoing social injustice that has been taking place seemingly unchecked for the last fifty years.

After obtaining the blessing, Eric shares typical goodbye gestures with AB, then makes his way to see more of his associates in the area that also are to have prominent roles within his overall plan. These friends are associates from his active-duty time with the Marines. During his two tours overseas, Eric made a reputable name for himself in the Marines. He had a distinct way of making friends and earning the respect, and oftentimes the admiration, of most who he came into contact with.

Eric met many different kinds of people who maneuvered through all walks of life during his active-duty days and the interesting readjustment time period that followed. When he was in the process of separating from the military, before his separation had been officially completed, he was told by one of his mentors to visit Washington, D.C.

He was told to visit an esteemed politician who could possibly have some employment opportunities for him while he got himself situated.

When Eric finished his contract with the Marines, he took his contract bonus payout and other funds that he purposefully saved up. This created a position of ownership in a multi dwelling apartment unit in New York. He worked that property and renovated it into a very nice-looking real estate investment. From there, he quickly grew to acquire four more. It wasn't long before all of his units were full of tenants who were reliable when it came to respecting his properties and on-time rental payments.

His real estate business continued to grow. The growth afforded him the ability to take additional steps away from the day-to-day and hire a property manager who saw to those dealings on his behalf for a percentage of the total take.

During that time of entrepreneurial zeal,

it was actually that politician who made that first real estate transaction possible. That politician was the esteemed, long time delegate of the District of Columbia, Demetrius Fortune. Based on their people in common and the respect that was shared amongst them, Delegate Fortune and Eric had initially experienced some slight difficulties in getting to learn how to get to know one another.

Demetrius recognized that Eric was a special individual with unique and remarkable character qualities. After that period of unease had transpired, Eric quickly began taking full advantage of learning all the innovative things Delegate Fortune had to share. The more they dealt with one another, Eric became more found of the delegate. Eric on more than one occasion partook in the very elaborate and well-known dinner parties hosted at the home of the delegate. Eric was seeing a great deal of the other side of life during his time working in the delegate's office.

Eric took that set of experiences, in addition to what he had already saved, and put into the building that the delegate had given him the information about. Working his big plan, Eric continued to save and build himself and his growing residual revenue streams up along the way.

Chapter 2

"LEGAL BRIEF"

It's now February of the year 2020. It's been two plus years of diligent adherence to the mission he'd been sent on. Michael spent those years researching and investigating into many law firms and their staff compliments. He also searched for the right firm with the right type of like-minded and devoted mission to take the merit of Eric's plan to where it needed to be taken to.

It has become time to take that research into the next phase. With two firms under the final magnifying glass, the best method of verifying if their groups would be best suited to move forward with is to initiate contact and interact with them. The next viable opportunity to better conduct this scrutinous endeavor is to participate in the annual Maximus Attorney Strengthening Conference that both firms respectively are scheduled to attend. This conference is a two-day event being held in Milwaukee, Wisconsin at the Hilton Milwaukee City Center.

Through his persistent and long reaching investigative efforts, Michael discovered that two of his top prospects will be in attendance for their respective firms. All that is needed to be done now is be in attendance and wait for the appropriate opportunity to approach both attorneys to set the table for the real examination, or create one impromptu.

Managing partner Sandra Sterling is attending the conference in the hopes of bringing developmental information back to her firm in areas of recent advancement in several areas of law being currently litigated and legislated across the nation. The firm she represents is located in New Orleans. Her team stands patiently in line waiting behind her for instructions regarding their accommodations and the group itineraries for their time at the conference. Each of their mobile phones are in full utilization as they wait for Sandra to handle that business.

Sandra is sternly attentive to several of the conversations at the front desk. She listens for anyone having to navigate around any unforeseen booking anomalies. She makes sure that she is in possession of any documents or credentials that she had heard being requested. She has gone through this process more than once before.

As a result, she stands before the front desk agent when it becomes her time and presents all that is required of her to successfully collect the set of room keys for her entire team. After completing this task, she walks away from the front desk into a corner section of the lobby and turns to her staff to dispense the keys. Once the keys have been handed out, they briefly discuss an early morning meeting in her room just before the time the first session of the conference is to begin. When they finish discussing that morning briefing, she too makes off towards her lodging accommodations with luggage in tow.

Once settled into her room, and her belongings have been properly stowed in their temporary homes, she returns to the floor of the lobby eager to begin the process of mingling and networking on behalf of herself and her firm more specifically. There is also the matter of finding something to eat. She takes great pride in representing her firm as she should, but she was hungry.

Sandra worked night and day fighting cases that were not simple whatsoever, while acquiring a more than satisfactory case record in regards to her many victories. She worked her way up the chain at the firm, through the myriad of glass ceilings that indeed existed, to become a partner. An indisputably respected partner at that.

Sandra didn't stop there either. After years of painstaking work applied to her craft and nurturing countless relationships within the firm, she was crowned the prestige title of Managing Partner by her sixth year with the firm.

After an hour or so of discussion and banter, she decides that the trip to Milwaukee itself has been exhausting enough that she now simply has to find something to eat, and perhaps even a stiff transmute drink to assist her transition into a more relaxed state of mind for the evening. She is hopeful that in doing so she can provide opportunities to consider the depth of the purpose of their attendance; she hopes to also observe her colleagues who are present more candidly as she sits off to the side so she can more precisely deliberate any ideas of approach. All so that she can approach the events slated for her morning with the appropriate attitude and mindset that comes from focus coupled with the appropriate amount of reflection to take on the tedium of the potential repetitious nature of the day to come.

She sits at the bar awaiting a table. While she's there, she orders the deep-fried soft-shell crab and a small bowl of their house special jambalaya on the side, along with a snifter full of Remy Martin Louis XIII. Her drink arrives shortly after ordering. Not so long after her drink arrives, the manager approaches her and informs her that a table has been prepared and is now ready for her to sit down. The manager assures her that her meal will be brought to her table, leaving her needless to worry. She listens to the jazz ensemble improvise into the evening. After several selections are played by the colorful musician ensemble, the manager returns, followed by the waiter with her meal.

"Excusez-moi mademoiselle, j'ai votre repas ... Aimeriez-vous que je vous fournisse autre chose avant que je vous quitte?" says the waiter with a slight Creole accent.

Sandra sits and enjoys the rich aromas coming from her bowl of jambalaya that she recognizes all too well. The next wave of scent filling her nostrils comes from the deep fried soft crab that she can detect with her eyes still closed. The rich andouille sausage bursts into the atmosphere with all of its enticing, natural native New Orleans flavors, striking her respiratory system like a slow-moving tank. Not left too far ahead of the unique and noticeable Cajun scents that remind her briefly of past trips to the French Quarters.

The snow crab's fresh ocean scent is smooth and not overbearing as she lifts her nostrils even higher to allow room for them to populate her pallet. The scent of the melted butter also is a much enjoyable accompaniment. She sits satisfied and quite relaxed with her right leg relaxed as it is lays across the top of her left foot. She takes her immediate mind from the matters of the legal world and begins to think about the multitude of matters within her personal life worthy of reflecting upon. First of which is tearing into this delicious meal hand delivered to her.

She eats and consumes several drinks as the soulful music sets as a soothing backdrop to a rejuvenating evening. Her next move is to linger at her table for an extended amount of time after paying her tab then make her way back to her room and prepare for the tedium of the next two days. Sandra has high hopes for what the conference could mean for her recent success in her field with her firm.

As she sits in indulgence, allowing her meal to begin its digestive business, and sipping methodically on her snifter, she is approached again by her waiter.

"Excuse me, Ms. Sterling. I have a gentleman that would care to join you at your table. Is this okay with you? He had just approached me just now."

Sandra, intrigued by the <u>announcement</u> of the request, instructs the waiter to bring the man to her table. Shortly after doing so, the gentleman arrives to the table escorted by the waiter.

"Good evening. I do hope I have not completely interrupted your evening and or your meal, either."

With her facial expressions betraying her, she releases a sleek grin as she takes in the physical appearance of her new acquaintance. The mysterious man extends his right hand out towards her, requesting her right hand to be extended back towards him, in the expectation of exchanging a modest handshake greeting with her. The man receives her hand and takes the crown of her hand's knuckles closer to his mouth as he leans in closer over the table to do so.

He places his lips onto her knuckles very slowly and sensually. A gesture set just shy of doing too much with the moment. He gives her hand back to her as she continues to blush. She grows even more curious as to why she was approached by the stranger.

"Please excuse me, Ms. Sterling. My name is Michael Crawford. I recognized you in the lobby earlier as I myself was getting settled in. I have followed a few of your cases through several law revues. Yale, Emory, Harvard, Marquette to name a few.

"The work you have done in the field of civil rights has been astounding, to say the least, in a relatively short time in the field. You have a few cases that have changed precedence. Some were in New Orleans, and a few went all the way to the Supreme Court with success. Come to find out that you're a remarkable beauty as well as a remarkable legal mind. It is definitely an honor for me to meet you at this conference, and hopefully I'll have the opportunity to become even better acquainted while we are here."

Sandra waves her hand in a directional manner to Michael for him to have a seat across from her at the table. Shortly after Michael takes to his chair, the waiter approaches Michael and asks him if he wants something to drink from the bar or something to eat from their kitchen.

Michael responds to the waiter calmly and politely, "My kind friend, I will pass on having something to eat since I have come to this table after food has already been consumed. I will pledge to strive to improve my timing moving forward, but I will request a snifter for myself. May you fill that snifter with a double shot of what this fine young woman is having? I believe it to be Remy Martin Louis XIII?"

Michael looks over at Sandra for her confirmation as to what she has been drinking. She smiles and nods nonchalantly back to him in agreeance. She reservedly remains a touch, surprised by his awareness of what she has been drinking without a bottle present beside her.

"How did you know what I was drinking, Michael?"

Sandra's facial expressions are beginning to sober up and grow more inquisitive and investigative than flirtatious.

"You can relax. I simply asked the bartender before I approached the waiter. You can send the waiter back to the bar to confirm if you'd like to. I will not be offended in you doing so. It is quite understandable, actually."

Sandra laughs slightly, then gestures for the waiter to do just that. It is necessary to confirm what this mysterious Michael character has just told her. Once the waiter returns and whispers into Sandra's earlobe, she looks piercingly into the eyes of her unannounced dinner guest. Her look can depict stern attentiveness, or that of the beginning of faint disbelief. Sandra's facial expression visibly returns to warmth.

"So, Michael, what *do* I owe to the pleasure of this visit? Instead of the great many other people in the lobby that would enjoy your company as well, why did you choose my table? What has brought you to choose me to spend this time with?"

Michael shifts within his chair with a distinct air of subtle reassuring confidence. He then leans towards the center of her table and stares back into her eyes.

He speaks, "I am primarily here for the conference. I'm looking forward to building relationships in our field and hopefully start some new and courageous legal work as a result of all the many different pioneers in attendance here. Hopefully, I can find my way into becoming a part of the kind of legal work that may indeed change the world. The kind that inspired me to become an attorney in the first place.

"I see myself in a rare position as an attorney with my life experiences and exposures that sculpted my approach to the law. I feel the potential stream of opportunities in this industry will lead to a landmark case in the civil rights agenda to become a real opportunity real soon. It could literally be another incident any moment of any day. I really do believe that.

"Hopefully, when I do find something this substantial, you would be interested in hearing me out. Maybe you and your firm could co-counsel with it. The glory and accolades for bringing home such a victory or to even make such a bold challenge would be ground-breaking enough if nothing else."

With that, Sandra raises her professionally maintained eyebrows and flutters the meticulously detailed eyelashes underneath them as she takes a few moments to allow what he has said to her to sink in. Then she runs her tongue between the crevasse between her lips from left to right before she makes a response to his statement.

"I will seriously take what you have said under serious advisement, Mr. Crawford. That kind of case sounds just like the sort of thing that our firm would be willing to be associated with, with its litigative efforts. I wish you prosperous travels, and hopefully, we can speak again during the convention. Perhaps even share a meal together. Of course, maybe starting it at the same time?

"I am going to retire for the evening. I sat here to ponder possibilities of this conference and my career. You have given me quite the inspiration to follow it into a nice rest this evening. I do look forward to seeing you in the morning if not at any productive point throughout what is set to be a rigorous day of legal theory. Good evening."

Sandra has taken an interest in Michael with his unusually stout physique for an attorney. When she finishes saying what she has to say, Michael leans in once again and kisses across the crown of her knuckle line of her bent hand once again. This time, there is a different, more elaborate, sense of sensuality in the exchange.

"Enjoy the remainder of your evening, Ms. Sterling. I will definitely be seeing you again with great anticipation."

Michael exchanges warm glances back to Sandra discreetly and respectably as he slips from the dining area of the bar until he is out of sight altogether. Meanwhile, Sandra simply works to fully collect herself before she departs the bar area herself and navigate back to her room.

The next day, the conference begins. Keynote speaker after keynote speaker. The podium supports many speakers who discuss various areas of law and the trending data of what cases are pivotal to the examined areas of law. Their decisions and current effectual precedence.

At first break, Sandra and two other junior members of her firm join together. The junior members role is to document the events and details of the conference overall. That's also the role of some senior members. They make their way to just one of the multitudes of tables full of food and refreshments for the conference members in attendance.

While Sandra is standing in the open foyer around the food on display, she leans her neck sideways. She is certain that she saw someone who she is certain resembles an old acquaintance from her law school days. She feels absolutely sure her premonition is a correct one, so she approaches the woman.

"Tanisha? Tanisha Kager?"

"Yes, that is my… name… Sandra? Sandra Sterling!!!!"

"Yeah, Girl, it's me! Wow! What has brought you way up to Milwaukee?"

"I am a junior partner with my mother's firm in Chicago these days. I graduated after you from FAM-U, passed the bar, then I went on a campaign to earn some experiences of my own. The result was me working for a few firms that operated in certain spaces I thought to be interesting to get my bones in the trenches on my own, separate from my mother's firm.

"After a few years of this, I spoke with my mother and father about crossing over to the family firm, and we worked it out. I have been working with the family firm for the last two years. I just had to work my ass off to earn my place with the firm's leadership. My mother is extremely hard on me. It wasn't until I made junior partner that she took a step back from how vicious she once was not too long ago. Now she is just demanding and hilariously determined to wade me through the waters into higher degrees of firm management.

"Anyway, I'm here to learn for the firm and for my own perceptive growth. Enough about me going on about my stuff. How have you been, Girl? How did you get here? What firm are you with?"

"I graduated and jumped right into my family's practice. Same as you, I worked my ass off to earn junior partner and fought like a beast to make managing partner. I earned my seat at the table as well. I am pleased with those accomplishments and ready to bring something big home for the firm. I am still ravenous for that case that will become that landmark situation. Hopefully even leading to equivalent legislation that the firm could also play a major role in developing. That is the mission for me. All day every day.

"I am excited now, though. Seeing you lets me know that this conference will be something more than a retention and discussion thing. Hopefully we are about to reconnect in here and keep it together moving forward."

They continue to chit chat during what is left of the break. The conference regains order and begins with the next keynote speaker. Secretly, Sandra is interested in the opportunity of seeing Michael in the crowd at some point. His offer was intriguing and coincidently just what she herself had been looking for to signify her career in a serious way. A case of that magnitude he had propositioned would be the catalyst for a very promising legal career. Just being a part of such legal work that handled landmark civil rights cases, let alone that case having connections to the eventual groundbreaking legislation, would create a profound impact on law itself. Instant legacy creation. *What could be any more enticing for an attorney?* she ponders.

After speakers exchange turns at the podium, the second segment of conference topics on social unrest with the justice system concludes. Judging from the reaction of the crowd, the matters discussed were quite impactful. From speaker to speaker, the whole hall suddenly erupted into small groups of separate conversations regarding the hot topic.

Soon after, the group is released yet again for lunch. Still, everyone is involved in at least one active conversation. Some more than one as they move from sentence to sentence between groups. From rehashing the information and standpoints shared by the speakers to their individual reactions to those statements, the energy in the hall is well past loud and rambunctious. Hungry and primed to consume, hundreds pile out into the lobby, heading out into the city for their break.

Sandra is fortunate enough to have re-connected with Tanisha in the confusion. Both of them and their respective groups join one another and take their lunch break with each other. They discuss the topic of racial discrimination at length. Everyone at the table just about takes their moment to chime in. They follow that conversation straight into how that discrimination has taken hold of the justice system that has just never been as equal, if ever equal, to the African American and Hispanic American communities historically.

The conversation grows even more heated in regards to the intensity of the comments and their deliveries. This recent case in Idaho with the state trooper who had shot and killed Miguel Childress during a profiled stop arises in conversation.

Without probable cause, Miguel was abrasively ordered to provide his license, insurance information, and registration for the officer at his window while the other officer had his gun drawn through the passenger side window as he scanned the rest of the vehicle visually for anything pertaining to criminality. As Miguel went for his glove compartment, he popped it open and from within, its contents popped out: a plastic knife and plastic gun that had belonged to his twelve-year-old son.

Miguel and his wife had taken the items away from his son earlier that week as they were in transit, and their son was playing with it in a fashion they did not approve of with his younger cousin. So, they took them and put them in the glove compartment as many other parents in that situation would have as well.

When those items popped out in the dark area without complete light from the dome light or the roving flashlight beam, the officer on the passenger side yelled, "Gun!" The officer on the driver side yelled as well for Miguel to immediately stop leaning towards the information he had been rudely commanded to retrieve in the first place. Miguel, unable to stop in motion completely as he was already over the top, past the climax of his lean towards his glovebox, tried to freeze. He just couldn't achieve a complete fast stop fast enough. Both officers shot him and unloaded their entire magazines into him from both sides of the vehicle.

He was left riddled full of those bullets, sunken deep into the driver's side seat saturated with that of his own blood. Lifeless, he sat in his vehicle. The disturbing element of this incident was both body cameras and the vehicle dashcam had recorded the events in their entirety, and the officers still were acquitted. They underwent no occupational discipline whatsoever. The nation of African Americans was collectively hurt as a result of yet again blatant disregard to justice in this matter.

The luncheon group discusses this matter as well. That topic takes them to the brink of extreme loudness. The matter is still semi-hot in the media coverage, and many are still extremely dissatisfied with the verdict.

As the team comprising of the representatives of both firms collect and migrate back to their respective transportation options, they begin to make their way back to the Hilton. The lunch break was long. They were given about three hours before they needed to return for the final symposium of the day. With more than an hour remaining on their break still to be exhausted, both teams arrive back at the hotel and begin to go about their own personal business in preparation for both the next segment in addition to their evening plans in the city.

Sandra and Tanisha find themselves standing in the main foyer openly joking with each other in regards to probably enjoying the conversations a bit too much at lunch and apparently eating more than they would normally have. At this moment, carrying the remnants of whatever is barely left of some type of wrap he had been eating, comes Michael.

"Ah, Sandra. Good to see you again. During the day hours at that. I must admit I am feeling good about this timing. How was your lunch?"

Michael closes the gap from where he first recognized her standing there with Tanisha and comes up and in close range of the two women. About four to five feet distance, he now stands as he continues to speak to Sandra who is shockingly still gathering herself as she too is happy to see him. Unexpectedly a little happier than even she had anticipated herself being.

"Excuse me. My name is Michael Crawford."

Both women sneak glances at one another as they both look Michael up and down as discreetly as they can, given the sudden insertion of his presence upon them. Tanisha is less discrete as she has just met Michael for the first time.

"Oh, I am Tanisha. Tanisha Kager. Very nice to meet you."

Michael shakes her hand and gives them both two business cards a piece and then responds to Tanisha and Sandra as well.

"Well, I am happy to meet you, Tanisha. As you can both see, I walk, talk, and eat almost around the same time often. I try to stay active for my practice. Seeing that I have fulfilled the previous requirement, Sandra, of finding you during daytime hours, maybe we can coordinate the three of us for a semi-formal dinner this evening."

The two women accept his invitation. Tanisha mischievously pokes Sandra in her back as she accepts. The three of them continue to speak on the subjects of their luncheon's many discussions as they walk around the lobby and lower levels of the hotel.

Chapter 3

"Lining Things Up"

While briefly back in the New York City area, Eric takes it upon himself to hit the old stomping grounds of Harlem. Here, he seeks out the company of his younger brother Dontre. Although Eric owns several vehicles, while in New York City and its surrounding areas, he chose a long time ago to refrain from driving. That way he will minimize the likelihood of having random interactions with local law enforcement.

Eric is prior military. Even with having that background, he's seen more times than he could stomach to count the police injustices. In all the communities he'd frequent and traverse through, he's witnessed police brutality, criminal actions, and harassment. Police brutality, criminal actions, and harassment and harassment against the very same people who those police officers were sworn to protect. Police brutality, criminal actions, and harassment towards those who contribute to their salaries.

Eric makes swift travels from the underground subway to the street surface along the legendary thoroughfare of Harlem's one hundred and twenty fifth street. He moves south east down one hundred and twenty fifth street until he arrives at sixth avenue. This street of historical lure, amongst many others within Harlem, has two other names: Lenox Avenue and Malcolm X Boulevard. The name was amended to add the moniker of being additionally identified as Malcolm X Boulevard in the year of nineteen eighty-seven.

Eric now finds himself at the corner of one hundred and twentieth street and Malcolm X Boulevard.

For a brief moment, he hesitates from turning right on one twentieth, and he quickly re-routes his direction to check Marcus Garvey Park. He follows a hunch that overcame him. Since it is a nice day outside, there is a good chance that Dontre is most likely in the park around his favorite section of the park— the chess table.

Eric can't resist the need to slow down in his stride once he arrives at the intersection of 120th Street and Mount Morris Park West. It has been a month or so since he has been back home and an even longer frame of time since he has been in this park or near enough to it to see it like this.

As Eric crosses the street into the park, he slows down and sort of soaks in all he can as he is still focused on finding his brother. Eric and Dontre, since their early youth, has a tradition of their own. They would work as tirelessly as possible to sneak up on one another out in the street.

Although Eric very well could have just called his brother on his mobile device and ask him to meet him at a specific location at a specific time, this method was just too irresistible for either one of them to disregard. They both take enormous enjoyment in catching the other off-guard. Growing up here, being caught off guard is a significant sign of not being alert. Not being alert can easily lead to one's death. It is seen as a sign of weakness. The inability to adapt and stay connected to an ever evolving and changing urban environment where what worked and potentially insulated a person at noon was obsolete by twelve o'five."

As Eric catches himself strolling through the park, off-point and briefly captivated by the sheer beauty of the park and the positivity in the scene of children playing with one another all around, he smirks and regains his focus on sneaking up on his brother. He approaches the area of the park where his brother has longtime enjoyed playing chess. He can see his brother and another individual sitting at the table active in a game. From what he can make out from what he can see from his brother's body language is that he had been in the position of advantage.

It is unclear if his brother has spotted him already, so he utilizes the cover of passing groups to inconspicuously hide behind the monument adjacent to the chess table and benches. He creeps along its perimeter in the hopes of sneaking up behind him fast enough to touch him before his opponent's eye contact shifts from Dontre onto himself, alerting his brother of his presence.

Eric's plan yields success. He manages to creep up behind the monument next to where they have been playing chess. Eric sneaks around with the quickness of a panther to just behind where his brother is sitting. Fortunate timing prevails to where Dontre's opponent's eyes are glued to the table as he is under the scrutiny of "check". This allows Eric to be able to very gently apply his fingers to the back of his brother's head with both the index and middle finger snuggly together, as his thumb reenacted the motion of a handgun's cocked hammer as he moved his thumb forward as a released hammer of a firearm would move forward as he whispers into his brother's ear, "Bang…. Bang…. Boy."

Dontre, still mostly focused on his pending victory, just responds without moving an inch...

"Shiiiiiiiiiiit. I saw yo ass enter the park, Bro. This fine individual sitting before me just asked for a more concentrated annihilation to where I was not able to disengage from the table and creep on you while you thought you was creeping up on me. I would have definitely got ya really good. Pull up for a few. This is soon to be over. I think I'm

ready for you today."

Eric shrugs his shoulder in slight disappointment as he introspectively back tracks his movements to remember if he was that visible. Afterwards, he snaps out of his mini tantrum.

"Well damn then. You got me. I have time to let you try. I owe you that at least since you scoped me out."

Dontre, upon hearing his brother respond and speak, smirks and moves one of his pieces. Then Dontre taps the button on the timer again.

"You looked real pedestrian-like as you were over there strolling through the park, Bro," Dontre says, while slightly chuckling. "Let me find out that after all these years that even though you done conquered these streets as a kid, went off and got back in not just one piece as a Marine, but decorated at that, to become soft and all nostalgic," Dontre jokes, continuing to playfully chuckle.

"I definitely think that today is my day to finally defeat you at this table. Oh yeah, I do believe today is that day. I need to finish this up so I can get you over here while you zoned out. I'll take that 'W' with no hesitation."

As he says that, Dontre visibly speeds up his pattern of move speed. He moves his knight to the "5D" position on the board. Then he taps the timer button with a different distinction than any of the previous times before then. His opponent, with a skeleton screw of pieces, is left with few options. His opponent moves his pawn located at "6B". The opponent mutters some disgruntlement under his breath as he reluctantly touches the timer button as he starts to begrudgedly await the seemingly inevitable outcome.

Dontre's next move is to bring his Queen up to the position of "7G". He takes his right hand to swoop up the now-captured pawn as his hand continues to glide towards the timer button as he remarks, "Check-Mate."

His opponent is not pleased with Eric for having popped up, encouraging Dontre to expedite his defeat. As he slowly gathers his things from alongside the side of him on the long bench, he mutters under his breath and gives Dontre his dap as he just looks at Eric with frustration.

"He didn't take that too well huh?" Eric asks Dontre.

"Oh, Jermaine? He'll be alright. He may be pissed at you though," Dontre snickers. "He hasn't won one yet. I will give him that he keeps trying. Shoot. I feel the same way with you. I ain't won one yet. I'm still trying to catch you slipping. Load 'em up"

"Is that right now?" Eric expels softly, as he sits on the bench and begin to inspect the timer clock apparatus all around its physical frame.

Eric looks at his brother with one eye enlarged and the other one mostly closed as he pokes at his brother slightly.

"Making sure you not trying to cheat me out here. Scoped me out in the park. You ready for your first 'W' today I see," Eric says, returning his brother's snicker.

When they finish setting up the board, they both pause for a moment in   discussion. "Michael started that move a while ago for me," Eric states as he moves his Pawn from "D2" to "D4", then taps the timer.

"Oh Yeah? I haven't seen Fam in a minute. How long since you sent him off to get that started?" Dontre asked, as he grimaced and then moved his respective pawn from "7D" to "5D", then tapped the timer.

"It's been quite a minute up to now. He had to find out a few things before he made his move."

Eric answers, before moving his pawn located at "C2" up to "C4", then taps the timer.

"That actually makes sense to me now that I think on it. I was wondering why I haven't seen him around for a good while now. I even went into his office more than once, and they told me he was out of town, each time. I figured he would get up with me when he got back home," Dontre replies back to Eric, as he moves his Bishop from "8C" to "5F", then taps the timer.

"Oh yeah. Michael been making that move. We started that like two years ago just to be sure we had it right." Eric acknowledged, as he takes his Knight from "B2" and relocates it to "C3", then taps the timer.

"Well since it's been that long, have you gotten any updates? I haven't heard from nor seen fam in that long now that you gave it a timeframe." Dontre answers back, as he places his fingers on his pawn piece located at "7E" and moves it to "6E", then taps the timer.

"It's been structurally cryptic, but yeah. We've been in constant communication and coordination since he been gone." Eric said as he picks up his pawn from "C4" and takes it to "D5", taking the pawn already there as he puts it down in the square, then taps the timer.

"Okay, sounds like he is making positive progressions on that move," Dontre answers as he grabs his pawn from "6E" and returns the favor in kind by taking one of Eric's Pawns as he replaces it with his own at "5D", then taps the timer.

"Most definitely. He is actually ready and about to take that first move. Setting off that business on the books," Eric replies as he runs his Index finger around the top area of his Knight stationed at "G1" briefly before he picks it up and moves it over into the square of "F3", then taps the timer.

"That's great news Brotha! Congrats on that progress." Dontre remarks while he hesitates slightly re-analyzing the board before he picks up his Knight at "8G" and moves it over to "6F".

Dontre looks upon his brother menacingly before he taps the timer with an escalated degree of spunk.

"Well it's about that time for me to go kick it with your boy. I need to know that you made that happen so I can make that move, and the ones along with it." Eric states, as he strokes his chin slowly in contemplation before forming a smile.

Eric, looks over his brother's face once more as he holds back a modest moment of laughter. He slowly shakes his head. Eric then took his Bishop piece from "C1", and moved it into place at "G5". After he does so, he tapped the timer with his eyes widening in antagonization.

"Which one of them is this?" Dontre asks, as he squints his eyes in distrust before he reaches towards the board to now grab his Bishop on "8F" and relocated it to "7E".

"Your guy in Atlanta." Eric replies, before he picks up his Pawn from "E2" and nonchalantly places it on "E3".

Eric reached for the timer and tapped the button.

"Oh. That's definitely not a problem. Make that move tonight, and go see him as soon as you need to. He'll be ready for you." Dontre utters, as he slowly watches over the board in focus before, he grabs his Knight from "8B" to "7D".

Dontre Then presses the timer.

"You seem to be awfully determined to snatch that Bishop. Well, I will make my way down to the 'A' immediately since you put it like that. Get that ball rolling really nice, and run the whole list down afterwards. Hands-on too." Eric says, as he re-positions his bishop from "F1" to "E2".

After doing so, he taps the timer button with amusement in an ever so slightly appalled manor.

"Say no more bro. I will line all of those other meets up. You straight." Dontre replies as he performs a Rook-side castle maneuver, moving first his rook from "8H" to "8F". He then moved his King from "8E" to "8G".

Dontre pauses momentarily, seemingly in the hope to see some indication of what direction Eric may be tempted to lean towards with his next move. Dontre, then catches himself and presses the timer once more.

"That will definitely work. That is just what I need to go down once I touch down. Things lined up, so I can say less and keep it moving." Eric exclaims modestly as he chooses to perform a Rook-side Castle maneuver of his own by first moving his Rook from "H1" to "F1", then by completing the maneuver by moving his King from "E1" to "G1". Eric presses the button on the timer afterwards.

"I haven't heard about Greg. What is his position?" Dontre asks, before he grabs his Pawn from "7C" and moves it to "6C" with confidence.

Dontre pressed the timer's button. He continued to look over Eric's demeanor in evaluation as he sat curiously watching his brother preparing to make his next move.

"Gregz is about to make his approach, and get his trip started real soon. He's been waiting and ready. So, any day he should be at it." Eric says, as he reaches for his Bishop stationed at "E2" and purposefully moves it over to "D3".

Eric reached into his pocket and pulls out a bottle of water. He opens the bottle effortlessly and begins to take a drink from it slowly and methodically, then taps the timer.

"Ok. I will spread the word for him too. For the link up." Dontre responses, as he sits still momentarily examining the board.

Dontre takes a moment to think further before he picks up his hand and hovers from the left corner across to his right, thinking almost aloud as to what his next move will be. Finally, grabbing his Bishop from "5F" and moving it to "6G" before he released his piece, and retracted his arm, tapping on the timer's button before fully retracting his hand and then returning his arm to his side. Then suddenly Eric moves quickly, indicating a pace increase in the time intended to make his move.

Eric then quickly grabs Dontre's Bishop located in the square of "G6". He replaced the piece with his own Bishop previously sitting at "D3". Eric after finishing his move, instantly dabbed the button on the timer.

Eric is now silent, and the same silence has overcome Dontre as well. Dontre then moves his Pawn menacingly from "7H" to "6G". In doing so he captured one Eric's Bishops in the process. Dontre slightly manhandles the Bishop as he snatches it off the table and aggressively pokes the button on the time as he grunts aloud for Eric to hear. Dontre then smashed the piece alongside the Pawn he'd previously collected to his side of the board.

Still silent, Eric takes his right-hand and relocated his Rook from "A1" to "B1" then took his hand along an expeditious motion to poke the button even faster. Just as he finishes, Dontre abruptly picks up his Rook from "8F" and firmly placed it back on the board at "8E". Dontre then poked the timer's button without haste.

Undeterred, Eric picks up his Bishop from "G5" and with an upbeat energy grabs the Knight already positioned at "F6" and replaced it with his Bishop. Then slapped the timer button with vigor. The entire time he did not discontinue the eye contact he had with his brother, taunting him.

Unaffected by the taunting, Dontre leapt in to grab his Pawn from "7G" to capture Eric's Bishop at "6F". After that, he presses the button on the timer as he then scoffs in Eric's direction.

Eric never took his eyes from Dontre. While he stared at the chessboard, he viciously picked up his Queen from "D1", then moved it "D3". He then tapped the button again.

Sneering his lips, Dontre humbly picks up his Pawn from "6F" and moves it forward one space to "5F". He presses the button in quick reluctance and sits, waiting for his brother's next move, significantly less assertively.

Eric moves lightning fast to grabbed his Pawn from "B2" and moved it forward two spaces arriving finally at "B4". Urgently pressing the timer, in eager anticipation, Eric sat teeming for his next opportunity to make his next move.

Again, Dontre with cautious discernment moved his King from "8G" one space down to "7G" and pushed the button slower than he had in previous times.

The two had stopped speaking back and forth for a few minutes now, as the game began to intensify. Eric without hesitation after his brother's last move grabs his Pawn from "B4" and moves it over to "B5". He swiftly poked the timer.

Dontre is growing all too leery of these familiar demonstrations of demeanor from his brother as the game progresses. He hesitantly picks up his Rook from "8E" and moves it purposefully to "8H" then promptly pressing the timer with remerging confidence afterwards.

Eric's response to that was to capture his brother's Pawn located at "C6" with his Pawn formerly located at "B5". Eric then tapped the timer with blissful energy. His gaze was unrelenting toward his brother sitting across from him at the table.

Dontre, still motivated in the fight, moved his pawn from "7B" diagonally down to "6C" where he used his Pawn to capture his brother's pawn. He then presses the timer with arrogance as he sneers his lips in a display of rebellion. He then took a moment to lean back in his chair as if to disregard the expected swiftness of his brother's next move, expecting his pattern to remain consistent.

Eric's response to that move was to bring his Rook towards his King from "B1" to "C1".

After Eric pushed the timer, he spoke: "Yeah, Gregz is about to step to Unc and bring him on with us."

"Yeah, that is what I was thinking to put you onto. That's a good look right there for real, for real."

Dontre takes his Rook from "8H" and moves it to "6H" in what he perceived as a threatening posture as he is smacked his lips, awaiting his brother's next move. Dontre paused momentarily before he tapped the timer.

"Yeah, like I said I see him bouncing to get that started no later than next week."

Eric, paused with a stern focus, moved his Knight from "C3" to "E2" methodically and purposefully. He took an additional moment to inspect the board, then leaned over ever-so slightly, pressing the timer like it was a finishing touch to a masterpiece from an artist's final stroke.

"Well let me know so I can reach out and get that link ready across the board." Dontre replied to his brother.

Dontre moves his Rook from "8A" to "8C". He carefully analyzes his brother's face for any remnant of an expression that would indicate something he can interpret in his favor from the move as he pressed the timer.

Eric doesn't say anything in response or even acknowledge what has been said by his brother. Eric grabs his Rook from "C1" with both his index finger and thumb. He then slid the piece across the squares edge into "C2.

Dontre brings his Queen across his side of the board from "8D" to "8H", pushed the timer, and then watched for his brother's next move. Eric does not waste any time before he moves in again. This time he takes his Rook from "F1" and moves it into position at "C1". Once he takes his fingers off of his Rook he reached over slowly and pushed the timer.

Quickly, Dontre moves his Knight from "7D" to "8B" back alongside his Queenside Rook. Dontre pressed the timer without hesitation.

"Reaching out would definitely be a good idea. We will need those connections to be made. That's really good. Do that" Eric blurts out quietly, as he pierces in to select his Knight sitting on "E2" to be his next move.

He scooped up the Knight and relocated it at "F4". He then engaged the timer's button before uncoiling back into his seat awaiting his brother's next move.

"I know you've been stacking the paper for this for a real long time. You said you were bringing on more support. What happened with that?"

Distracted by the sudden move of Eric's Rook, Dontre took his Rook from "8C" and moved it to "8D" near the Bishop at "7E". Dontre cautiously touches the timer afterwards as he stared at the board in a contemplative gaze.

"You already know I been stackin' on this from the time I left Paris Island. I knew then I had to make all this worth something more than just what it was sold to be. I was quite fortunate. Found some people, Mikey found some people, and you found more people. What we were able to bring together was a group of committed cats with a purpose. Straight committed. We good on that tip, D. When I tell you we good, we're really good. You played a serious role in getting us ready for go-time. Just continue to follow the script."

After speaking, Eric took his Pawn that was on "G2" and brought it a square over to "G3". He pressed the timer really quick. Dontre then moves his Queen abruptly from "8H" to "7H" before pressing the timer.

To that, Eric's response was instant. He grabbed his Rook from "C1" and moves it over to "B1". As he tapped the timer, he drew his hand back to the table behind his King's row and begins to tap rhythmically.

Dontre taps his fingers across the edge of the table close to his chest as he observes the table and board. After a moment or two of contemplation he reached over the board, picks up his Pawn from "6G" and moved it to "5G". After holding his hand with his fingers extended slightly over his released piece, he reached over to the timer and poked it.

Eric only took a short moment between seeing Dontre's last move, and moving into the execution of his next move. He grabbed his Rook from "B1" to "B7". Eric appeared rather resolute in his decision to do so. Eric tapped on the timer and seemingly prepared for his Dontre's next move. Dontre responds in kind by grabbing his Bishop on "7E" then putting it back down onto the board at the coordinates of "6D".

The game intensified. In response to Dontre's previous move and casual demeanor, Eric moves his Knight from "F3" over to "G5" with sharp focused cunning, as he snatched his brother's defenseless pawn. Dontre had seen this turn many times before now. He immediately became circumspect, but it felt behind-time.

Dontre's opportunities to surmount a victory seem all too unattainable to him at this point where the vibrations of games played in previous times became felt and oversaturating to his senses as he fought within himself to not allow it this time. This time he still felt that he had an opportunity to win. Dontre moved his Queen from "7H" up a space to "8G" retreating behind his King.

Unfortunately, Eric took advantage of an exposed vulnerability and moved his Queen from "D3" to "F5". Where in doing so he captured another one of his Brother's Pawns in the act. Dontre grabbed his Bishop from "6D" and hovered it over the location of "4F", where he then grabbed Eric's Knight stationed there with a fierce focus amidst waning confidence.

"So, it's all coming together, is it?" Dontre remarked trepidatiously in a somber tone as he looked upon his brother who was sporting that all too familiar smirk. One that by this time in their lives was all too apparent what was coming next.

Still smirking barely visible enough to recognize Eric moved his Rook from "B7" to "F7". The result of doing so was the capturing of Dontre's Pawn. Dontre, now initiating his best attempt to at least stalemate his brother takes his King from "7G" to "8H".

"I definitely would refrain from considering anything at this point. Is the game confirmed or accomplished?" Eric replied to his brother. Dontre just smirked in response as the air seemed to be rapidly released from his sails.

Eric grew more and more confident with each passing sequence of moves that the game was undoubtably about to unfold upon his brother unfavorably. Although the game began with Dontre basking in his initial over confidence in his ability to get a win as if that were the only feasible outcome. Dontre was beginning to find the avoidance of the grim reality of the game's outcome was about to find its conclusion momentarily.

Eric made his next move. He picked up his Queen from "F5", moved it down to the square below at "F4". In doing so, Eric then captured his brother's last remaining Bishop. His brother's response was to take his Knight at "8B" and move it to "7D". Eric then grabbed his Rook at "C2" by the tip of its structure and slid it upward on the board to "C6" where he captured yet another Pawn.

In seeing this, Dontre appeared emotionlessly displeased as he picked up his Rook at "6H" and moved it under the protection of his Queen by placing it at the coordinates of "5H" where the Queen stood watching what was left of his army at "8G". Eric then dusted off his lap and looked around the circumference of the table for any uncollected belongings on or below the tabletop. He reached into the game area and then picked up his Rook from "C6" and then cautiously pondered with it in his hand as he twirled it about between the primary grip of one finger to the next within the same hand before he sat it back onto the board at "C7" one space over.

"You ain't shit, Bro!" Dontre exclaimed. He then placed his King piece onto its side and got up from the table in disgust.

Hearing that being blurted out from his brother, Eric begins to smile and make light of the looming situation. This game was about to undoubtably unfold upon his brother who was initially over confident in his ability to get a win in this game. Dontre is now realizing that he is about to find its conclusion momentarily.

Dontre knocks his king to its side across the board slowly.

Dontre speaks to his brother inquisitively, "Well, with all that lined up, what about the final series of moves? I imagine you're already ready for what that will look like."

"I think I am. I believe we have both prepared for that if anything first before everything else had been brought into play."

The both of them stand up from their seated positions and embrace briefly before Eric maneuvers himself, indicating his departure is soon to come. Dontre, seeing this from his stance and posturing, speaks out to his brother as he has the opportunity to before Eric's impending departure.

"I am proud of you. Both Mom and Dad would have been proud, Eric. I look forward to the day that allows me to see you again. I love you, Man."

Eric embraces his younger brother firm and long. They hold one another for a lengthy moment.

Afterwards, Eric makes his way through the park. He makes his way back to the north side of the park, opening out at Fifth Avenue and 124th Street. From there, he makes his way briskly towards 125th Street and 5th, as he ventures off into the crowd towards the number six train subway line. Briefly before he reaches the staircase leading down into the subway tunnels and gate, Eric grabs his mobile device and makes a call to his brother's contact whom he'd be soon meeting.

"Hey, Johnny. It's Eric. I am Dontre's brother. Will you be in town near Atlanta within the next few days?... Great. I will be there as well. I hope to be able to obtain a portion of your time while I am there. Will that work within your schedule?... That's fantastic! Look forward to seeing you in the A."

Chapter 4

"UNCLE EZELL"

On the corner of President Street and Utica Avenue, in the Crown Heights section Of Brooklyn New York, we find Ezell Brown holding court at a table set with chairs to it outside the corner stores surrounding him. Ezell carries out much of his business on this tabletop. Has been doing so for many years. Quite a few decades actually. He has several interlaced arrangements with each shop owner of the intersection and along Utica Avenue where he had their overall approval of him doing so.

Ezell is a former member of the Kings Paper Street Gang that has been notorious from the mid-fifties to the late seventies until their leadership had been decimated from federal charges that led to crippling indictments throughout their rank and files. He has cultivated several lucrative relationships from those days that outlasted the gentrification of what used to be the Crown Heights of his day.

Ezell served time as well. Ezell joined the Marines during the Vietnam War, served two tours, then returned home where he reconnected with the Kings Paper Crew. Or what was left.

He served a ten-year bid for murder, racketeering, promotion of prostitution, and conspiracy to engage in organized crime about six years after his return. He had kept wealth from his time in the streets and the utilization of wiser choices in how he invested his money. As a result, he was able to negotiate a more tenable term of imprisonment from having a highly reputable team of attorney's retained and aggressive on his behalf. Ezell was more than able to afford such advocacy because he was quite wealthy.

Ezell had ownership in over thirty businesses off of Utica Avenue and other sections of Brooklyn. These investments either came from him bankrolling their conception, to him having the keen eye to recognize opportunity himself and put younger people who had passions for that particular field of business over the day-today operations. In those arrangements, he normally acted like a franchisor. He would retain a franchisor fee from their payroll each month, like a dividend for a publicly traded company would disperse quarterly.

Ezell was just extremely discrete in the manner in which he carried out his lifestyle. He picked up these discretionary behaviors from his experience in catching those cases and having had to leave the streets for those ten years that the state wanted to be thirty.

While he was gone, his elaborate and difficult to trace financial empire was able to cover the costs of caring for the five women he had been dealing with and the children he fathered with each woman. The women were so well cared for during his time away. They were also respectful towards Ezell.

The women transformed their relationship with him. At one time in the beginning, before Ezell was incarcerated, the women were competitive for his affections and indulgences. But they grew to working together hand in hand. Together, they learned how to deal with one another.

They took some of what each of them had been given monthly from him plus the business that he gave them to manage for their own chance at earning supplemental money from what he was dispersing to each of them. The women put all that money together and helped each other out.

This was indeed the lofty plan hatched by Ezell while he prepared to serve his time. He saw the potential benefit if he was able to have his influence over each of the women. He knew the advantage of bringing them under the understanding of the efficacy of trusting his vision, despite their then disdain for one another over emotional issues of envy and jealousy. He knew that their feelings would distract them from having seen the advantage on their own.

So, Ezell would arrange to have the women come visit him in a pattern to where they would inevitably run into each other coming and going from the facilities he'd be housed at. Over time, between his words and their constant dedication to visiting him, they grew to develop a unique comradery based initially on self-interest. Later, they gained the awareness of the opportunity to have more together than separate. The "bag", as it is referred to, became the best unifier of all.

Ezell is holding court on the corner of President Street and Utica Avenue as he has been doing since about a month after his release. He has a table that is foldable and is broken down when he is done for the day. Whichever one of the many neighborhood children that is there that day breaks the table down and places it inside whichever of the businesses nearby for the next day. Most of the buildings on that corner,

Ezell either owns or has a stake in the business leasing the space from him, or both.

As Ezell is sitting under his large table umbrella with his paper and laptop, Bluetooth device activated, and normally in use, He is cheerfully excited to see his younger sister's son Gregory stroll up. Gregory used to be one of those kids who did a variety of chores and tasks for his uncle, like fold up his table and roll his chair into one of his designated businesses at the close of his day.

Ezell is nearing sixty-eight, and he has always enjoyed his nephew's company. Especially since Gregory took reception to his uncle as well. Gregory started out in his early twenties running a laundromat for his uncle. Greg made it profitable by making decisions that derived from listening to his uncle from his early years spending time around him. Gregory also played a big role in raising some of Ezell's children through mentorship while Ezell was incarcerated. That mentorship was also an integral part of Ezell's plan on bringing his women together. Through the children, too.

Gregory grew to take on several other managerial roles in many of his uncle's business throughout Brooklyn. Gregory had an affinity for Harlem as well. It was where his father had been from. So, he would spend as much time there around his father and his side of the family as well. This is how he and Eric met one another early in their respective youths and grew to be more brother-like than mere friends.

Gregory would bring Eric out to Brooklyn, and Ezell would have fun showing them both different things about the streets, women, life in general, business, etc. Ezell loved Eric as well. He could see for himself that their relationship was real and without deception or corruption. They indeed in his eyes were brothers. So, he dealt with Eric like he was his nephew as well.

"What's the good word for you today, My Nephew? I am happy to see you this morning!"

Ezell exclaims out to Gregory immediately as Greg comes into view after rounding the corner of Utica Avenue and President Street.

"Good morning to you, Uncle Ezell. How are you feeling today? I hope you're feeling as energetic as you always come across, Old Man,"

Gregory responds back playfully to his uncle.

Well, within the respectful constructs of their relationship. Ezell is a punchy individual and raised his young mentees to be punchy, yet respectful as well.

"There are limits," he'd always say. "Once you know and understand them, operate within them, not around them."

Gregory laughs, then meets his uncle at his table. They embrace in a hearty hug. Ezell ends the embrace by tapping and holding firm onto his nephew's shoulders as he briefly looks him over with gleeful eyes. Ezell's face grows less jovial as he looks around his surroundings and gestures with his hand for Gregory to take a seat across from him at his table. One of the kids nearby caught the inevitable moment of the request, and had already been in the process of bringing out an additional chair to the table where Ezell is.

As the chair arrives, the young person speaks loudly but briefly all the same, "Here you go, Mr. Brown."

"Thank you, Sammie. Catch!"

Ezell tosses a very small rolled up bundle of bills towards little Sammie that is probably about ten bucks in a rubber band. As Gregory rolls his chair into position before starting to sit into it, he takes in a breath. Once seated, he begins to speak. Greg understands that his uncle just rolled out a red carpet for him, in a manner that many do not receive. He realizes how busy his uncle remains. Whether Ezell was reading, speaking on his phone, on his tablet trading, or some other degree of entrepreneurial pruning of his portfolio of business involvement, Ezell is a busy man.

Greg has to not disregard the allure of the pleasantries, but respect the time he has been given and get to it so as not to overstep those famous boundaries. He of many knew better, and had been taught better directly from His uncle. Gregory was his famed and respected top pupil more or less. An example to kids like Sammie who are well aware of who he is.

This is one of those unspoken moments where he is going to be teaching a supportive class on what it calls for to be an apprentice to Ezell Brown.

Gregory speaks, "Unc. We had a conversation a few years back where I told you about something me and Eric had been strategizing. You told us it was bold and potentially dangerous. Do you remember that conversation?"

Ezell nods his head to say yes after a few seconds of contemplation on the matter. Then Ezell moves the newspaper that had been sitting directly under him away to the side as he begins to respond to his nephew.

"Yeah, I remember that. It apparently has come to that time where both of you have made some moves in that plan like we had discussed, huh?"

Gregory nodded and responded, "Yes, Unc."

"So, that means the part we played together in that plan that we discussed is what you came here to verify with me now. Is that about it?"

"That's it, Unc. What do you say? You still down for that trip?"

Ezell reclines back into his chair as he looks upon his nephew with a blank stare. Gregory himself is unable to completely interpret his expression. After a very brief moment, Ezell waves his left hand into the air again. Then Sammie returns.

"Get Chris for me, Sammie."

"Yes, Sir, Mr. Brown"

Sammie runs off, then disappears around the corner onto Utica Avenue. Ezell closes his laptop and grabs his newspaper. Then he leans over the table towards Gregory and speaks to him.

"I have been wondering when you two would get around to 'our' part. I won't even lie, Nephew. I was beginning to think y'all had changed y'all mind and decided not to go through with it. I wouldn't have thought any different of either of you. It was surely an audacious plan. But since the day you brought it to me, I set aside some contingencies to accommodate what I have going on in the event that this moment was to actually come to pass. Give me a few minutes, Son. Let me get a few things together. Then we can roll, Nephew."

Three cars pull up to the curb, and Sammie jumps out the rear passenger door and runs back to where he was across the street. But before he does, he runs up to Ezell, and Ezell gives him another rubber banded tip. Next, from the remaining three doors, Christopher, Lavante, and Tyree rise from the vehicle's now opened doors.

The three men are in their late twenties. Christopher is Sammie's older brother. He once played a similar role in his early youth as his younger brother plays now for Mr. Brown. Christopher speaks out to Mr. Brown as he and his group walks up to the table, shaking both Ezell's and Gregory's hands.

"Good morning, Mr. Brown. What would you want me to do?"

"Chris, I need you to get the Green Team together and initiate our two-month protocol. Can you commit to that today? I realize it is last minute. I know we understood that when it was conceived it was constructed as a plan that if ever implemented to be a last-minute activation. Even still, you know how I am, and I just want to make sure we're good here before I head off. I can activate another group. Rotate the order?"

Chris smiles, expecting Mr. Brown to say what was said and simply replied to his mentor, "No, Mr. Brown. We have been ready for the possibility of getting activated since you gave us the game plan. We will hold it down."

"Okay, then. Everything is in order. Get with Basil at the Gyro shop. Get with Deyman over at the convenience store if we need to go to Yellow. We are about to leave now. Hold it down, Chris."

Ezell rises from his seat. Sammie comes back with a few of his young friends. Sammie instructs them on how to fold up the table. Sammie watches as they carry it off with him. They follow behind, rolling both chairs into the convenience store. Sammie gives instructions to them as to where to take the table.

Gregory stands next to his uncle, and they walk to the curb at the intersection. Gregory watches, slightly nostalgic, as the young men assume their respective positionings across the intersection in his uncle's absence; and as the children with Sammie take to the business of cleaning the corner of any trace of what Mr. Brown has left behind.

A blacked-out SUV pulls up to the curb in front of Ezell and Gregory. Ezell gestures for Gregory to take shotgun as he reaches for the rear passenger door. Once they are both secure inside the vehicle, the vehicle pulls off from the curb in between the vehicles moving up the street.

It isn't long before the vehicle has pulled up in front of a brownstone building. Ezell has owned many in the Borough, but this one is the one he had lived in with his family of families.

Ezell goes inside by himself, telling his nephew, "I will not be long."

It only takes him about ten minutes to go into the building before he is back out of the building making his way down the steps of his brownstone. Carrying an olive-green military issued duffle bag, he carries it to the rear of the vehicle. The driver opens the trunk and Ezell returns back to the passenger door he exited from, opens the door, and re-enters the vehicle.

Ezell then gestures to his nephew and speaks into the rear of the vehicle over his shoulder, "Do we need to grab your things?"

"Actually, no. I will kinda cover that as I go."

"Sounds good."

Ezell then taps his driver on the shoulder and instructs him as to where he wants him to go from there,

"Take Utica down to Linden. We're going to South Jamaica next."

The driver takes his direction and then proceeds along the most efficient route. Ezell grabs a phone handed to him by his driver and begins to dial into it. When the phone begins to ring, Ezell waits for the other end to pick up the line. When they do, he begins to listen attentively for what is said before he responds.

"Good morning. I need to speak with India please… Hello, India. This is Ezell. Yes. I will need to fly out on the very next jet. I have two guests along with me… Thank you… Okay, the next available departure will be ready by eight tonight? That will be fine. Thank you very much."

Their vehicle makes its way along Linden Boulevard and onto South Conduit Avenue. From there, they merge onto the Belt Parkway. After a few miles along the Belt Parkway, they take the service road exit re-entering South Conduit Avenue. From there, the driver prepares to take the left onto New York Boulevard, more recently known as Guy R. Brewer Boulevard. The vehicle then proceeds up Guy R. Brewer, crossing through Rochdale Village, then across through Baisley Housing.

As they pass through the housing area and across Foch Boulevard, they arrive next at Linden Boulevard. After making the right onto Linden, the driver is then instructed to make a rather quick left onto

O'Donnell Road, a dead end street. The vehicle is instructed to stop at a house along the rim of the cul de sac at the end of the block.

As the vehicle comes to a stop, Ezell exits, and is about to head towards the door on the side of the home. Before he departs to do so, he leans back into the vehicle and speaks to Gregory.

"I will be back in a minute."

Ezell goes to the door, knocks on it, waits a short while, then as the door suddenly opens, he goes inside the home. Ezell remains inside the home for about twenty minutes. After that, he exits back out of the home. He is now accompanied by another individual. Gregory instantly recognizes the individual for who he is. It is one of the older brothers of his mother, Dante. Both Dante and Gregory are quite pleased to see one another.

"Nephew! It's been too long. Just spoke to your mother the other day. I am glad and excited to see you. It's been way too long. Busy mutherfucka," he laughs, as he reaches out to hug Gregory.

"I see this is where I can find your ass at now, Unc! I'm on your trail now," Gregory also laughs.

In the background, Ezell receives a call on the mobile device given to him by the driver earlier.

"Hello? May I help you?... Yes, I do have the proposed flight plan. I am sending over now. Thank you."

Ezell then pulls a second device from out of one his pockets and begins to type into it. After a short series of texts, he puts the second mobile device into an internal pocket of his clothing, a different pocket from where he placed the phone given to him by his driver.

Dante puts the bag he carried out of the house with him into the rear of the vehicle as its tailgate opens up in front of him. After placing his duffle bag into the vehicle, he goes around to the rear passenger side door, opens it, and hops inside the vehicle smooth and spry like he isn't even close to being in his upper forties.

Ezell makes his way back to the rear driver's side door and climbs in himself. Gregory and Dante speak affectionately, catching up from the last time they had the opportunity to speak in person. Ezell tells the driver to pull off. The SUV makes its way back down the block and turns right onto Linden with the intention to follow the path previously travelled back towards the Belt Parkway.

As they finally reach it, Ezell instructs the driver, "Hit JFK, Man."

The driver nods and places his attention and awareness back into what is required to safely and proficiently traverse the infamously quick reacting New York City traffic. As they arrive at the junction between the Belt Parkway and the Van Wyck Expressway, the driver turns south on the Van Wyck and proceeds to the South Service Road, making their way towards the destination of General Aviation Layne.

As the vehicle turns into the parking lot adjacent to the hanger for the private jets, the driver grabs the two large duffle bags. Gregory takes one of them from him as they continue towards the building in between them and their flight. They sit in a corner of the lobby looking at some maps. They briefly discuss areas of interest as they await the attendant to inform them that their plane is ready to be boarded.

Chapter 5

"Bold Proposition"

The Maximus Attorney Strengthening Conference has come to a conclusion. It is a strong day at that. The conference was packed full of several hot, relevant, and more importantly, controversial topics. These topics prevented anyone in attendance from not having strong opinions and viewpoints, whether they were shared or kept silent and pinned up. The speakers also shared several emerging perspectives on what was taking place in the field, in addition to developing precedence and tactical approaches to the ever-occurring change and need for adaptation.

As fate would have it, Michael finds himself in mid-consumption of a cold beverage as both Sandra and Tanisha are making their way from the conference hall followed by their respective legal teams. They too find some delight, some surprise in running into Michael again amidst the several hundred people in attendance.

"There cannot be too many more coincidental meetings before I start to consider that there is a more deliberate and purposeful probability at play here, Mr. Crawford. I hope you're not that sloppy, all due respect and everything. I deduce all day. So, I can imagine you must as well," Sandra smirks, with inquisitive confidence to Michael.

Michaels laughs, "Ahh haa! So, I get a preview of your sense of humor, do I? That was charming, indeed. Next time, I will seek to avoid failing to file with the clerk's office of my intentions to enjoy something cold on a hot afternoon after a stuffy conference full of discussion that would leave the moistest of mouths parched. For that, I will perform better moving forward indeed.

"Now, if I may continue to say what I was originally compelled to say before your prompt and necessary reminder distracted me almost completely from saying, for several reasons the personal need I have for the avoidance of incriminating myself must not divulge: What time will we all be meeting for this evening's meal?"

The ladies look at each other in mid-blush. Sandra more so than Tanisha. But Tanisha is blushing because of her awareness as to why Sandra is blushing, although it is reluctantly beaming from her face. Their respective legal teams glance into their little positional triangle, all having been able to see Sandra far from her usual stoic self.

Sandra quickly collected her bearings and responded to Michael, "That's right. We did make preliminary arrangements for the evening, didn't we? Excuse me. I had forgotten that we had. I was distracted myself. We had a very active day with much discussion. We can meet in the lobby around seven thirty? Will that provide you enough time, Tanisha?"

"I believe so, Sandra. Will that work for you, Mr. Crawford? Seven thirty…?"

Michael drinks the last portion of his beverage before he places the canister into the trash receptacle behind him.

"That will work fine. Very well. I look forward to seeing you both in a few hours' time."

The three of them part ways. First, Michael. Then after a brief and lighthearted discussion, the two women go their separate ways into the hotel towards their accommodations. They seek to first relax and collect themselves after an interesting day in regards to what had been presented, and the discussions thereafter with the additional emphasis of preparing for what is to be an intriguing evening for sure.

Michael reaches into his jacket pocket and pulls out his mobile device. He continues to make a call. As he is walking through the front of the lobby on his way to exiting the building altogether, it is clear he has reached someone on the other end of the phone.

"Alert the sponsors. Their services will be needed as planned this evening," the voice on the other end of the phone says.

Then, as he ends that call, he continues to type into his device: Eric: Sponsor meeting set. Coordinate.

Smoothly, he places his device back into his jacket. All of this is done without causing him to miss a rhythm in his stride as he treads through the hotel with methodical purpose and cunning awareness towards his environment. His next destination is unknown. He simply steps outside the hotel, and his driver has purposefully just arrived at his location with impeccable timing. The kind of timing that draws attention all to itself due to the smooth synchronization of the two events moving so closely to one another. Not the usual thing by far. Certainly, not something typically seen in Milwaukee without screaming wealth of a proportion hardly seen.

He swiftly opens the rear passenger door, and just like that, he vanishes into the vehicle, leaving nothing left to see but the tail lights for anyone in the moment to catch how it all happened. Turn after turn, the vehicle makes its way through the somewhat bustling Wednesday afternoon mid-day traffic of their downtown section. Finally, the vehicle double parks. Michael reemerges from its rear cabin, out onto the street as he makes quick work of the distance between him and the destination's door.

Michael pulls the door open. He slides in between the cracked opening that was created. The atmosphere goes from the faint honking of horns and slight odors of exhaust fumes to the sultry sounds of jazz music and silverware colliding with ceramic plates and conversation. Upon recognizing Michael by face, the host quickly pounces in front of him to lead him back to the rear of the house where the manager had been sitting in his office in between tours of the dining hall and facilities.

"Good afternoon, Sir. I gather we will be accommodating you and your party this evening?"

"Yes, and good afternoon to you as well. Have you what I asked in place?"

"Sir, we have prepared your space as you have requested. If you wish, I can permit you to inspect all the elements of your request to ensure that they meet your specifications."

"Of course. Let's go and see what we have prepared."

The three men promptly exit the crowded office and embark on a hastened pace through the food preparation area through a series of rooms and hallways. They reach the private dining room set aside by the establishment for special occasions. As they reach the threshold of the room's door, Michael reaches into his pocket, grabs a manila envelope, and hands it over to the restaurant manager.

"This envelope is a specific set of instructions in addition to the ones you have already carried out. I will have my people come shortly upon my departure to execute them precisely and stand in place until I return this evening. This team of mine will not leave the establishment until I do this evening.

"As discussed, your discretion is expected as part of your compensation for the booking. Your hospitality in these matters is most appreciated, and we will hold our end of the deal on your behalf with that other thing as discussed."

As Michael hands off the manila envelope to the manager, he reaches back into his pocket and retrieves his mobile device. He dials a series of key strokes into the device, then applies it to his right ear.

"The room has been secured. Send in the tech unit to secure the premises for this evening," Michael orders.

He then turns and softly shakes the hand of the manager. Michael and the host leave the manager, and the host continues to escort Michael back to the front lobby by the bar. This is where Michael sits, enjoying a drink or two until he receives the notification on his phone that his team is in place, and the room has been secured for phase two.

He continues to slowly consume his beverage until there is nothing left but its straw. With the room full of a mixture of cologne, perfume, and the aroma of Italian sauces and seasonings filling the room, Michael lingers momentarily before he reaches into his pocket yet again to grab his phone and text a quick message.

He stands up from his barstool and grabs his jacket from where it had been hanging over the rear of the stool. He puts it back on. Just as he completes that task, the host acknowledges his appreciation over many things. Most of which is his patronage, however brief that it was before stepping aside and allowing him to move past him towards the door.

Michael gives the host a generous tip as he passes by. He does so discreetly through the cup-fashion, putting his palm to the host's palm, walking by one another.

Sealed with a firm and warm pat on the shoulder, Michael tells the host, "Thank You."

Similar to what took place at the hotel, Michael steps outside the restaurant. By the time he reaches the curb, his vehicle service has also arrived. Once inside the vehicle, Michael makes a few more stops in the vicinity before rounding back to the hotel. By now, nobody at the hotel remembers the slightly conspicuous fashion that would describe his earlier departure.

The city simply moves too fast to truly remember and hold a place to reconnect the two occurrences of his comings and goings. He exits the vehicle and hurriedly makes an immediate jaunt to his room. Once there, he gathers his belongings and packs them neatly into his travel bags. He walks over to the night stand and picks up the receiver off the telephone base.

"Hello, this is the front desk. How may we assist you today?"

"Well, yes. I do require the bellhop to come to room 587 to take my luggage down to my car."

"Not a problem at all. The bellhop has been dispatched and will be there shortly. Are you also checking out?"

"No. I will not be checking out just yet, but thank you for asking."

Michael returns to the lobby where he can see many people still meandering about as there is still about an hour and a half left in break before the conference resumes on its closing push. He goes to the hotel's restaurant hoping to find something quick to eat before returning. It does not take long at all for the host to find him a seat. Even less for his waiter to introduce himself.

"Bonjour monsieur, Parlez-vous français gentil monsieur?"

"Oui. Je fais, mais je préfère parler en anglais. Veuillez continuer comme vous le feriez en français. Ne me souciez pas de répondre en anglais. J'aime plutôt entendre votre français. Me donne beaucoup de souvenir de mon temps à Paris il y a longtemps."

"Tres bien Monsieur. C'est très apprécié par vous. Je m'appelle Jarad. Que puis-je vous faire boire aujourd'hui? Seriez-vous par hasard prêt à passer votre commande également? Si ce n'est pas pressé, prenez votre temps."

"Jarad, Nice to meet you, and yes, I would like some ginger ale on the rocks. As for my meal, I would like the crawfish po'boy sandwich."

"Très bien Monsieur. J'aurai ce droit. Merci de votre compréhension."

The waiter shuffles off into the kitchen first, then doubles back to the bar to grab his beverage. He returns almost instantly and delivers the beverage to him. As Michael finishes thanking him, he transitions into prowl mode and takes his own time to observe and survey the room around him into what he can also see of the lobby as well.

From there, he is able to see many of the lawyers he had come to recognize across the two days of the conference. He takes a degree of enjoyment watching the other men and women in his field of expertise go about the business of attending conferences and networking as they discuss their current caseloads and complain about the hours they have to work each week. He has not been directly in the usual swing of things for about two and a half years after making the moves he has been making with Eric.

He sits there sipping his ginger ale, reminiscing over the nostalgia that he enjoyed over his passion for the law, his firm, and how all of these elements truly were invigorating him all over again in Milwaukee of all places. He knew exactly what he was doing, what his role within it was and what was expected as a gain, an accomplishment in its predictable conclusions. The team, from its highest-ranking members to its soldiers on the ground, had been waiting for these events to move forward for a good while now.

He sips more of his drink until Jarad, the relatable French waiter, returns with his sandwich. There are a very arousing set of fragrances emanating from his plate. So much so that he is forced to pause for a moment.

"Thank you, Jarad."

"Mais bien sûr. S'il arrive un moment où vous décidez que vous avez besoin de quelque chose d'autre, n'hésitez pas à me faire signe. Voulez-vous autre chose à boire? Peut-être plus de Ginger-Ale?"

"Yes. This time, may I have both a ginger ale on the rocks and an orange juice without ice, please? You have been most helpful."

As Michael sits with his beverage, he pulls out his mobile device and logs into an app that permits him to securely communicate with his team in place at the restaurant. From there, he checks the status of the network link and texts a few concerns for security to his team.

What is left on the agenda for the conference is the closing speaker and the networking social. Michael remains in the bar area during the final keynote address. He listens to the speech via his mobile device as it is casted live over the intranet provided by the conference organization.

When the speaker concludes their time at the podium, several of the attendees start to depart the conference hall. This mass exodus results in a brief flooding of the lobby. Groups of them opt out of the networking segment that is to follow. Largely due to their predictable attempts at getting ahead of any presumed traffic that might ensue from so many people trying to leave the hotel around the same time.

Still, Michael remains where he is, sitting, drinking, and observing the crowds, hoping to spot either Sandra, Tanisha, or any of their respective staffs. Eventually, after a period of time elapses, a few recognizable figures begin to emerge into the hallway coming from the conference hall.

That's one of Tanisha's people, Michael thinks to himself. *There is another. And here come some of Sandra's people. They may have been all together as they were apparently departing,* Michael continues to contemplate.

He is correct. They had been leaving together. Now is the opportunity to confirm and reconstitute the enthusiasm amongst the parties for the meeting set to take place in just a few hours' time. Michael departs his table and makes his approach.

"Michael?" spoken softly by Sandra, as she maintains about as much professional bearing as she can muster.

Between herself and Tanisha ever so faintly between slight facial expressions, discreet smirks, and eye movements, it would suggest the two of them have a separate understanding of things regarding their opinion of Michael.

"I had just mentioned your name to Tanisha during the networking segment. We were looking forward to have seen you, and here you are out here."

"Yes. I admittedly chose to watch the final speaker give their speech over a drink and a light snack here at the bar. I was hoping to catch you both here like this as I was keeping a watchful eye over the traffic coming through the hallway. Definitely was trying to catch an opportunity to continue to build on our last conversation," Michael replies quickly.

"Michael, did you just admit to stalking the two of us and our staffs?" Tanisha quickly asks.

Michael clears his throat. "It would appear so, Ladies. You have me dead to rights. When you have a strong opportunity to fulfill so much within one campaign, I would be remiss not to utilize tactics some would consider…aggressive, even relentless. I will claim the accountability of being exposed there."

Both women take a unified moment to nod their heads in acknowledgement of his humility and accountability. Their slightly jovial conversation begins to return to its professional purposes.

"Noted, Mr. Crawford," begins Sandra.

"What are the plans for this evening? When will we get to be better briefed on your industrious proposal?"

"Hopefully to your collective taste and aesthetic approvals, I have arranged for us to first have a meal at a local establishment, then I will unveil the proposal. All that remains for the moment is to find out how much time do you both need to prepare? I have cars waiting when you give me the word to take you there and back if you have not yet checked out. They could also take either of you wherever you need to be upon the hopeful successful completion of my evening's agenda."

Sandra looks at Tanisha inquisitively. Tanisha returns the gesture. Both looking for some facial idiom that would quickly communicate to one another that would ideally go unbeknownst to Michael as they improvise a jointly agreeable decision without making it obvious. Finally, when this maneuver has failed to produce something within the window of being remotely inconspicuous, the women break silence.

"Well...I don't need much time. Will this offer be extended to just the two of us or to any members of our staff as well?" asks Sandra.

"The room fits twenty-five, so I think that should be enough for us all if you believe that everyone needs to attend. My conversation is aimed for the two of you. It makes little difference in who else is present as long as we can agree to respect confidentiality, and I don't say that to imply you do not have trustworthy staff. Just keep the communication between the designated parties."

"Understandable, Mr. Crawford. I do not have an issue with that concern. It is your proposition. You should have an idea of how it will best be conveyed and to what audience. I cannot speak for Tanisha, but what I can do is just bring a few of my staff. The others would not serve a purpose as you have suggested and would probably just rather go to their room and handle whatever details they need to have addressed before we depart the hotel and head back to the office in the morning."

Sandra, once finished, looks over to Tanisha, waiting for her to chime in on the matter.

"I agree. I will just bring a few with me as well and let the others go prepare for check-out in the morning. We can be ready in about a half an hour. If that works for either of you, I will go see to keeping that time and handle a few odds and ends before we meet in the lobby for your car to arrive," Tanisha replies.

"That works for me, too with the half an hour," Sandra agrees.

"Great, Ladies. I am grateful you both have been so accommodating in these matters. Even more the reason I am certain we can find a pathway to make what I have prepared to share with the team to come to fruition. I will clean things up at my table and get ready to join you both. I have two cars already awaiting instructions from you both. I will text that information shortly over to you so you can manage your own individual ride experiences."

The three come to an unspoken point of agreement and go on about conducting the business at hand. Michael returns to his table where he cleans up after himself.

"Excuse me…"

After a short-delayed response due to being slightly preoccupied with other guests, a staff member answers, "Yes, Sir?"

"Can I get a box and the check, please?"

"Yes. I will get that right now, Sir."

Michael collects his belongings. With some of his sandwich still hanging from the side of his mouth, he begins to make his exit of the hotel.

The evening grows darker as the effect of what was last seen of the sun has finally faded for that day. The sounds of traffic filling the background vehicles traverse the city. Michael's vehicle arrives to the valet area. His keys are politely handed to him, and his door opens. He then begins to place his collection of belongings into the rear seat. He hops into the driver's seat before he quickly darts off away from the hotel.

Michael makes a stop to freshen up and change clothing. When he finishes this task, he makes his way to the restaurant to meet with his team and check on the operation status of the network and so on to include other areas of concern before his guests are to arrive and the meeting is to begin without interruption or flaw.

The host and the manager of the restaurant meets him at the rear entrance to the building as he enters.

"Good evening, Mr. Crawford. We are on schedule, and the room is just as you left it. The kitchen has a cook dedicated to fulfilling any orders that would come from just your room. I have also set aside two bus staff to see that there will be zero delays or interruptions to a high-quality demonstration to service," says the manager.

"We were thinking that it would be more suitable for the ambiance set aside for you and your guests to have them utilize the rear and private entrance when they arrived. Your thoughts on this?" asks the host, looking on for both Michael's and the manager's approval.

"That's actually not a bad idea at all. That will definitely work for me. Can this be carried out without causing an undue strain for your crew?" Michael responds to the host while asking the manager the follow-up question. "My guests should be starting to arrive in about thirty to forty minutes. Please have your people escort them from the rear entrance as suggested into the dining room. Here are pamphlets I would like each of them to receive upon entering the hallway to the dining room.

"I will be in the kitchen, and I will remain there until I get a confirmation from my team that both cars arranged to transport my guests have arrived and they have been fully escorted into the dining room," Michael continues.

"Yes, Mr. Crawford. If these are your wishes and instructions, then this is what will take place. We appreciate your business and support of our business," remarks the manager.

As they speak, one of Michael's tech team walks in and begins to set up a very small but tall tripod. Another team member hurries in, running a few cables to the tripod's base and up long its pole, then placing a medium sized monitor on its apex. The two continue to set the monitor up. They start the video feed of the rear entrance hallway leading from the entrance to the door of the designated dining room for their meeting as well as the dining room was in full display. All is done rather quickly and effectively efficient.

Michael and the manager continue to speak as the manager is slightly distracted with the swiftness of his tech team in the demonstration of their expert competence. The manager is also astounded in how none of this activity even seems to register across Michael's facial expression. Michael is unfazed, like this is all normal.

A third tech team member rushes into the corner of the spare kitchen where Michael and the manager are and brings a tall bar stool that has a cushioned seat with a cushioned backrest. The tech positions it right to the side of Michael, appropriately positioned in front of where the tripod was just erected.

Michael then gestures with his fingers to one of his tech team to engage with one of the kitchen staff. When the tech team member does so, he understands what is being communicated. This becomes obvious when the culinary staffer brings Michael a simple roll sliced open with some type of meat and sliced cheese within it. The staffer also brings a small apple juice pouch.

The video feed is now live. Michael sits on his bar stool and eats through the small four-bite sized sandwich he was given as he watches for the arrival of his guests. The tech team leader enters into the kitchen.

"Vehicle one is four minutes out. Vehicle two is at an estimated six minutes out."

"That is what I wanted to know. Thanks," Michael says, as he pats the tech team leader on the shoulder.

His team leader hands him a small short band radio for further communications before he departs the room. With the pouch of apple juice becoming constricted from the force of the vacuum being created within itself as Michael sucked its contents beyond dry, and producing that increasingly loud but familiarly distinctive sound of the pouch crumbling into itself, Michael watches the first car pull up to the rear door.

"It's a go, Sir," remarks the team leader.

"Roger that, Team Leader. Let's get them in nonchalantly. They are not to know all of us are here. May shake them up," replies Michael.

"Copy that."

The vehicle's driver's side door opens, and the driver walks around the vehicle to open both rear passenger doors to allow the occupants of the rear of the vehicle to exit the vehicle. One by one, the four guests proceed to follow the host into the building as they peer around the rear of the building and entrance. After being escorted through the hallway, the occupants of the first car are now entering into the dining room. It is Tanisha and her group who arrive first.

By the time they are finding their desired locations to sit, the second vehicle, presumably Sandra's vehicle, has arrived. Once Sandra and her group are escorted into the dining room, the host enters in once again to ascertain as to what will be drunken by whom. Michael remains in the kitchen observing.

"It is time, Team One," Michael softly speaks into the handheld radio.

He then departs his barstool just as two tech team members break down both the chair and tripod faster than in which it took them to erect both structures. Michael tosses the crumbled-up pouch he was just drinking through into the trashcan by the side of the door. Taking the servers' tunnel to the room, he enters with his hands stretched out to welcome his guests.

"Welcome! Your presence here tonight is most appreciated. Now that we are here, I must inform you that I am speaking to you all as an agent for the interests of my clients. They have retained my services to broker an arrangement to initially just seek out excellence in the field of civil rights litigation. Without a mere shadow of any doubt, this is who you all are and what you represent in my esteemed opinion.

"Since our initial meeting, I have taken the time based on the powerfully positive first impressions made to conduct a very thorough research into only your legal careers, private practice, and with your respective firms. My research vindicated my first impression and validated my value to my clients for having an eye for remarkable legal skill as well as talent.

"I stand before you all and your senior partners and feel honored to be at this moment in our time in this life. I feel the chills like perhaps that of those in the presence of Martin Luther King and Rosa Parks as they strategized their iconic next moves. I do believe what is on deck is just as revolutionary to the overall cause and intention of our forefathers into fighting for all of our collective civil rights."

Just about each guest move and

shift about into their seats as Michael speaks.

"First, as you all think on the framework of the purpose explained briefly as to why you were invited here tonight, I want you to relax and remember it has been a rigorous couple of days here at the conference. Please allow the wait staff to serve you this evening's meal. During which time we can further discuss the purpose of our gathering."

With that being said, Michael walks up to greet Sandra first. After shaking her hand, he then turns to Tanisha and does the same. Once those personal exchanges are complete, he leaves the room behind the multitude of servers coming and going also through the tunnel that leads directly to the kitchen.

Pro forma to the normality of the field, Sandra, Tanisha, and the group of their respective peers take their attention from fervent curiosity in what their host had to share in regards to the purpose of the evening to delight in perusing through the decadent menus provided to them by the wait staff. The group grows more relaxed and comfortable, with drinks being ordered in moderation and excitement to choose their entre from the tempting menu.

When the food comes out, so does Michael. He has the remains of a second sandwich hanging on the corner of his mouth before his finger places the last piece back into his mouth. The group grows excited to eat seeing their food closer to being set in front of them.

"I hope the food is to your liking!"

He sits in a seat set to the side by a separate table by his team. One of the wait staff brings out a modest house salad and some honey mustard dressing on the side.

"Would you like croutons, Mr. Crawford?"

"No, thank you, Ma'am."

Forks are making contact with plates and the group is enjoying their meals. There is laughter and light conversation.

"What do you feel is needed to gain some traction, some progress in what we are seeing in regards to putting an effective end to police brutality?" Michael asks both Tanisha and Sandra.

"With what just happened in Utah and Idaho more recently, I am curious," continues Michael.

Realizing that he does not want to interrupt their ability to respond, he leans back into his seat as he winces his eyes and pokes out his mouth to show he does actually realize it is their time to respond.

"Good to be curious. Lord knows I myself and those of my firm have that very question on all of our collective minds, Michael. The issue has not changed. Challenging individual incidents is one thing of the normal process of tort litigation. Where as to achieve constitutional change at the federal level then to mirror that success on the individual state level has always been the true issue and quagmire of civil rights. The field saw sweeping advancement decades ago, but haven't seen any substantial growth in the blight of police brutality from the onset of this legal crusade," responds Sandra.

"I agree, Sandra. These are longstanding issues that do not seem to have simple or easily accessible solutions at the moment. I believe we are closer now than we have been before due to the recent increase in polarization of so many blatant examples of brutality across the nation. We just as an industry need to find a collective approach to take to Washington. Sponsor the drafting of new robust and more importantly 'effective' legislative documents that can be then lobbied into strong bills that can in turn develop into actual enforceable laws that will then need to have the equivalent degree of scrutiny placed upon their enforcement through more lobbying to see it all the way through the gate into normalcy. Then take that success to each state and see it through. Then and only then we stand to finally vindicate the efforts initiated by many of our foremothers and forefathers who had far less access and significantly less education," replies Tanisha.

"Wow! I knew you guys were sharp. My research said you were; your respective command presence has confirmed that as well. Now that we get to sit here and actually communicate on this subject, I am getting the chills while listening to the collective passion and intelligence in how you both convey your legal brilliance. Truly, this is a rewarding moment. I agree with you both.

"I agree with you both to such a high degree of accuracy. What would either of you care to tell me if I told you that accomplishing the totality of what you both just shared is why I essentially brought you here? No, no, no. I mean what if I told you that I came here to find legal minds such as yours to share just the exact opportunity to create just such a series of accomplishments?

"I, again, represent a client that has arranged for you to collaborate between your two firms into the endeavor of creating the infrastructure for just the exact groundbreaking set of legislative goals. My client has also taken great lengths to collaborate with many influential and wealthy investors to make the retainer for such work a fund like the likes of most law firms have rarely seen if ever for such an undertaking. Leaving no stone unturned in the process. But if you should discover one as a potential stone to be turned, let it be known, and it will be!" Michael chuckles.

"Before I turn the conversation over to more qualified minds, are you at least interested?" Michael asks. "I know that you cannot express any official levels of commitment without conferring with your partners. But before we can continue, I will need everyone present to fill out and sign these non-disclosure agreements for what will be discussed. My notary is here and will stamp each of your documents as you sign them and present identification."

Michael's team leader then unsheathes his license and stamp case. Once each document has been filled out, signed, and stamped, Michael instructs his notary to collect the documents and store them appropriately. He does just that. Then, Michael uses the radio given to him earlier.

"Bring me the big screen," Michael says softly.

A few seconds later, another member of his team brings out a rather large sixty-five inch television screen on a cart without any wires to be easily seen. As that team member tinkers briefly with the remote, another team member brings Michael a tablet. Michael utilizes that tablet to connect and control the functionality of the television on the cart.

"Thank you. Please dim the lights now," Michael requests.

As the room grows less lit, Michael goes through a serious of screens after he successfully casts the screen of his tablet to the television.

"Ladies and Gentlemen, are you ready for the next step? I just want your undivided attention before I begin."

No one objects to the commencement of what is to come next, so Michael initiates the control device to open the desired application on the tablet— a teleconferencing application. When the application comes fully online, there are seven active participants to the conference waiting on their arrival into the room.

When the group in the room is able to see just who these seven individuals are, each and every one of them are astounded. Some grab their table napkins attempting to clean any food that is still clinging to their faces while others seek to straighten out their attire and ensure they are more presentable.

"Ladies and gentlemen of the board, please address the group. I believe they are eager to hear the proposition we have been brought together here to share with them."

Chapter 6

"Atlanta"

As his jet taxies into the hanger at the signature terminal of Atlanta's Hartfield International Airport, Eric shuffles through his phone with focus. He grabs his windbreaker jacket and begins to check his ears to ensure that his discrete earbuds are secure in place. Eric exits the plane.

Once outside, he first looks around the area. He is able to see clearly in the hanger with curiosity and observance. Then he takes his first step followed by several more down the flight of stairs to the ground with a distinct rhythm. His transportation is already parked in the hanger.

A meek, studious woman exits his vehicle wearing a dark blue knit business skirt with a light blue pin striped dress blouse and dark blue heels. Her hair is long and curly. She has an attractive face adorned with a deep maroon lipstick.

She walks over to Eric. She hands him the keys to the discrete non-luxury sedan before she continues to walk past him and into the rear passenger seat of the fully tinted town car that is parked in the hanger on the side of the sedan she got out of.

Eric takes the keys and without hesitation opens the vehicles driver's side door. He climbs into its cabin and presses lightly onto the gas pedal, causing the vehicle to loudly purr its engine. He repeats the action one more time before he applies his seat belt, grabs his wallet out of his pocket, and places it in the center console for easier access.

One of the technicians in the hanger brings his luggage— a single duffle bag— out to the car and places it into the trunk as Eric is playing with his gas pedal and the vehicle's engine. Shortly after he does so and recloses the trunk, Eric places the gear into reverse and departs the hanger, throwing out a friendly gesture of acknowledgement with his hands to the technician as he drives past him.

He quickly speeds through the initial area of the front side of the hanger. He makes his way onto Toffie Terrace as he scoots along. On Inner Loop Road, he finds his way to Virginia Avenue where he makes a left and into the city limits of College Park. By this time, he shuffles through his phone and dials in a contact for his phone to call. It is Johnny Garneir. After a few chimes of the ringtone to play, the call is answered.

"Hey, Big E! I was wondering when I was going to get the call. I figure you just touched down, huh?"

"Yeah, that's right. Not far at all from where D told me we'd be linking up at, too."

"Well, shoot! Pull into the garage in the backyard. There is a stairwell I had put in when I got the place that leads to the basement where we are at. It was a real bitch putting all that concrete in, too without bringing a ton of eyes on what we were doing over here. When you get down the tunnel, just open the door. I can see you anyway once you enter the tunnel," Johnny laughs.

"Alright. Say less. I will see you in a minute."

Eric follows the instructions provided and pulls into the yard. He drives around the circular driveway to the adjacent driveway that leads to the rear of the house. Once there, he proceeds down the staircase under the storm door lid. Eric finds himself navigating a dimly lit cement framed corridor. He can't help but notice that along its ceiling, there are ports for exhaust. He finds it peculiar given that the design seems like it was poured concrete.

He continues to walk the gauntlet until he finally arrives at the steel door blocking any further travel. He quickly realizes that he still has his ear buds logged in his ears. He takes them out and returns them to their case, and then puts that case in the interior pocket of his windbreaker. He pulls on the cold steel handle of the unusually large steel door that is twice as wide as any normal door he is accustomed to seeing in the civilian side of life.

Customary goes out the window in his mind as he looks around the bomb shelter tunnel he was in, in Southwest Atlanta of all places. As he finds himself slightly tested in pulling the door away from its frame far enough to create an opening for him to walk into, he sees Johnny and several of his friends. They're sitting around a table that on one side is a wall littered with about ten medium sized screen television monitors. The very thin kind. Whereas the other side of the room is a series of lockers and equipment to perform maintenance functions next to a door that looks like a munition's locker. His associates are dressed in a mixture of different color neatly creased battle dressed uniforms and BDUs.

"There he is! Did you like my bunker tunnel system?" Johnny laughs. "When was the last time I saw you? It had to be when we all were in L.A. for that Lakers game against the Knicks."

"Johnny, why are you playing with me? You know damn well we didn't see no damn Knicks game in L.A. Like we gonna go all the way out there to watch them get washed. We last was together on that rooftop in West Baltimore when Philando opened that corner store. When you almost fell off the roof because you tripped over that dark colored bottle none of us saw until you tripped over it. Dontre is the one who was next to you and caught you."

"Ahh!" Johnny shouts rather loudly. "Okay. You got a real good memory, Bro! Too damn good if you ask me," Johnny remarks, as he shakes his head in disappointment. "Welcome to the A! Dontre wouldn't tell me what you have going on over the phone. Seemed important. So why don't you fill me in?"

"Not a problem. I know you. I don't know your friends. We need to talk in private. What do you have down here, Man? A freaking wartime arsenal? Stay ready so you never have to get ready, huh?"

"Without a doubt. You taught your brother, and he taught me!"

"Well, let's go check out this locker you have here as we kick it for a few."

Eric flings his left arm ahead of him, between himself and Johnny, gesturing for him to lead the way since it is his bunker. Johnny laughs, then lets out a partially deep sigh as he looks upon his friends with a look of slight embarrassment as he leaves where they had been off towards the munition's locker room.

"Wow, you really out did yourself with this. What don't you have in here? M-4s, A-Rs, M-16s, AK-47s! Nice! You have a whole crate of those FN-F2000s! Very impressive. Before I get any further distracted in this militia wonderland, yes, I have something huge taking place.

"Only family in on this one from the strategy board. No one else. There is way too much at stake to gamble on unknowns. My very being here in your home, or one of them, is a detriment to you and yours. We will need plausible deniability, and after we link up today, we need to scatter the breadcrumbs far and wide. All over the damn place because they will be coming behind me. It won't be immediately, but eventually. When they finally do get around to checking under this stone, we don't want anything here that can lead them to another stone if you pick up what's being put down, J.

"Sounds heavy, Bro. What the hell you got going on, Family? This sounds interesting like a motherfucker.

"I know. Interesting ain't got shit on this. This is the sort of thing that leaves a scar that stays forever. Forever on the face of the B.S. we been dealing with as a people for before any of us was born into this world.

"Alright, alright. Tell me already, Big Bro. I'm going crazy waiting."

Eric leans into his right ear as he put his right hand on Johnny's left shoulder. He whispers into his ear for about five minutes. Almost with each word uttered, Johnny's facial expressions go from visible variants, ranging from mild shock to full on astonishment.

"Hell yeah! Let's make this happen, Bro! What exactly do you need from me?"

"I am glad you asked. What I need from you is to make some friends. Friends that can facilitate some areas of the game plan. In such a way that even after several contingencies, we will still have plausible deniability when the alphabet boys come through. Because it will not be a matter of it they will. It will definitely be a matter of when."

"Alright, E. Say less. I know some of the old crew that's still scattered around the A. Many of their contacts will fit that bill, and we can play off one another just like old times. Your brother taught us well and did right by you in the process. They'd love to be associated with you just because of Dontre. Let's hit a few corners."

Eric leads this time as the two men depart from the gun laden equipment locker. The group of Johnny's associates are still patiently waiting when they remerge. It is at this moment that Johnny speaks.

"I'm out. I'll be back later this evening, pending traffic. Finish what we had got started, and when I get back, we can move onto the next one."

Afterwards, it is apparent that Johnny has forgotten something. He speaks to one of his people, "Grab me the grey duffle."

One of his smaller associates with a gold tooth raises his eyebrows at the mentioning of the color, and then walks off quickly to one of the rear rooms Johnny didn't get to show Eric. After a moment or two, he returns and tosses the bag to Johnny once he is about seven feet away from where he is standing.

"You can leave your car here. My guys will move it discretely into the front garage. Or better yet, we can have it driven back to a place you'd find more appropriate. Plus, we can't be seen where we headed in that thing no how," Johnny says, shaking his head in disapproval.

"That's fine. It was just a rental, more or less. I like the service, Li'l Bro. In and out, real smooth. Just how I like things."

Eric follows Johnny as he climbs a few flights of stairs into the main foyer of the home. Through the foyer, they pass through the contemporary designed kitchen making their way into the main garage. Upon Eric's entrance into the garage, he is impressed to see what Johnny is eager to show him to be their method of transportation as they hit the next series of streets along their path to move along with Johnny's area of involvement in his plan. A 1963 tan on gold Buick Skylark with the soft pearl convertible top. The classic Dayton's rims at about twenty inches wide with the Vols tires to match. It definitely makes for a sweeter ride than what he rode in with.

"You like this one?"

"Yeah, it's real nice."

"Let me have my guy bring your bag from the back up here."

Johnny shoots a text, and within a few minutes, one of his guys come to the garage door from the same kitchen door with Eric's bag from the trunk of his car. The friend walks to the trunk. As Johnny presses the bottom to open it, he places both of their duffle bags into it and closes it.

Johnny disappears back into the house as the garage door is sliding open as the motor engages from Johnny pressing the pad on the clicker he has in his hand that is attached to the keys. They leave the garage, and soon after that, the property. With the music blaring classic blues hits of the seventies and sixties, the two make their way along Main Street into East Point.

"We got one local stop, and we out."

"No problem. Do your thang. You got point on this one."

They turn off Main Street onto Irene Kidd Parkway. They make the right onto Gus Thornhill. They slowly turn right onto Harris Street before making their final left onto Washington Road. The destination Johnny is seeking is next to the corner lot, near the intersection. After they shut off the music, they pull up the hill into the yard and park the vehicle under the car port. Then they exit the vehicle and walk up to the door under the car port. Johnny knocks on the white, but stained, metal screen door.

Behind it is a solid six panel wooden door. After both of them wait under the carport for someone to answer the door, it takes no longer than a minute that the wooden door is slung open. Instantly, the aroma of popcorn is strongly identifiable from within the home. A rather stocky built African American male stands before them. His facial expression goes from being obviously surprised at the also obvious interruption to relief as he squints briskly before he fully recognizes Johnny standing in front of him.

"What do we have here? You standing at my door? In broad daylight at that? This must be good. You know we are not supposed to be around one another. Seen being around one another is the main thing."

"So, you know this is real then. Shut up and let me in so we can get this over with. If I could have called you, I would have. I know you wouldn't answer that call, so I came over so we can chop this up!"

With sudden agreeance across his face, he stands aside and allows them entry into his home as he looks each and every way around from the doorway in case anyone is paying attention to their arrival. He is not alone. He and his son are watching a movie. It is obvious they have come to a pivotal part because the film has been paused, and his son is leaning at the edge of the couch waiting on the return of his father.

On top of the television is a small glass box on a base frame. Inside of it is an ankle bracelet monitor. The kind that is placed on a person's ankle while under house arrest. The base frame has an engravement. Both Johnny and Eric gaze over it as they walk through the living room and past the television in mid pause. The inscription reads, "Never again".

"Tell me what it is, Johnny. I figure it's something big because you're here. I figure it is something serious because you have this guy with you. I can't put my finger on the name, but he looks really familiar, so I know I know his kinfolk. I know I do. What is this all about? You see we just sitting here getting some quality time in before he starts to smelling himself like we all do at around that age."

"Okay, okay. Look. You nailed it. Flat on its head. This doesn't get any bigger than anything we've ever done or spoke on. You happy now?"

"I already knew it. Too many random parts to this visit. Go on, Bro. Keep going."

"Well, let's go to the other room. This is your ears only stuff. I want you in on this. But you will not be a direct part nor a key role. Just not directly involved because I know you done with that side of things these days. I know you still have your network and connects, so that's what we need. You can say no, but I need you to say yes. I know that you can be trusted either way."

"Stop stalling. C'mon. Follow me then. Give me a few, Zion. I'll be right back. Don't do me dirty."

The man leads them both back deeper into the house, into what looks like an office converted from a spare bedroom. He closes the door behind them all and gestures for them to have seats in the two chairs. He sits behind his desk and pushes his seat back up against the wall as he leans slightly back.

"Out with the thing, Johnny. You're torturing me, and you know this."

"First, not to be rude, this is Eric. You should see his face as familiar. This is Dontre's older brother from New York. Eric, this is Tim.

"Tim, Eric does have a gigantic move that is serious and unlike any shit you've heard before. It's freakin' bold, and it is going to require all imaginable and some unimaginable hands on deck to make it happen.

"Eric has a plan that makes it look like a walk in the park. He has a contingency plan like seven anomalies deep. All that I am asking is that you first hear him out, then hear what your role is in it all. After that, if you with it, then you're with it. If not, you already know what I need from you at that point."

Johnny's face becomes grim as he speaks the last part. Apparently, communicating something more than just words as he speaks them. His face becomes sterner as he speaks again.

"This is for all the marbles, Dude. What's it gonna be?"

Tim sits and looks at Eric as he twists his face up slightly. He then looks in the direction of the door as if to consider Zion and the household as he thinks momentarily.

"We good. Tell me," Johnny says, with a stern look emerging of his own in his expression back at Johnny.

Eric looks at them both discretely. He acts like the fly on the wall to a certain extent as they go back and forth as awkwardly as they were. He figures the awkwardness is in relation to a code that exists between them both in regards to the fidelity of their discretion and silence or the eventual secrecy of whatever was discussed. This is a positive thing to see. Something he already knows Johnny understands the utter importance of.

Johnny grips his hands on the ends of the rails of his chair. "Alright," he says, and gets up from his chair to walk over to Tim who is still sitting.

Tim looks at this with shock, and then he looks over to Eric to see if he is shocked as well to better gauge how shocked he ought to be. Johnny makes it around the desk, leans into Tim's ear, and begins to speak softly into it. As he does, Tim's facial expression becomes more blushed the more Johnny continues to speak. He looks upon the face of Eric with the same slightly intensifying execution of his facial reactions. As Johnny senses these occurrences, he continues to speak. While he turns his eyes over at Eric, watching his reaction to watching Tim's facial cues sent towards him makes Johnny nod, then turn backs to Tim. Whatever he says to him next produces a completely solemn look upon Tim's face. It is then that Tim nods his head once more, then pulls back away from Johnny and gives him a hand-dap type of handshake.

"On. We gonna do this, and y'all gonna make that happen. I'm with you, Bro."

Johnny, after embracing his handshake, leans in again after saying, "This is what I need you to do."

Then just like that, Tim stands up, the two men share a hug preceded by an additional handshake-dap, then they separate and walk towards the door. Eric stands up and follows them. When they arrive at the door, Tim stands holding the door, allowing the two of them to exit as he closes the door behind them. Both Eric and Johnny walk through the home, back through the living room, and out of the door.

On his way through the living room, Johnny gives a similar handshake-dap to Zion who embraces him as he walks close to the door before he leaves. Tim looks at Johnny, then Eric, and nods his head in a symbol of acceptance and agreeance with them both.

Tim says, "Eric, good to meet you. Your brother brought us all up around here— our crew anyways. He is a real dude. I respect him, and I won't let either of you down. Johnny, I will hit you through the usual channels moving forward."

Johnny hops over the door frame of the vehicle still exposed by the convertible top being let down on the vehicle into the driver's seat. Eric walks around the rear of the vehicle. Johnny has already started its engine.

They pull out of the driveway and back onto the road. They make their way back onto Main Street and take it north until it becomes Lee Street. They continue on Lee Street until that turns into West Whitehall Street South West. Eric enjoys the music and the journey through Atlanta's historic core neighborhoods. They're ethnically historical for both civil rights history as well as amongst the strong hip hop culture that has been bred here over the last thirty years that creates music unique to any other in the genre.

Curious still, Eric taps Johnny on the shoulder, and Johnny turns the music down as they come to a stoplight at the intersection of West Whitehall and Ralph David Abernathy Boulevard.

"Tim was looking squeamish back there for a few moments. How did you turn that around? Do you believe that he can be relied upon? Not just to make it happen, but later when the dogs come sniffing around? That ankle bracelet and that inscription may be an indicator that he may not be ready to step up for this move…"

Johnny moves his mouth as to consider what Eric has said before he responds to the heart of his curiosity.

"I reminded him of what life would be like for him without the support of his community. Any community. We have all taken some loses. Some more than others for works in the past. Works he is still benefiting from. His family benefits, too. I just reminded him that his indirect involvement, although crucial, will not be the degree of involvement that should leave him forgetful to what is at stake if he folds. Whether he puts in the work we require or not. He saw the big picture.

"Dontre's name holds weight here in Atlanta. His name holds weight in many circles connected to the several circles here alone. Your name is hallowed here because Dontre let it be known. He remembered. We don't leave no one behind. Never have done it, won't ever do it. He will be reliable. If we need to establish a contingency in the event that may not be the case, so be it. But he will have to make his mark either way."

Eric looks at Johnny. There is silence. Eric looks up and away as to think about what Johnny said, and then he nods his head in return before turning the music back up just as the light turns green again. Johnny makes a left at the light once green, and they drive past the infamous "Peaches" strip club before they make the right back onto Lee Street South West. From there, they take the right turn veering onto the onramp towards the Ralph David Abernathy Freeway heading eastbound on I-20.

"We need to see one more guy while you're here for that additional impact of your presence. Then I will take you back to your jet. I know you got to keep it moving out here," Johnny tells Eric.

"Okay. Cool."

Eric sends a series of text messages out with his mobile device to have the plane and flight plan prepared for his next departure in advance.

Johnny and Eric proceed along I-20 until they come to exit "60B" which is Moreland Avenue, northbound towards Little Five Points. As their vehicle travels up Moreland again, Eric just takes the time to soak in the energy of the cities he bounces between as Johnny jots through one area to the next. Eric takes extra delight in watching the members of the community just coming and going along with their day-to-day lives as he contemplates what he is about to undertake on their collective behalf. On behalf on the frustrations of so many who look like himself here and in other cities similar to this one across the country and in many respects across the globe as a whole.

When the vehicle approaches the intersection of Mansfield Avenue North East and Moreland Avenue, the light again switches to yellow, and then finally red, stopping traffic north and south bound on Moreland, while opening up movement east and west along Mansfield.

Johnny takes his right hand and pulls down on the vehicle's turn signal lever. The light turns green again. Johnny turns right onto Mansfield slowly as he turns down his music and brings the convertible top back over the top of the vehicle. When their path comes across Felder Avenue Northeast, Johnny makes a left and then pulls the vehicle to the curb just shy of the corner of Felder Avenue and Druid Place Northeast.

Johnny and Eric both exit the vehicle. Johnny presses a button on his after-market remote start and alarm keypad; it chimes rather distinctly. Johnny recognizes and is recognized by a walker-by as he does these things. They embrace and exchange a dap-hand-shake-hug before Johnny asks the man, "Is Lewis in there?"

"I am sure he is. You know what time it is right now. If he isn't up there, I am sure he isn't far from finding his way here."

With that, both Johnny and Eric take to the corner as they approach it and the entrance of the yard that sits across from Freedom Park. There are about ten individuals already standing around in the yard congregating amongst themselves. Seeing this, Johnny takes his mobile device out and sends a single text with it before he puts it right back into his pocket. Moments after that text has been sent, the door is opened wide, and Lewis sticks his head out of it.

"Johnny? C'mon!" Lewis shouts.

Lewis' declaration of acknowledgement doesn't get any reaction from the group of men and some women standing in his driveway or sitting on his steps as he speaks. Johnny looks up, nods his head to acknowledge his invitation, and he and Eric follow Johnny into the yard and up into the house. Once inside, it is clear that the crowd is merely a part of the small party he apparently has going on within his home.

There is a basketball game on the television, and the festivities seem to be centered around the television. Lewis gestures for the both of them to have a seat on one of the couches with open spaces. The game is in its fourth quarter. They both sit and watch the remainder of the game with the modest sized crowd. Eric looks on and is again slightly nostalgic over how the group in his house is obviously enjoying one another's company like many house parties he witnessed as a child long ago.

He takes additional moments to take in discretely and inconspicuously the way so many of the people would smile, laugh, joke, and move about in happy energies all the same. He is blissful despite his stoic demeanor. Eric is well aware it may certainly be some time before he would be so carefree and without the concerns that will soon be his only reality. Despite all of his trainings and experiences that lend him great advantage in these forecasted dealings to come, he just decided months ago that during these kinds of moments and the opportunities they present, he was going to stop and smell as many of the roses and their individual petals as he realistically could within pragmatically applied reason.

The game continues. It is close. The score is close, coming in to the final two minutes at 98 to 103. As the nail biter game comes to a climactic end, the crowd grows excited and reacts with celebration. There is drinking and hugging, shouting and high-fiving.

Johnny gets up and whispers into Lewis's ear. Once he does, Lewis gets up, grows serious in his face, and invites them to come with him to the rear of the house. Once there, they descend down the staircase that lays behind the opened door by Lewis. Down in the basement, there is a finished set of spaces that is surprisingly quiet from the commotion taking place upstairs.

"Johnny, what you got going on?" Lewis asks, curiously.

"There is about to be a move made so bold that if you don't play a part, you won't ever forgive yourself for not doing so. Straight like that. I know you, and you know me. This is as real as it gets. All real OG hands on deck. There is the old code applied: If I tell you, I may have to kill you. Secrecy is not even a game. You've proven your integrity with me, out here, everywhere. This isn't a test; it's a call."

"Drop it on me," Lewis replies.

Johnny stands up and walks over to him. Putting his arm over and around his shoulder, he speaks swiftly into Lewis' ear. Eric can see vividly that Lewis is instantly excited as he pounds his fist into his other hand with high enthusiasm. Quickly, he leaves from under the arm of Johnny and runs up into the personal space of Eric and gives him a powerful handshake, dap, and hug as he pounds on his back in high approval.

"I'm all over it!" is what Lewis says.

Johnny grabs him and speaks. "I will hit you through the usual channels as to how and when I need you to move, moving forward."

"Not a problem! You let me know whatever whenever! Yeah, Boy!" Lewis exclaims, pacing back and forth in a short-repeated path.

"Did you speak to Tim, too? He a little skittish, with reason, but his resourcefulness is top notch," Johnny says.

"Yes. I saw him first."

"Good we got the A on this level of it, Man."

With that, Johnny, Eric, and Lewis shake hands, then Johnny and Eric head back up the stairs with Lewis trailing. They maneuver back to the car and head back down to the airport hangar. Eric gets a text message while in Lewis' basement that his plane will be ready in two hours for take-off.

"Come with me to Detroit, Johnny. I have a few crews already in place. After that, we can hit the other spots on my short list. What do you say? I will have you back in a few days," Eric says.

"Damn. I'm with it. Let's roll through my other house so I can grab some things?"

"Whatever you need we can grab on the road. Better off getting a taste of moving like that, minus the jet, in preparation for what's to come. I don't want you that entangled, but if that becomes the case, better off knowing you got the basics from me on how I do this. Again," Eric says, laughing, "minus the jet."

Johnny agrees, laughs with Eric, then makes a few texts as they continue onto I-20 en route to the airport. Detroit it is.

Chapter 7

"Proper Channels"

It is a partly cloudy, but remarkable day with still an enormous amount of visible sunlight as Ezell, Gregory, and their commercial flight touch down onto the tarmac of Los Angeles International Airport. The sky, even through the small and limited view bubbles they call windows, is bright and vibrant. As the two wait for the signal from the flight attendant crew to prepare to disembark their plane, already Ezell is reaching for his phone.

His first move is to pull his earpiece from out of his jacket pocket. Once he does so, he logs the piece securely into his left earlobe. Ezell reaches into his pocket, searches with his fingers for his mobile device, grabs it, and begins to press upon its screen. Gregory puts his left hand across the front of Ezell's body gently with some minimal degree of force as he presses upon his chest with his forearm. Ezell takes slight exception to this gesture silently with just a facial expression that appears to be waiting for the communication to explain his reactions. Gregory's only response is to take the middle finger on his right hand and touch his thumb with; his index finger stretches out and slightly waves back and forth as he gestures for Ezell to be patient for a few more moments before he makes whatever call he was preparing to make.

Gregory looks around and finds the time as an opportunity to pull out another phone from the inside of his thin jacket. Gregory grabs a small package that contains a new SIM card. While balancing the two, he breaks open that package. Still balancing the items between both hands with delicate and meticulous care, he then pops open the side port on the new phone to expose the SIM card tray from within it. He places the new SIM card inside the tray and pushes it back in discretely.

He keeps an eye on his surroundings for any potential passenger spending more time than need be over observant of what he was happening to be doing with a vigil and keen awareness. When he completes that task, he grabs the phone in an unusual fashion. He grabs it with an awkward grip as he applies a slightly enhanced emphasis in the position of his grip. This action hard reset the device and the screen begins to undertake a process of reboot unlike a typical reboot cycle.

Gregory continues to press the screen as different prompts appear. Once he is done, he turns the device off and restarts it. Once that is done, he takes the packaging that he has in his hand from the SIM card and puts it deeply into his thigh level cargo pocket. He grabs the next SIM card and starts the same process with a second phone he also pulls from his inner pocket. With an additional effort, he slips the first phone he just completed working with into the coat pocket of Ezell's right side.

Ezell had been watching him low-key as he did it all. Ezell watches a little longer as Gregory continues to move swiftly with the operations of performing the next series of tasks before him. When Gregory finishes the second phone, he reaches into his inner pocket once again to feel around its contents before grabbing at something slightly. When his hand is fully removed from that pocket, it is holding a small Ziploc bag.

He puts his other hand into his pants pocket and pulls out the mobile device he had been using and turns it completely off. He removes the battery and places a piece of aluminum foil he had in that small Ziploc bag. He wraps the piece of aluminum foil around the first phone from the pants pocket completely then places them both back into the Ziploc bag and places it back into his interior pocket.

He then looks over at Ezell with his eyes extra widened and nods his head to see if Ezell had picked up on the instruction. He then gives Ezell the second small Ziploc bag for him to do the same with his other phone. Ezell's eye pauses, then opens wider after a short delay and he follows suite to wrap his device and stow it back in the bag provided.

Ezell then reaches with it in his hand into his inner pocket and lets it go into its contents before retracting his hand and then grabs the phone that was just put into his pocket and begin to turn it on. Once it is completely on, he plays with it for initial familiarity. Once he is through with that, and deems himself able to navigate its functions, he then reinitiates his original attempt at making a call. After dialing a series of numbers into the phone he had some difficulty in drawing from his mind, he presses the phone and seems to be waiting for the call to connect.

"Flipp? … It's E. We just touched down. I am grabbing the car, and we can figure out where we are going to meet. I figured we can get it in over at that In and Out spot you took me to that we saw that guy at before."

Flip responds with a remark.

"Yeah, that will work. See you when we get there."

The sky, glowing brightly, displays too many hues of blue, white, and grey to consider completely. With more palm trees visible than where they just left by far, they both in their own right takes in the scenery change with welcomed appreciation for the atmospheric differences to home as they make their way from deboarding their plane to navigating the maze of terminal possibilities to where the rental car agencies are housed.

The two men find their particular rental car agency and find the line for the attendant is lengthy. One by one of several, they wait their turn to be seen and serviced. Not much needed to be said, this is Ezell's show. Ezell is not a big talker by far. He is a to the point minimalist that isn't fond of the extras.

There are still several people in front of them in the line. They continue to wait, for the most part of the time, in silence. It is not an uncomfortable silence, either. Gregory is all too familiar with the personal tendencies of his uncle. Ezell is comfortable around his nephew, and the two men stand in line with their minds occupied in their own distinct thoughts, as one by one, they are next to be seen. Now, they are being summoned to the next desk ready to assist a potential or existing client.

"Hello, how can I serve you this afternoon?"

"I am here for reservation number D345678T23410," Ezell speaks sternly and without wavering.

"Thank you for the reservation number. Let me put that into my system and find your reservation, please."

As she types into her console and continues to engage with it, the two men stand motionless and patient. Her head is turned away from them, and her face is completely focused into her screen and keyboard and mouse area. After a brief delay stemming from her computer usage and waiting for her system to respond, she pulls her chin back up in the direction of Ezell. She smiles brightly with her white teeth encased in her impeccably pink gums, showcasing a gorgeous smile as she speaks once again to him, "Mr. Brown, here is your contract. Please look it over carefully. I will need two forms of identification and your method of payment, please."

Ezell reaches for his rear pants pocket and pulls from within it his wallet. As he presents her the credentials and payment she requested, he continues to remain more stoic than anything as he gives her his full undivided focus as the transaction is still being carried out between them. Gregory, however, is scanning the room as he stands aside Ezell. Greg shifts his stance to accommodate this continual scan of the general rental hub lobby for any and every out of place glare or behavior he can register discretely.

When the receptionist returns to Ezell his belongings, he collects them just as proper and returns them to their original places in his wallet before replacing it in his rear pocket securely. The attendant gives him instructions to report to the vehicle garage. Showing him a map of the facility, he thanks her, then turns to Gregory, and they are off on their way to now retrieve the vehicle. The walk is about seven minutes from the desk they left to the elevator landing before the curb of the garage.

Ezell stands with his eyes beaming over the multitude of vehicles on display for selection throughout the allotted area to choose from. He selects the mid-sized SUV. Mainly due to it having a moderate size and dark tinted windows unlike most of the other runner ups to his attention and larger purpose. The both of them casually hop into the SUV, taking turns. Ezell first with the assistance of Gregory purging the data of the vehicles' in-dash computer before driving off and turning off all Bluetooth connectivity.

Ezell puts the vehicle into reverse, and they are on their way to departing the area of the airport. There isn't an awful amount of traffic as they make their way to its exit and start to cross over and under the tentacles of South Sepulveda Boulevard onto West Century Boulevard into South Inglewood. As they cross over the 405 Freeway, then South Inglewood Avenue, they are close to the burger spot that Ezell had mentioned to Flipp over the phone earlier.

The eight-lane roadway is a refreshing sight. The hustle and bustle and unmistakable vibrance of the city is slightly invigorating for them both to see. They do not discuss it, but it is obviously something pleasing to see for them both as they cross one intersection to the next as they approach the stadium area. Almost there, they both break their silence as they witness what appears to be a full-grown tree in the middle of the eight-lane road. It is sitting in the medium area like it is there with no intention of allowing these vehicles to prevent it from doing what it does.

They are both amazed and taken back from the sight of it momentarily as they press on.

They take note of all the stores and their names that are newly introduced to them as they pass each section where their brands and titles are plastered across several billboards and placards in the seemingly never-ending series of strip malls, and their sign monuments visible to their eyes as they continue to move along West Century Boulevard. Much different from New York, the architecture and the colors are more adobe and clay, mauve and white in each structure they pass.

As they reach the light at Club and Century, they take the left and navigate the curves until they arrive in front of the restaurant that is their destination.

"Good! I am starving!" remarks Gregory.

"Who you telling, Nephew? I can tear something down right now. Its gonna straight jack up my gut, but, Man, I don't have a taste for nothing else right now. C'mon, so we can be done before he comes through, or at least be started."

With the SUV placed in park, both men step from within its cabin and make way through the parking lot into the building. Gregory takes more time to do so. He catches up to his uncle's position due to his prolonged observance of the surrounding area and the movement of traffic and pedestrians alike. He embraces the difference in scenery as he soaks up the rays of the sun glistening off the edges of the tall palm trees erected over the sidewalks stretching into the sky with their vivid shades of green.

"I told you," Ezell mentions.

Gregory kind of trots up to where Ezell stands as he holds the door open for his nephew. Once inside the building, there is only one person in line, so they make haste to be second. After their food is ordered, they sit and get themselves ready to eat what they have ordered as quickly as possible. When their order is announced to be ready to pick up at the counter, Gregory springs up and speeds over, grabs the tray, and bounces back to their table. They begin eating.

Shortly after, Flipp comes through the doorway. He takes a careful examination left to right of the dining area with stern curiosity before he recognizes Ezell. His face becomes warm and friendly at the sight of Ezell. He puts his arms up and spread them wide as he gives a heavy double nod of his head and neck as he makes his way to where they are sitting.

"What is good, Shun?" Flipp comments with laughter in his voice and a smile erupting all over his face, unable to not laugh as he makes his obvious coastal dig at his old friend.

Ezell stands tall and meets him a few feet from the table. "What it do!" Ezell says with an amused look on his face before the two embrace one another. "Flipp, this here is my young nephew Gregory."

Flipp and Ezell release their embrace of one another. They give each other a hand-dap-like handshake as Flipp is in mid-route towards embracing Gregory as well in the same fashion.

"What it is, Nephew?!"

"I'm straight. Good meeting you after all this time. My uncle has told me a lot about you. From inside and when y'all both were out and re-connected. He told me you one of the realest he knows. That's a huge statement coming from him. Got to respect that."

Flipp looks over Gregory with approval and gives Ezell a pat on the shoulder before he speaks. "You Raised this one right I see. I hear you all in him. That's another blessing, My Brother!"

"C'mon, let's sit back down. You two was eating, and we doing too damn much up in here right now anyways," Flipp remarks.

The three of them find space at the table and they sit down. Ezell and Gregory are just about finished eating. With the edge taken off from their meal, Ezell does not waste much time cutting to the chase with Flipp.

"So, were you able to buy me some time, Fam?"

"I was. We got to link with four members of the board I have strong ties with. I just kept it what you told me, and I got the advisor with me on keeping it all tight. Big Homie knows, too, but he waiting to see what you do when you get your shot. It's on you now, Bro. I got you to the lake; you got to swim it out from here."

"That's love. Well, I sure as hell ain't come to sink, Flipp. Let's make it," responds Ezell.

The three collect themselves and swiftly depart the fast-food eatery. Returning to their parked vehicles, Ezell and Flipp continue to quietly discuss matters. They make their way through the parking lot before forking off where heading to their vehicles require change in the paths they are walking.

"What's up?" asks Gregory once they are completely back in the truck.

"Flipp was explaining to me how a few things have changed as expected. Nothing remains the same. Life is always making changes.

Flipp was the top enforcer for his whole crew before he got knocked. During the time he was gone, one of his guys made some moves and slowly became more influential than the rest of that tier of the crew. He now sits next to the big homie as an advisor. We have his ear and the ear of Big Homie as a direct result. You got favor. What we are about to present has favor. That's about it. We are about to follow him to one of the current cat's spot who enforces, and from there, we gonna catch a ride to the meet."

"Aight, bet. Sounds like that's ideal. Good looks again, Unc," answers Gregory.

Ezell, who is now sitting in the front passenger seat is watching the movement of the vehicle Flipp is driving in. As he observes Flipp's ragtop Convertible Chevy rise up from its hydraulic suspension system, he cannot help but notice a set of matching white Durango SUVs at the intersection. They are heading eastbound on West Century in both the left and right lanes. They took an apparent disdain to his presence in the parking lot.

Check those two Durangos at the light Fam. They were all up in your ride, Ezell texts Flipp fast as they follow him out of the rear of the parking lot back onto Club.

Good looking Homie…You and nephew fall back extra hard and keep it like five to six cars off me. Straight up, Flipp responds to the text.

"Your man got the connect, huh, Unc?"

"Yeah. Before he got locked up and we had initially met, he was one of his group's top enforcers. He had a great deal of pull then. When he got out, we moved a great deal of work back and forth as he fought to get back his position. He never lost the respect, just that position. He was always seen as clutch, though."

Flipp pulls off at the green light, leaving burnt rubber beneath them and a deafening screeching sound along with it before they whip a long U-turn across the traffic heading westbound. Cutting off traffic as they perform this stunt, men begin to emerge from both the front and rear passenger windows of both vehicles. Some men are draping themselves over the roof with hand guns and assault rifles pointed at Flipp's car as he approaches the intersection. Flipp is as prepared as he can be.

He flips his wheel extremely forcefully to the right. The vehicle responds by swerving its body to the right as its rear swerves to the left forcibly. He brakes the vehicle to a hard stop. Flipp crawls over the seat out of the car on its passenger side before they get to shooting at him and his car. With the passenger door still flung open and Flipp bracing himself for cover behind the rear passenger's door, he can see his glove compartment a few feet or less away from his reach. With pretty much perfect timing, he reaches for the glovebox and snatches it open long enough to grab two hand guns, two magazines, and a round object, pulling back to his cover before the barrage of bullets ensues.

Ezell and Gregory sit in their vehicles with no weapons, in shock as the scene plays out right in front of them. Ezell is infuriated he is without any means of protection for himself or to be able to offer assistance to his friend.

The group of younger men draped in clothing makes it clear that this is a gang related attack. The gang pauses to see if they got him. At that moment, Flipp looks through the fortunate angle provided to him through his rear-view mirror and can clearly see their positions. He chucks the round object at where the two Durango SUVs are stopped at. He waits a few seconds before he stands up quick. He shoots the closest one directly in his chest with three quickly released rounds before he sinks back down as fast as he rose up for more cover.

A moment later, there is a huge explosion emanating from where the two Durangos are. In the explosion, the remaining gunman is sent flying to the pavement from the blast close to across the intersection. Glass falls to the street from several areas, and more shattered glass is all over the place. Luckily, the only vehicles caught directly in the blast are the two SUVs involved in the attack.

Flipp stands up tall and quickly runs to the last gunman and shoots him clean in the skull before he ransacks his own vehicle. He sprints off to Ezell's SUV, and as he gets in, he shouts, "Let's go! Let's go! Get the fuck out of here!"

Gregory takes off, speeding around the SUVs engulfed in flames. He continues to speed off westbound on West Century where he comes across the light turning green as they reach the intersection at South Doty Avenue. There he whips the left, rushes along its path, and takes a sharp right on West 102nd Street, almost jumping the curb as he navigates the end of the turn. Slowing down at this point, they cross South Prairie Avenue and proceed down the block until they reach the corner at South Freeman where they made the left.

Once they hit 103rd Street, they make the right. Before long, they pull into a driveway that has a long, overgrown bush. The bush is the length of the property and about fourteen feet tall and about four feet thick centered at the gate it has grown over. As they pull into the yard, the garage opens up. As they drive inside of it, the garage closes. They are safe now from any potential police patrol and any search for the make and model of the rental.

Gregory and Ezell hop out of the truck along with Flipp. Ezell and Gregory stand and wait for Flipp to make the next move. He walks around the rear of the vehicle with Ezell walking behind him. When he gets to where Gregory is standing, he speaks.

"Y'all wait here. I will be right out," Flipp says, visibly aggravated.

"That was insane, Unc! I was thinking he was a goner. He did that, though!"

"Yeah, he has definitely calmed down a lot since I last came out here. He would have stayed longer and did more. When he was done, he might have dealt it out with the police, or he would have left on foot into them streets. We not far from his home now. He would have disappeared all the same then as we did today. That grenade was a nice touch, too.

"That explosion was insane! I am still surprised we got out of there without getting bagged," Gregory exclaims.

The garage door slips open long enough for Flipp to poke his head, neck, and shoulder through. "Come on in," Flipp says, quickly.

They both take heed to his instructions and proceed to follow him into the home. While inside, they are whisked through the kitchen where there are about twenty or so individuals standing around.

As they move through the home, Flipp tells them, "Don't worry about that rental for now. I will get you guys a next car to ride around in. A completely different one for the time being."

By the time they reach the door, there is a different tinted out SUV pulling up to the curb. They step out of the house, onto the porch, and then straight to the rear of the vehicle as several of the people who were just in the house with them look on. Flipp sits in the passenger seat of the SUV.

The driver pulls off from the curb and then speaks to Flipp, "What the fuck happened, Man?"

"Them fools tried to peel my scalp back! What the fuck you mean, Dawg? That shit didn't go as they expected either, though. I recognized them fools, too. I know just where they were from."

Ezell and Gregory sit mostly silent as the two upfront discuss the shooting.

"Good thing your peoples didn't get caught up in that. They just got here!"

"Yeah. Them fools got flame broiled over there, Dawg. Fucking with me?" Flipp chuckles, menacingly.

The vehicle moves along at a quickened pace as they travel eastbound back to Freeman Avenue. They hit a left there, then speed along until they reach the corner at Lennox Boulevard. They take a right heading towards Hawthorne Boulevard.

The car is silent from conversation at this time. The driver turns the radio up to where the music is blasting, and the base within its melodies create visible vibrations in the rearview mirrors.

When the vehicle reaches Hawthorne, the driver makes a left and takes it to them onto the eastbound on-ramp of the 105 freeway.

The traffic is considerably tight, but the movement is still going at about an even sixty-miles-per-hour as the average rate of progress in the close to bumper-to-bumper situation around them. They remain on the Freeway until they reach the exit labeled "5".

Once off the exit and waiting at the light on the corner of the three-way intersection at West 120th Street, Flipp turns to Ezell. "We are almost there. I am gonna go in with you. Your nephew will be straight out here with my dawg. He will no doubt be straight. Get your shit together as we get closer. This is for all the marbles."

When the light turns from red to green, they take the left. They continue until they reach South Van Nees Avenue, where they take a right southbound on it. From there they make a left on West El Segundo Boulevard. At the corner of South Western Avenue, they make a second left and take that all the way up northbound to West 111th Street. They take the second left onto South Hobart Boulevard and then turn at the first corner, making the right onto West 110th Place.

About midway through the neatly landscaped block, the vehicle stops and parks in front of a yard. The yard is slightly elevated from the ground on a higher mound of earth than most of the homes surrounding it. There are a few other homes similar to it on the block that they pass before they stop. The concrete driveway is very wide. Wide enough to fit possible three cars side by side as it goes all the way back to the rear of the house where a detached garage stands. There are at least twenty men and some women standing around in the rear area in front of that garage as they pull up into the driveway and drive around to the back where the crowd is.

The driver stops the vehicle and places the car in park. He turns the music off and hops out the car to greet the group of stern-faces standing around where the car is parked. Next to get out of the car is Flipp, then Ezell, and finally Gregory. Ezell stays moderately close to Flipp at about the distance of six to seven feet as he too goes and greets the group.

Flipp continues to share his tale of how he almost got smoked on his way over there with moderate enthusiasm and more annoyance. The driver annotates his sentiments with short one-word confirmations like "insane", and "exactly" as Flipp runs through the basics of what had taken place.

When he is done, he points in Ezell's direction and waves his hands for Flipp to come closer. "Then my dawg from New York who was here to set this move up scooped me up, and we boned out of there."

The crowd looks on with slight approval of the involvement of the New Yorkers in their midst.

The driver tells Gregory to hop out of the backseat and hop in the front. Gregory easily complies to the instruction since the seat has been vacated.

Flipp takes the lead, and Ezell follows as he walks through the group to the steps that lead to the rear door. As they walk through the kitchen, it is surprisingly empty. The dining room, however, is not. The table has several seats, and all of them are filled, minus the chair at the end closest to where they entered the room.

The man sitting at the other end speaks up quickly. "Have a seat, Ezell. Let's talk."

Flipp stands aside and provides a clear path for Ezell to take his seat. Ezell nods his head respectfully to acknowledge the invitation. He then takes the seat out from where it sits from under the table and sits down. He then pulls himself slightly forward towards the table.

"Okay. We are here to listen. Not often do we hear outsiders. Definitely not at this table in this fashion. We expect you got some heavy shit to lay down. So lay it down and make it count, Brother."

As the gentleman at the end of the table speak, the heads of all present go from attentively listening to him and looking in his direction to looking in Ezell's direction awaiting him to speak.

"I appreciate the gravity of having this opportunity set before me. No disrespect to the power wielded from this table in all; however, I am merely a messenger. I won't even attempt to glorify myself as anyone other than that. I come on behalf of my nephew. He is the one who forged this plan from the basement of his mind. Because of my ties with my brother Flipp that started in the pen that then continued back out into these streets and because of plenty of money made by many of us here I can only imagine, I am able to speak with you now.

"I got to reach out to similar groups after this and have the same conversation with those I can reach with the time I have to do these things. I do not have to remind you about situations like Rodney King and countless others who were brutally beaten by the police, and only to have those police who were in many cases recorded on video doing these things to us, get away Scott free for it.”

The group mostly nods their heads in some minimal degree of agreeance as he speaks.

“This has only grown more aggressive, and the police have grown even more indifferent to this pattern.”

He pauses briefly to clear his throat as he is becoming more passionate about what he is saying to them. He envisions the several cases and news stories that dominated the media over just the last twelve months.

“What my nephew has planned is a response to this pattern since protesting hasn’t provided an acceptable outcome or more less deterrent to this epidemic. His response will not be something simply or easily attained. His response will require all of our people in positions of organizational strength and demonstrated, unwavering intestinal fortitude on all sides of this gang thang to come together for this one unified cause that affects not just us as adults, but, unfortunately, more frustratingly, our children.

“The police do not seem to differentiate nor give a fuck whether they are killing us in these streets or our children in their cars or at their schools or in their own homes. In their own playgrounds. This shit is bad all over this motherfucking country, and many of us stand as the underground leaders of our respective communities.

“What I am is mainly due to me being a product of where I live. Where I was forged into steel. Right here. Just as you are here right now. There is no larger threat that has ever existed against our lives than these evil police who talk that law shit and that justice shit and then fuck us in the courts, then shoot us dead in the streets for reaching into our pockets or even moving while Whites can shoot at them, attack them with weapons other than guns, and they somehow find their way into the back of a squad car with no injuries from that interaction majority of the times."

The man sitting across from him at the other end of the table interrupts, "Okay. So just what are you proposing? You're not being clear as to what it is you want from us."

Another speaks to Ezell, "What is your nephew's plan? What is it you want from us?"

Ezell takes a second to collect himself as he looks around the room, unsure of how to completely gauge the two responses. Undeterred, he continues to speak directly to their questions. "At an appointed time in the future when other pieces of the plan are properly mobilized and in position, when the next incident of police brutality takes place— and we all know there will be a next one— there will be a planned protest.

"At this planned protest that will take place in several cities across the nation that are strategically advantageous to the plan, we will strike at the police in a way that will have never been done before. Period. This will send a message that will speak to the world in volumes. We will take an approach in completing this plan to where if we all play our parts, all that will happen is there will be a huge increase in police presence in all these cities in the aftermath of the incident.

"There will be a degree of backlash. The plan leaves it to leave breadcrumbs that lead vaguely to myself, my nephew outside in the car, and my other nephew out on a similar mission to put together the execution of the plan in addition to the preparation for how what's to follow goes down. You are asked to play a role in that part as well."

The group looks around at one another in astonishment after Ezell answers their question in boldness. There is some clamor amongst them. Then another one on the opposite side of the table from the man who spoke last speaks out as the rest of them continue to clamor. However, when he begins to speak, the group becomes silent and attentive once more.

"That's a bold request! You want us to put ourselves at risk and into the target of the police— not for money, but to just fuck with the police? I can't speak for us all, but I still need to hear more about exactly how your nephew plans on accomplishing this shit with our assistance, what exactly is 'our' assistance, and how will we communicate about the 'appointed' time and shit. But I like this shit! Fuck them crooked ass police and this crooked ass system!"

Many at the table grow pleased with his statement and show visible signs of their agreeance to what he has said. The man sitting across from Ezell also shows facial expressions as his fellow council member speaks. Same with the one who spoke before he had said those inciting remarks.

Then the man sitting across from him turns back serious and turns back facing Ezell and speaks again, "Alright. We will get with Big Homie and discuss what we will or won't do. When we make a decision, we will reach you through Flipp."

Flipp taps Ezell on his shoulder. Somehow, he understands the tap to communicate the meeting is over, and it is time to go now. Ezell then stands up, looks in the eyes of each person at the table and standing around it, and gives a respectful nod before he turns, walks back through to the kitchen, and out the back door. He stands on the porch looking upon the group of people still standing within several sectioned off mini groups within the larger gathering with just an air of acceptance.

Flipp puts his arm over his shoulder affectionately as he speaks to his friend. "You did good. Made them think, then imagine. I think you even got them excited. There is still much to happen before I get the opportunity to talk to Big Homie who already knows what it is. He just needs the council to be on board so He can make the rest happen without putting himself in a jam. Let's roll."

With that, Flipp passes by Ezell who is still soaking up the experience before he too ventures back down the steps towards the SUV they had come in. Upon sight of Ezell exiting the house, Gregory blows a slight sigh of release. Immediately after, he smoothly reaches for the door handle and opens the door as he steps out of the front passenger seat. He stands at its opening until Ezell returns, gives him a handshake like "dap", and the same to Flipp.

"Thanks, Flipp."

Then they all return to their respective doors, open them up, and enter the vehicle. The driver cuts the car's motor on, and the music shoots back up to its previously high decibel. He places the gear into reverse, moves his foot from off the break to the gas pedal, and back and forth as he moves backwards along the driveway back into the street.

They travel back to South Western Avenue where they take that to Imperial Highway. They make the right, heading west onto it. When they reach the corner of Crenshaw Boulevard, the light is green and then quickly changes to yellow. They rush and take the light just before it turns red. At the on-ramp back onto the 105 Freeway, they take the westbound entrance.

Once safely on the 105, Flipp turns to Ezell.

"Okay. So, this is what we got going on. I am going to take you to the airport. There, your rental will be there waiting for you. I got a guy who drives for one of them online car dealers. He had an empty slot on his trailer, so we put a cover over it and loaded it up for you. It is being transported to a low-key gas station nearby the airport that is pretty much off the radar by prepared measures that are pre-existing to our needs. When we get there, we will unload the truck from the trailer, and then you guys can do what you have to do from there."

Ezell is pleased. So is Gregory. Ezell reaches his hand out to him as he gives him a handshake like dap.

"Thanks again, Fam," Ezell replies.

When they arrive at the gas station, it takes place exactly as Flipp said it would. Before they depart the vehicle, Ezell leans forward touching Flipp on his shoulder. Flipp turns around to acknowledge Ezell after he tapped him. When he does so, Ezell pulls a thick folded manila envelope out of his pocket and gives it to him.

"Where are you guys headed next?" Flipp asks.

"First, we will shoot up to Oakland where I am gonna link up with Bug and Scoot. Then I will hit Kansas City, Chicago, Milwaukee, Detroit, Dallas, then Houston. All with the same message. I am checking one brother in each city. One at a time. I just booked our flights on the highway.”

“Well handle your business, Man, and remain safe. I will be in touch with what the next move will be. I know you need all of us out here on board, so once the big homie signs off, we gonna reach out to the other big homie and work down to their council the same way. This time it will be them both speaking on your behalf. Judging from the reaction you got today, and some of the other unmentioned benefits from the move we discussed and haven’t shared just yet, they will be motivated,” states Flipp, as Ezell and Gregory get in their rental and depart for the airport entrance as the sun is starting its descent from the sky.

Chapter 8

"Billable Hours"

The television monitor's large screen becomes cluttered with boxes from within the video conference platform as the many other participants become visible across its screen, one-by-one. Michael is sitting next to the screen on its right in his barstool looking over the small crowd as they each have their own distinct individual responses to what is taking place on the monitor. When the eighth and final conference square becomes visible, there is one face amongst the eight that is obviously more recognizable to that crowd than the others in the videoconference. The easily recognizable face is none other than the extremely popular attorney in the civil rights field. He has been retained for at least twelve out of the last fourteen cases where the families sought action after the police department and their state for the events that led to the demise of their respective family member at the hand of law enforcement.

It is Na'Quan Bishop. There are a few moments of soft commotion shared amongst the guests. Bishop only deals with strong cases that are slam dunk opportunities for success. Both for the families of the victims as well as the lucrivity for the firm.

Bishop, as well as each other participant, also has visual capability of the crowd in the dining hall. He looks over the room sternly as they clamor discretely; they are able to maintain their demeanors and professional bearings.

"Welcome! Good evening to you all. On behalf of our client who shall remain nameless at the present time, Michael has gone through a great deal of effort and evaluation to find you. He has gone through a great deal of effort to arrange for this meeting. He has taken great measures to bring you here this evening.

"Today, as I stand before each of you, I stand as the face for the overall purpose of this gathering and the eventual face of how our time will be spent during the upcoming months. So, you choose to join our journey. We must maintain our pact of confidentiality with our client and the necessary plausible deniability of anything we would have to legally disclose to law enforcement. We are here with three purposes and those purposes alone: to investigate, to evaluate, to determine through facts and evidence the most efficient strategy of approach for the legal question that has meandered and lingered over the heads of the entire justice system for over more than four hundred years and counting. Sad to say, however true this is.

"We are the front line of the most evasive allotment of justice in existence throughout the history of this could-be great nation that definitely should be great at this particular junction in time. We should not have had to be the ones to see this through. It should have arguably taken place for us to witness in our early youth. But the perpetual violence and egregious acts taken against our plight murdered those who were most vigilant in that fight of those times.

"Just in the last seven years, we have painstakingly witnessed the untimely deaths of forty-seven of our brothers and sisters. Not by hands of citizens that would be better compartmentalized as the run of the mill criminal statistics for a municipalities COMSTAT statistical renderings. No! These forty-seven deaths were in fact murders, executed by members of the law enforcement community all across this county. The same men and women who have taken oaths to serve and protect the community have neglected the value of our collective, melanated lives for as long as there have been law enforcement entities in this nation.

"A temporal coincidence I think not. Judging by the collective dossiers and the activities associated with them, neither do any of you present based on your litigative histories. This is why we are here. Why you are here? I need you.

"The remaining members of this conference panel are prepared to pay for the entire costs of the work I plan to enlist you, and the might of your respective firms to engage alongside me in, as we take on a fight that needs to be left unscathed no longer."

The remaining people displayed on the screen look upon Bishop as he speaks with reverence and unmistakable agreement.

Bishop continues, "Besides just myself, we have Meredith Pendleton, a woman of notable business acumen and success."

Meredith waves her hand before the eye of her camera.

"Some of you may or may not know Tre Jones. He is more affectionately known for his stage name of 'Double Up'. He has created for himself a most profitable career in the music industry over the last seven to eight years."

Tre puts up a "peace" sign with his index and middle fingers with his thumb leaned against his ring finger quickly for the camera.

"Also with us is Jazmine Stokes. She is another successful entrepreneur that has dedicated time and commitment for our execution."

Jazmine then waves at her camera in suit.

"We have Samuel Stevenson with us as well. He, too, is a successful entrepreneur with exacting ideals in these areas we will be focused on."

Samuel puts up his fist for the camera with a stoic expression across his face.

"Many of you may recognize Francis Stallsworth, two-time league champion and six-time MVP famed athlete."

With his introduction, Francis chooses to spin a complete three-hundred-sixty-degree spin around in his chair for the camera with a constant grin on his face.

"You should surely recognize Ms. Melinda Bradshaw. The media mogul that owns several television networks and a news outlet."

Melinda merely nods her head as she releases a smile for a moment before she retracts its wrinkles back into the serious look she is most known for.

"And finally, a woman who I need least to introduce, Tiffany Robinson. Former Miss Universe and esteemed Hollywood thespian."

Tiffany makes no other action but embellishing that trademarked smile upon the crowd. Bishop looks to Michael at that point. Michael takes his cue and takes to a pacing stride in the view of the television screen as he begins to speak to the group with the faces of the monitor watching behind him.

"As Na'Quan mentioned, we have a considerable war chest to operate from within. Over twenty million dollars in the initial reserve. That will cover billable hours, filing fees, and other discretionary expenses we may encounter. There is more behind that. We just have to remain vigilant on our budgets and the transparency of those expenses for the obvious reasons.

"What we will be looking to do is take what is provided to us moving forward with the collective actions of the law enforcement communities in regards to how they handle our communities as a whole. We all know that eerily we will undoubtedly experience several more police abuse of power incidents. There is no real deterrent set by the law to discourage these rogue departments and their rogue agents from doing these things again and again at our expense.

"We will need to have our ducks in their row for the time when we will be called to act. We will need to attack cases that are pre-existing as well as that special case that fits the bill that has yet to take place. We will fight these cases all the way up through the courts.

"The ultimate goal is diverse. We will seek significant landmark remedies for the families while also seeking landmark precedence in state courts as well as making a push for federal precedence. Hopefully reaching the supreme court in arguments. Ultimately, we will engage in separate lobbying to have legislature in place to be argued on the floor of the senate and ultimately signed into ratification by the president.

Whomever that may be at the time this all comes into fruition. This is the overall long-term plan and goal here."

The group is now interested and quite attentive with their alert attention span.

"So now that you know, feel free to finish your evening in the ambiance of the dining area with your meals. Since you now have much to discuss amongst yourselves and later when you return home to your respective offices with your firms, I will not expect a direct response from you here and now. However, I will be checking to hear back from Michael as to who responds, when you respond, and most importantly, how you respond.

"I wish you all a good evening, not only from myself, but from all of my colleagues present as well. Take this proposal in its initial form most seriously, as you take it up the chains of your firms to the decision makers. We hope to reconvene at a later date."

With the group of conference members across the screen sending their visual departing gestures for the camera, one-by-one they disconnect from the call. Michael then signals discretely to his technician team to wrap up the audio-visual equipment. Once the signal is transmitted, Michael returns to his stool and waits as he watches the group interact amongst themselves for a long moment.

Sandra turns from her team towards him.

"That was interesting. There is a great deal of mystery to this. Undisclosed clients and endless bags of money. I almost find it hard to believe that this is about civil rights and not something else. Is this about something else, Michael? I think that is something we would all like some reassurance on.”

“All I can re-assure you on is that what we are doing is strictly legal work. Trying to sift the data and find that one case primed to make a difference in precedence. Hopefully, several cases that in totality raise the legal standard and force executive execution of the rights already verbalized in the constitution, just not realized…as of today.

“We are not engaged in any active act of nefarious acts taken place or planned to be. Our scope is strictly legal. We may find potential cases where we may represent those who participate in civil unrest, criminal vandalism, even battery or its lesser form of assault. We will potentially evaluate the value as it pertains to our goal on a case-to-case scenario.”

Sandra turns and looks at Tanisha. The both of them find little to argue with his rebuttal. Still with a singular eye fixated on Michael, she lingers as she takes it back over towards the attention of her colleagues. They eat, discuss the opportunity, and enjoy the remainder of their meals.

The group is now preparing to depart. Sandra lingers behind to discuss a private matter with Michael. They share that conversation separate from the group in lieu of departing the dining hall and back to the car service vehicle that is awaiting their arrival.

Tanisha comes over to where they are having their discussion and grabs out to Sandra’s hand. She grabs it affectionately for a moment before exchanging a mutual gesture of their goodbyes for the evening.

“I’ll be calling you in a few days,” Tanisha says to Sandra.

"We will be in touch for sure. I envision my firm seeking to embark on to the next step here."

Michael shakes her hand properly. He then nods as she turns and goes about her way to the car waiting for her in the rear of the building. Sandra shakes Michael's hand as well, and they say their farewells. Michael stands motionless as he looks upon Sandra as she departs, watching her until she walks out of the room. When she is gone, he mixes in with his team wrapping up their usage of the space entirely.

As he works with them in doing so, he then goes into the hallway leading to the kitchen where he runs into the host. Michael hands the host a thick envelope and shakes his hand. Michael then departs with his team into the SUV they have parked in the rear of the building as the final suitcases are being loaded onto the rear of the vehicle.

The owner of the restaurant rushes out of the rear door just before the vehicle begins to pull off into the evening.

"I just was hoping to catch you so that I can tell you how thankful we are for your business. Please return to us when you visit our great city again. We appreciate you greatly."

"Your service and hospitality are legendary of no matching. My experience in the fulfilment of this evening's purpose was due to the excellence provided by you and your staff. Thank you, My Friend," responds Michael.

The two men shake hands through the opened window of the rear passenger side of the vehicle. The owner walks back into the building, and the tinted window of Michael's door slowly closes. The truck then slowly pulls off from the pavement and heads into the evening.

At the next hotel he has arranged to be his accommodation for the next few days, he is sitting around with some other community leaders as he arranges for a mobile barber to come visit him in his spare room of the joint suite he has reserved.

Some of the invitees begin to arrive to the suite. The barber, being amongst the first, comes with an assistant who is pushing a dolly with a large appliance looking box on its body. When the assistant passes through the door and sets the dolly down where Michael's associate and mobile barber instruct him to, it is clear that it is an actual professional barber chair he has brought into the suite. The assistant departs the room. The men converse as he departs.

"Okay, okay! We got a professional barber chair! That's what I'm talking about. Class," one individual says loudly.

"Can't truly get a haircut and not be sitting in a real barber's chair. Something about that, no a lot about that, literally doesn't sit right with me," Michael responds, chuckling.

"I appreciate the invite for such a warming and intellectually intriguing event. Rarely have I heard of anyone so randomly offering such a gratuity of service. This is nice," responds a second individual present.

"I'm sure, just like everyone here, we all know Michael, but I cannot say I know the rest of you by sight, let alone by name. My name is Phillip Wright. I own a tuxedo rental shop and men's clothing store downtown on Menomonee. The Wing Tip. We've been there for twenty years. My uncle was there fifteen years before I took over the shop."

The men in the room nod and acknowledge his blanket introduction to the group. The barber, whose name is Stephen, begins to pull his clippers out of the case he was given by his younger assistant Jamal. His equipment is clean, new appearing, and of a shiny exterior. The metal on several of his clippers glisten as it is struck by the different angles of the lighting from above in the suite as he pulls each piece out of the bag. Once he is setup and ready to start cutting, he spins the chair around to test its spinning capabilities. Once Stephen is satisfied, he gestures for Michael to take a seat.

"Alright. I am ready for you, Brother."

Michael stands up from his seated position in his chair. He strolls over to the newly positioned barber's chair and sits into its cushion.

"Just give me a 'one' all around. Give me a sharp line and points. I will keep the mustache, and you can get rid of everything else."

"No problem."

While Stephen is beginning his process of carrying out Michael's requests, Jamal sits in the chair Michael left behind. The other men in the room begin to converse amongst themselves as they watch the smaller television that came with the room. The television is apparently set to one of the local news networks.

"…In other news…President Brad Ace makes a statement in support of law enforcement in regards to yet another incident of alleged police brutality. When asked what his plans were to address this systemic issue of overlooked importance, he simply replied, 'When there is evidence of wrong doing, my office will take the necessary precautions in evaluating any wrong doing. However, my office stands with law enforcement and the dangers that they encounter dealing with that of the criminal elements as they protect our nation, state by state, city by city, and street by street'…"

"See! That's that shit right there. We are never going to get any serious recognition from the fucking government for how these police be violating out here!" says a guest.

"What do you expect that man to say? He has said from the moment he stepped on to the scene he was down with the police. He has no need to give a fuck about what they do because they ain't doing it to him, or his children, or anyone he naturally comes into contact with on his day-to-day.

"Don't forget how he went all loud about them young kids like twenty years ago before he even got into politics. His weighing in influenced that jury into giving them kids all that time, and they didn't even do the crime. He was never even charged for the liable or defamation of character for putting out all those ads at the time condemning those boys. Not a peep; not an action filed. That was up in New York at that. One of the most litigious states in the country, and not one attorney went after that man for that bullshit he kept stirring up!" says another guest.

"Yeah, you right. That's fucked up. Make you think that this shit ain't never going to change. With Ace and people in positions of power like him, they are always pandering to an audience to push whatever their agenda is whether it is a short term or a long term agenda. Most people end on the receiving end of whatever the propaganda is of the day. What

I do is immediately research what resolutions just got or being brought to the floor in Dc or in a few states depending on the time I have when I get the inclination. Most times these bizarre things are happening when serious legislation is being pushed through its process. While we keep seeming to fall for the okie doke and they remove one or several liberties we weren't fully taken advantage of away as we quarrel over frivolous shit. Like the morons this system already touts us to be. We just prove them right often. Sad as shit but we do. Look, we well into the two thousands, and we still dealing with this Rodney king type shit. They still Emmitt Till'n dudes. It just doesn't get no media coverage until it do," Stephen says.

Jamal just sits with his head spinning on a swivel as the grown men around him converse.

"What make matters worse for me is that it just don't seem like we seem to have figured any of this shit out yet. Most of us don't have a plan on what we want to do in life. They got the game rigged in many regards.

"Don't get me wrong. I am not saying that brothers don't be out here making these choices that put them in the position of being locked up. That's not where I am going with it. What I am trying to point out is there are several factors to what comprises of these brothers' day-to-day lives through their environments that have a huge role in them seeing these decisions that lead straight to either the penitentiary or to the grave. That set of circumstances wasn't just stumbled upon and just happened to be the predicament by happenstance. They created this system where we find the inner city ideal, don't even matter whether that is the west coast or the east or in between.

"Look at Milwaukee. All this shit the same, Dawg. Take their own labels and break that shit down. 'Projects'. 'Project'. Sounds more to me like an experiment.

"Ivy league schools have exposed all of this in several reports that have been published over many years. Bottom line. This is, again, old news, but we steady falling for this okie doke as a people. Most of us, if not all of us here right now, found ways out and have achieved success in different forms. Many have not. Young Jamal here is still in that fight in determining which path he will ultimately take.

"You ain't lying. But I know first-hand that the game being played is on some serious, real-deal next level chess shit when you break it down. Well, at least when I broke it down. I see we went through hell to just have a seat in their schools. Many followed those opened doors and went the education route only to discover that more often than not, that on the other end of that door was more discrimination. Got a degree, but can't even get an interview, let alone a job in respect for whatever you went and obtained a degree in.

"So, they went and created affirmative action. That was a program that did have its merits in what would seem to be in the right direction, but like in everything this system does, it coincidentally neglected to address the issue that caused a need for programs like affirmative action. Negative and biased corporate culture that breast fed bigotry and segregation of a new kind. Jim Crow's family still alive; they just stopped giving them names. No name, no proof, more or less.

"So, you can have a program like affirmative action all you want. The culture of any office will always dictate the vibe and atmosphere of those dwellings and interactions amongst the staff. They willingly and knowingly introduced an instigative sub-culture within the dominant culture to create a disdain for such programs. Basically, dooming their perception from their inception. So, what was a common result? Who wants to go to school, put in the amount of work it takes to go all the way to still be seen as less and still have to fight three times as hard to make the average salary and be seen as less each step of the way?

"Promotions? Get passed on. Or if you get it, could not have been because you busted your ass to get it and get there. No. It had to be because you're a product of affirmative action. Diminishing every accomplishment and disregarding the efficacy of your contributions. Who wants that?

"They do not teach the difference between Ivy league, HBCUs, and traditional colleges and universities. Not in the public school system, home school systems, or at home, sadly. Not in our homes anyway. A complex myriad of confusion, disinformation, and misinformation! How is a young child supposed to navigate around that with any probability of success? That's just the education issue. Don't let me even get started on the pipeline to prison, Dawg. Shiiiiiiiiiiiit!!" Stephen continues.

"Well, let me stop you right there, Bro. Definitely no disrespect, but I came from these streets, and I made it out. Before I did, I made probably every common mistake one could make out here. I hear what you been saying. Don't get me wrong, I do. I agree with much of it, too. All I am saying is that more emphasis needs to be placed on a person's decisions. There is always context to our choices. There are several factors that create our fucked-up environment that lead a motherfucker to making some dumb ass choices, no lie.

"However, brothers out here know one thing before anything else: independence. We start out disobedient because we want to be. We want to buck the system and do our own thing. We not trying to follow anyone overall. We definitely not trying to follow no one that has not shown themselves to be in possession of a successful working knowledge of 'a path'. We've all morphed into that Missouri shit— that 'show me' state shit.

"There is a direct connection to what you saying and what I am saying. Most of the cats out here do not seem to see that there is a negative cycle. There are too many cats that are actually making money out here. That's what we all do here in this country. Make money at the next person's detriment.

"You too lazy to cook your own meals? No problem. There are shops lined up both sides of every block in every city ready to charge you for a home cooked meal. Sometimes not even that, just some quick food. Someone profits from seeing an opportunity at the expense of their target audience.

"How many kids have some parents who keep them in the fly fits only to have financial aid as their means of going to college? All them old clothes in the trash by then or are on their way. We need to be more real about the consequences of our choices. Both the immediate gratification fulfillment and the potential, if not eventual negative backdrop to those choices.

"We as a community definitely seem to be dense about this reality. Don not even get me started on why our communities do not invest in life insurance coverages and living trusts to ensure the growth and prosperity of their families. Like I been saying, we stay doing the same things generation to generation. Overall Failing. Those that do make it out that paradigm, just like many who are forced to capitulate into the corporate culture that demeans their value, turn and make no efforts to reach back to bring any of us through the door they got into. Instead, they shut that motherfucker and look at you the same way that those in power look at them. Straight brainwashed and indifferent from the result of the trauma it took for them getting wherever they feel they arrived at. I just want that to be said since we discussing this shit. Cannot leave that part out," says a different guest.

"What are your thoughts, Sir? Aren't you some kind of a lawyer?" Jamal asks Michael. "You haven't said much."

"I'm just listening. I think all of you are on point. Each of you are just speaking on the elements of the matter that you're most directly affiliated and experienced with. It all connects. What's not clear is what's next? After all the marching, all the talking, begging, what is to be done?

"Do folk go about it by redressing their elected officials? That part you guys haven't spoke on nor how that avenue began or is currently being re-developed into even a thing. It wasn't a thing a year ago, now it is becoming one.

"And how couldn't it be a thing now after we have seen the first Black president, regardless of how you may or may not feel about his potency? Just the visual alone has to mean something. We all can imagine to realize what it must have been like to be Black of melanation, and having to be that while governing everyone, and the strong political gravitational pulls from this side, that side, this ambition to the next. Those seeking control over what's scarce, and the profit in having that control, even if just briefly. It's definitely a non-stop machine that preluded him and will dominate the meta-dealings of Washington, D.C. for the foreseeable future.

"Again, if you have two grand in ya hand, what will you do? What you invest in says what you about. So, will you buy something that benefits you today? Fix something from the past, like debts? Or will you be bold enough to gamble on making that money and the opportunity count for something larger? Now substitute that two grand and replace that with your time," Michael responds.

The men all have to sit back in their seats and ponder the epiphany Michael just made them see as he weaved them through his point. There was a moment, a brief one, where all of the men in the room sat still, nodding to themselves and making their own peace with what Michael just said.

"That's real," most of the men speak aloud, while some of the remaining men utter, "Word."

Jamal then picks up the remote and changes the channel to a basketball game. The men grow excited. They start to shout at the screen when one of the players break off his defender and catches a windmill dunk with an aggressive effort to damage the rim with the dunk. They continue to shout as the player hangs onto the rim and spins along its curve. The player turns his frame back towards the defensive side of his court before he releases his grip on the rim, staring at whatever players from the opposition that were within his gaze. He does so intimidatingly.

Michael's haircut is complete. Stephen calls the next man up to the chair.

It's a typically bustling Wednesday morning. The firm and its staff are swarming through the office. From the lower entry level attorneys and clerk and their assistants to the junior partners, each body is in rush mode as the upper echelon get ready for their nine a.m. meeting. Their big weekly meeting today just so happens to also be their quarterly meeting.

Mostly every seat within the rather spacious contemporary themed hall is occupied. The projector has been cut on and the two remaining seats to be filled is that of the chairwoman and one managing partner. In the other room that houses the chairwoman's office sits both Sandra and her mother Arleen Sterling.

"Have that report delivered to Stan when Marly gets it completed. Set up my lunch with Phillip at Catch 35. Send my agenda to the conference room now.

"Are you ready, Sandra? I am excited. This is merely a formality, and I cannot see there being any real resistance to the merits of your proposal. Just some vetting will be the focus of any response of additional questioning. The name of Na'Quan Bishop alone will be the closing factor before you begin.

"That reminds me. Delores? Make contact with Mr. Bishop's assistant so we can confirm his availability for that segment of today's meeting. We want his video feed to be punctual and timed properly."

"Yes, Madame Chairwoman."

"Delores?"

"Yes, Madame Chairwoman?"

"Make sure you also have Vivian Kager and her conference team ready to be brought in as well to the conference. Keep William in IT abreast of the importance of this feed, and let him know that the signal strength needs to remain smooth and uninterrupted. I do not care what resources he needs to access in doing so. Let him know his fiscal budget and employment depends on this being the outcome of today's reliance on his department."

"My apologies, Ms. Sterling. Shall we go next door?"

"Yes, Ma'am. I am right at your side. After you, Madam Chairwoman."

The cherry wood wainscoting suddenly opens up, and a well-blended door reveals itself from within the wall. Through its opening walks through both Arleen and Sandra Sterling. At their entrance, the occupants in the hall stand erect. The chairwoman stands at her seat, grabs her gavel, and hits its block with it. The occupants then take their seats and await her opening statement to the room.

"Good morning, Team. Good morning, members of our esteemed board. Today is more than a meeting. Today will be more than a quarterly briefing. Today will be one of those days where pivotal actions are pronounced on this floor that will hold within their content as the framework for a potential set of priorities and aspirations that this firm was founded under, and goals that have defined our practice for over the sixty years of our incorporation.

"Today we each will have a seat at history in its inception. We will still conduct briefings pertaining to the details and itineraries of the agenda for our weekly and quarterly topics of coverage. Before we delve into the normal set of business, I give the floor to your managing partner Sandra Sterling. So, she can introduce this segment of proposed potential and that possible opportunity for accomplishment for the firm."

Arleen takes to her seat and watches as Sandra walks from her side to the podium between the long mahogany conference table with all of its meticulous engravings of design and craftsmanship and the tall and long window overlooking the Chicago River.

Sandra reaches the podium. She lays her thin designer briefcase across the top of it, opens it, and pulls from within it a folder. She has a Bluetooth laser pointer in her hand. She begins to introduce one slide after the next to the board of statistics. The slides are of criminal justice cases from the previous quarters and years in regards to the volume of civil rights violations conducted by law enforcement officers in the state of Illinois. There are also cases from other key states with staggering numbers and percentage increases from one quarter and year to the next. She continues to go through these figures. She brings awareness to how they have fought as a firm many cases and won many cases collectively in these critical areas of constitutional infringement.

"The next logical step forward is for our firm to take the fight into Washington, D.C. in the form of Constitutional reform. Now is the time for change to federal law, and after that, its robust unrelenting enforcement. With that, I ask you all esteemed members of our board to listen to a proposal.

"Historically, this is neither the time or venue for such a thing to be introduced, let alone pitched. Yes, this is a true fact and normal set of procedure in these patterns of our operational behavior and activity. I need not remind you of how last year we saw more brutality cases. Blatant videotaped incidents that demanded our legal minds to step up and step in for litigative relief to the countless families affected.

"There is no other name more regarded in this field of civil rights enforcement than that of our esteemed legal colleague Na'Quan Bishop. Today it will be him, not I, to communicate this proposal of partnership in bringing that advocative lobby effort to D.C. for the long overdue execution of protection from the Constitution over this area long neglected in regards to rogue law enforcement and complicate law enforcement agencies who condone, and sadly in some cases, support perjury and acts of violence and intimidation towards members of minority communities in of all places, the United States of America. Ladies and gentlemen of the board, I present to you Na'Quan Bishop!"

The attention is then drawn to the enormous projection field boundary behind the head of the conference table, behind where the chairwoman sits. Sandra uses a remote-controlled device to initiate the blinds to electronically close shut, producing a very dark atmosphere. The projection device is then turned on and the signal becomes visible onto the wall behind the chairwoman.

The brightness of the projected image mirrors from the desktop it receives its image from, three windows populate the screen's landscape:

all separate videoconference feeds through an application that facilitated three different instances of connection. As the video conference members feeds become connected, it is revealed to be Na'Quan Bishop in one window, Michael Crawford in another, with a screen displaying a similar large conference hall to their own in the third window.

In the first two windows, both men are dressed in impeccable style and their backdrops matching their debonaire styles of professional couture. In the last window of the conference hall is about twenty equally well-dressed individuals seated in a functional set of order.

"Good morning! Good morning, Falcon Legal Firm board members! Your image has flown high above the legal community, setting standard after standard, and precedence after precedence in our field. We continue the fight of many before us. I started my firm under the premise of observing the increasing need for legal representation in our most neglected and abandoned communities due to unethical actions by the very same law enforcement professionals that have been sworn to oath to uphold an unwavering stance of defense for the people from those who seek to violate ANY right provided to us by our highly glorified and justifiably so esteemed Constitutional values. And it's the Law of the Land!

"I am merely an agent. Yes, I have fought tirelessly and continue to endeavor into the fray for this Constitutional issue of no meritable match. This long thirsted, still unquenched desire to achieve homeostasis in the form of justice and the pursuit of equivalence in the happiness obtained in its delivery is still at hand and in high demand!

"Let's get down to the details! We need to find a case that we can ride to the Supreme Court! A case that exists or will soon exist that falls within all applicable statute of limitations that will allow us to work in unrivaled diligence to make the flagship issue of how egregious an injustice many suffer under every day as a result of the ineptitude of this system of government that have failed to produce remedies to the declarations of independence echoed through time from our forefathers and the justice system that have yet to be fulfilled and delivered to the very people these tenets were prescribed to centuries ago! Let us not loosen the grip on the opportunity to finally bring some successful conclusion to these accords!"

All participants sit in awe of Bishop's speaking. He can visibly be easily viewed and received as a captivating speaker.

"The proposal is simple. The endowment set aside by my client will compensate every useful billable hour on the expedition of achieving some justice long overdue to the people who have been trampled upon by a system of oppression and indifference. All that needs be done to accept such a contract of retainership is to respond in kind. Send me and my firm a letter of intent to collaborate on pending litigation regarding the pursuit of civil rights legislative reform. My office will be awaiting your individual or collective response. Have a blessed day. I will remain in conference for any follow up questions either board and its members may have for me."

Arleen speaks, "Any member of this board after hearing the proposal in its initial form are required to submit their vote as to how we shall proceed. Yah in favor of collaborative involvement in seeking to define and develop a legal strategy to accomplish these presented goals as part of a team. Nah for those who oppose our involvement."

She presses a button on her tablet, and the members of her board receive messages on their company tablets. They cast their votes as they receive their message. During this time, although not saying much, Vivian Kager instructs her board of the same pending vote in session.

"Ladies and gentlemen of the board, please now cast your votes on the measure of agreeance to collaborating to conduct a partnership in this manner with this firm."

With the votes casted, both Bishop and Michael sit in undisturbed silence as they await the results of the voting between the two legal teams.

"We have an outcome," announces Arleen. "We have agreed to move forward."

"The vote has been processed, and we have decided to move forward as a group," announces Vivian's treasurer.

"We are familiar with your method of preparation. Mr. Bishop, reach out to us when you are ready to begin. We are ready to work on whatever matter you deem viable to come to the conclusion proposed," remarks Arleen.

"Agreed," replies Vivian, quickly.

"Well done, Team. Me and my partner that was also brought together by our client will continue the work of procuring the proper case information for both of your teams to sink your teeth into. We will be in touch. Michael here will make all periodic contacts to keep things copasetic in the communication exchange," Na'Quan says.

The screen closes, and the day continues as per their normal activities for the content of their morning meetings.

Chapter 9

"On the Move"

Eric and Johnny are sitting next to one another on another of Eric's private flights. As they taxi, they stop in preparation to disembark from their plane.

"Johnny, these next few moves are going to be quick and surgical. I will need for you to let me know where your people are now so I can have the jet ready. We will be in and out rather quick. Hit your people up in advance, and let them know we will be coming to see them for a quick conversation of importance, not a reunion."

As Johnny says this, he dismantles a burner phone to its circuit board and reassembles it. Then he places a new SIM card into it before he resets the phone and hands it over to Eric.

"Here. Make those calls and texts with this. Just for the calls while we are here for here only, I mean," Eric instructs.

"Not a problem, Big Bro," Johnny responds, as he takes the new phone from Eric.

Eric watches as Johnny sends out a few text messages. Then the new phone rings aloud.

"Hello?" responds Johnny, once he pushes on the phone's screen and places it next to his ear.

Eric reaches in his pocket and gives Johnny a pair of Bluetooth earbuds. "Hold on one sec, Bruh," responds Johnny to whoever is on the other line as he configures the pairing of the ear buds to the new phone. Once he achieves success in doing so, he continues with the conversation. "Hey, Shark! Yeah, it's me. We here. I will meet you at the tire shop. Give me about twenty minutes or more to get there. Let's just say give me forty minutes so you don't have to sit there waiting on me," Johnny chats.

Eric looks upon Johnny as he completes his call.

"Okay. Let's roll."

Like the previous time, there is a vehicle waiting for them to exit the plane and take them to their destination. However, this time their luggage remains on board the plane. Once they exit the plane and down its staircase, they immediately enter the rear of the vehicle. Eric gestures to Johnny to address the driver to their next destination as he nods his head and shifts his eyes in the driver's direction while looking Johnny eye to eye. Johnny takes the facial cue and does just what he perceives to be an instruction.

"Good morning, Sir. Can you take us to the corner of Nevada Avenue and Conant Street? Thank you," asks Johnny, politely.

The driver cautiously departs the hanger and makes his way to John D. Dingell Drive. They enter onto the Detroit Industrial Freeway, Highway 94, eastbound. The driver speeds along Highway 94. When they arrive at the exit for Telegraph Road, the driver's GPS notifies him of several traffic accidents on his current route. The GPS offers a solution in the form of an alternate route suggestion.

The driver opens the partition glass and speaks, "Do you approve of the suggested route change, Sir? Taking the Industrial Freeway to the Southfield Freeway, then 96 Interstate Expressway eastbound to West Davison Street?"

"That should be fine, Brother," Johnny replies, as he looks upon Eric's face for him to interject.

"Carry on, Man," Johnny continues to speak to the driver. "That will work. Hopefully, we can make better time that way."

The two men sit in mostly silence as the vehicle turns onto Southfield and makes its way along its path to Interstate 96. After they merge onto 96, the driver takes it until that road merges into West Davison Street.

"Turn right to McPherson Street, and the house is on the left at the dead end," Johnny instructs through the partition glass.

A few miles after Davison Way turns into the Davison Freeway, the car turns right onto Klinger Street and down to McPherson Street. As it approaches the dead end, the vehicle stops. Johnny grabs the phone given to him by Eric and sends a text through it.

"Hey, J! Come on in!" bellows a man at the door through its fabric screen.

"What's going on, Man?!" responds Johnny, as he and Eric depart the vehicle. Eric turns to the driver as he comes to the window.

"Turn it around, and keep it running, Brother," he says into the car to the driver.

They both meet with the man at the threshold of the door.

"Shark, this is Eric. Eric, this is Shark. I told you I was stopping by on some serious business. We here. Let me in," Johnny says, decisively.

"Okay, okay," responds Shark, as he clears the way for them to enter. "Head to the right. That's where my living room is."

The house is small, simply laid out as far as decorations are concerned. There is a rather decent sized section of the larger wall dedicated to honors Shark must have received during his time in service. He gestures to them that taking a seat on the sofa is what he wants them to do. The sofa is old and worn out, so when they sit on it, the cushions engulf them deep within its limits. Both men pull themselves from its grasp and sit on the fringe of its edge. The home smells like stale potpourri.

"What the big deal, J? Just get on with it," barks Shark.

"Nah. That's not how this is gonna play out. You already know the drill. Do you have any issues with getting dirty? Old school shit. We've already discussed dirty. We don't go there until you tell me that," responds Johnny, with a slight scow to his tone.

"Man, just tell me what the fuck it is that you driving at! You already know I am down with you and any serious shit you'd come all this way to tell me. So, stop fucking with me, Man," answers back Shark in a higher scowling tone.

"I need you to get with some of your vet dudes you've told me about that been having that itch. We need some interdictionary tactics laid out when I send the word on the operation. We doing this shit for the people this time. These police done went way too far and for too damn long," Johnny tells him.

"That's right. About mutherfuckin' time, J! About mutherfuckin' time. I always thought it would be Cash who would suggest some. You weren't far behind on my list of who would do crazy shit like that. But about fucking time. Let me know when and where. Definitely let me know what I need to get and do to be ready."

"I just told you. You should pretty much have an idea of the basic gear to do that. Get it in small spurts off the grid. I'll be in touch. There is absolutely no room for fucking this up. Do it for Rexxo! I'll be in touch, Shark."

Johnny stands up and starts walking out of the living room back to the front door with Eric trailing behind him.

The two jump out of the front door with a quickness and walk briskly down the walk path, back into the vehicle. The vehicle takes them back to the hanger. It is off to Milwaukee from there.

Before they climb the steps, Eric turns to Johnny and says, "I'm gonna need that burner I gave you now."

Johnny doesn't hesitate to pull it out of his pocket and hand it over as he watches to see what is to happen next. Eric grabs it respectfully, opens it up, then takes the SIM card and battery from within it. He puts them in a potato chip bag given to him from the driver and places the SIM card that was in the phone and its battery inside before handing that bag back to the driver. Then he pulls out a different SIM card and a new battery and re-inserts both into the mobile phone before he gives it back to Johnny. After Johnny takes the phone back, they both step out of the vehicle. Within a few seconds, they are back onto the plane, awaiting takeoff instructions from the flight crew.

As the flight crew goes through their procedures and checklists that have to occur before takeoff, Eric is already on the phone. "Hey, Mikey. We about to roll through Milwaukee. Hit me with that intel of who to follow up with. Stay aware and remain on point. I know you heard what Ezell and Gregz went through. This shit real everywhere, Man. Don't get caught slippin' out here."

Eric sits quietly as he apparently listens to Michael speak for quite a few minutes without responding at all. He just listens inventively.

After a short while, Eric responds, "That's still a great deal of good news and spectacular progress. Good shit, Fam. Good shit. I hope to follow up behind you and solidify that link. We all may need that shit before it's over. I'm gonna lock that shit in, too."

After that, Eric grabs his phone, disassembles it, and performs the same exchange of SIM card and battery. He hands the items over to the flight attendant who then places them into a chip bag she created by emptying the contents of a bag from the snack bar. Johnny doesn't say a word about any of these things, but he is still just as impressed as if he couldn't stop talking about the whole trip so far.

Before too much longer from through the window from where they both sit, it can be seen that there are members of the ground crew removing the chalks from underneath the plane's wheels as they are preparing to depart the hanger and onto the taxi lane towards the runway. Shortly after this series of actions commence, they are in line for takeoff.

As their plane starts its sprint to optimal speed before attempting takeoff, the two men just sit in their own separate zones of contemplation. Eric is calculating what's left to be done, with whom, and how.

Johnny is soaking in what has taken place so far while anticipating what is to come. All the while Johnny is in his own vibe of amazement and confirmation. For so many years while he served with Dontre, he heard him rave on about how awesome of a guy his older brother was. Not simply due to him being his older brother, but the grandiose way in which he just lived and carried himself. The things he would endeavor to do. Johnny is just in awe himself seeing this vision play itself out, slowly confirming the sentiment for himself.

"We both have people to see here. We are going to make it quick checking them all. We heading to Houston after this," Eric says to Johnny.

Johnny turns to look at Eric, and then he looks out the window as he shows an expression of agreement.

"I'm waiting for the next battery and SIM card," Johnny mentions with humor as he extends his hand holding the burner phone towards Eric.

Eric smiles, then laughs. Eric then reaches into his pocket and grabs out a mini-Ziploc bag that has those items inside.

"This time I want to see you swap them out," Eric tells Johnny.

"Oh, okay! Gimme those bad boys. Nascar pit stop style," Johnny responds with some excitement.

Eric watches over Johnny as he attempts to detach the existing battery in its place. Johnny grows slightly frustrated as he is slowly realizing he is unable to remove the part as swiftly as Eric had done. He is certain he saw each step.

Eric reaches in, "Take this and …pull that towards you…"

"Ahh, okay. I think I may have it now. Put it back like it was so I can try it again, Bro?"

"Okay," responds Eric.

Eric takes the device and makes sure it is how it would have been before he started to take it apart. This time, Johnny does get it off.

Shouting, Johnny says, "Yeah! That's what I'm talking about. Thanks!"

Johnny doesn't have any issues taking out and replacing the SIM card. Once he finishes exchanging those parts, he hard resets the phone and waits for it to come back online. The flight attendant approaches Michael with another chip bag, and he puts in both the swapped-out parts from Johnny's phone as well as those from his. This time, he takes the chip bag and begins to get up and get ready to exit the cabin of the plane.

As the two exit the plane descending down its staircase into the hanger, the vehicle they are about to utilize has its driver ready at the door, holding it open. As they enter the vehicle, Johnny once again instructs the driver as to where to head first.

"First stop: Montana Avenue and Seventh Avenue."

The driver starts to pull out of the hanger. The vehicle speeds across College Avenue and takes a right onto North Chicago Avenue. When they arrive at the traffic light at Marquette Avenue and Tenth Avenue, the vehicle takes the left onto Marquette.

As the vehicle draws closer to the designated intersection, Johnny leans forward to the back of the driver's seat and begins to speak again. "Pull up to the house right over there— the one with the brown truck parked alongside it. No. Just park in the alley between the homes."

When the vehicle parks in the alley behind the first detached garage, both men exit the vehicle. Johnny is in the lead position with Eric cautiously following. They walk behind the garage to the back door. Johnny texts with his phone, and shortly after doing so, the door opens, and a slender man appears.

"Come in, Johnny. Who is your friend?"

"This is Dontre's older brother."

The gentleman's eyes grow larger upon hearing who Eric is.

"No shit! Ain't that some shit. Eric, right?"

Eric nods with a smile as the man speaks with him. The man then turns around and extends his hand out towards Eric, hoping to shake it.

"My apologies, Brother. Dontre was a hero to us all. You, you were the hero that our hero couldn't stop talking about. Your brother sure does love and admire you, Man. My name is Theo; these guys call me Cash. So, what is it that y'all need from me, Johnny? This got to be some real shit.

"We need you to get your vet crew together. The real ones you told me about. And we need you to link up with some guys we will send your way. Get them up to speed on the latest interdiction tactics. Like that time we all got shipped over to Qatar.

"Oh…y'all on some real devious shit! I like this fucking plan."

"Good. I will hit you up through the normal channels with that language Boots developed in Karachi."

"Not a problem. Keep me tuned in, Brother. Let me round up the fellas."

Both Johnny and Eric turn, beginning to make their way to the door. Cash was already grabbing some of his things as he planned to leave behind them. They move with hastened purpose as they cross the backyard and hop back into the vehicle.

"Take us to 6025 South Meadow Court," Eric tells the driver as he sits, attempting to become more reclined into his soft leather seat.

When they arrive at the address, Eric opens his door, and begins to exit the vehicle. Johnny steps out as well. Johnny looks around the cul de sac. He observes all the flowers and neatly groomed properties draped with several displays of vividly colorful flowers and bushes. Johnny wonders to himself how someone living here would want to help them, let alone risk all of what he is seeing to legitimately do so. Johnny quickly catches himself and realizes he is working with Eric on his objective, and not the other way around. Eric has already proven himself as formidable and quite tactful.

Eric approaches the door, pulls out a key, and inserts it— to Johnny's surprise— into the new looking bronze doorknob where the key hole sits.

"A friend of mine purchased this home a few months back. He knew I would be in town, so I decided to make use of his generosity," Eric informs Johnny, as he catches a glimpse of his shock in him having the key to the door.

"You're everywhere. I guess the better question is, '*Where are you not at?*'" Johnny asks.

"I'm sure there are a few places that could serve as an answer to that question. I'm certain of it," Eric responds in jest.

Eric walks through the home with a familiarity that gives Johnny slight suspicion regarding Eric's initial demeanor about his familiarity with the home. Eric disappears upstairs into the home briefly, then returns back downstairs with a cordless landline phone in his hand. The phone looks different than the usual cordless phone from Johnny's view. It has a dark plastic piece attached to the lower half of the phone. The attachment looks as if it is not permanently affixed to the phone itself, but connected in some manner that Eric does not have to touch it for it to remain secure where it is positioned.

Eric begins to press numbers on its illuminated keypad. The phone's dial tone is then heard vaguely, and it is followed by a distinct ringing sound.

"Hey. Yeah, it's me. I was about to order some lunch. Did you want to share a meal? Okay, I trust your taste. Bring it over after you're finished picking it up. I will just wait for you to arrive," Eric speaks into the phone.

Eric shoots back up the stairs as he obviously is working the attachment with his hands, detaching it from the phone itself.

"What is that, Eric?" asks Johnny, finally.

"Oh. This is a voice augmentation device. My buddy prefers that I use this on his phone whenever I come here and need to use his phone. I definitely agree and see the value in using it. He had it made for his house phones.

"That's wild. Why would you even need to do that? Hold on. If that thing changed your voice to where it apparently doesn't sound like you at all, then how did whoever you were just speaking to even know who they were talking to? You didn't seem to even discuss that, so what's up with all that, Eric?" Johnny asks, with a different trace of intrigue in his strained tone.

"Okay." Eric turns back facing downstairs where Johnny is standing and looks at him with interest.

Eric's eyes widen with part curiosity, part paranoia as he slowly skips back down a few steps of the staircase closer to Johnny. Eric observes his facial expressions and body language more precisely as he draws closer and continues to speak.

"We've been swapping phones for the last twenty-four hours, and you have doubt as to why I would seek to augment my voice when speaking on a landline, Johnny? Are you unaware as to why, or is your inquisitiveness coming from something else?" Eric's tone sharpens and makes Johnny for the first time uncomfortable.

"I truly do not get what you doing, or why we've been swapping out parts in these phones you gave me completely. Off-hand, I can only assume it's some type of method of preventing being tracked. That's all I got. As to how what we've been doing facilitates that for you, I have no clue. To the actual details, I mean. That's just not exactly my thing. Seems like it's definitely your thing. So, by all means, if you care to explain and stop creeping me the fuck out, please go right ahead," Johnny responds, as he still is uncomfortable, but just to a lesser degree as he waits for Eric to attempt at educating him.

"Most cell phone carriers operate within an encrypted in transit user to server to user method. Which means that if I send you a message, whether through voice or text, and that message goes through the carrier's server, it is sent to the end user of the transmission. The problem here is that once that information hits the server, that server filters and processes it. It also in most cases makes a copy of the transmission for its records. Those records can be accessed typically unbeknownst to either user by anyone who can decrypt the server's language. From there, voice analyzation can be utilized to make voice print certifications and identify you by the voice pattern they have tracked on you, or anyone for that matter, since you first spoke into a phone.

"What we are doing, Johnny is dangerous for us both. I have made many efforts to maintain our inconspicuousness. I have apps installed on the phones we have been using that utilize an end-to-end encryption. That mean that our transmissions are stored at the endpoints of each transmission, and never in mid-transit like through any undisclosed server or intermediary location. We also have features installed into the operation of these phones that utilize an unhackable end-to-end encryption as it receives and sends transmissions.

"So, since the land line here," Eric says, as he points to the cordless phone in his hand, "does not have these features, the best we can do is augment our voices and prevent the potential eavesdropper working underground or even above ground for the Central Intelligence Agency, A.K.A. the C.I.A. or the N.S.A., better known as The National Security Agency down under N.O.R.A.D., which means North American Aerospace Defense Command.

"These are very real agencies that leave very little room for error in these matters. They remain relentless. If we slip, they will track it. Then find you after they aggress anyone who knows you with dungeon time for conspiracy to commit God knows what illicit criminal activity they can devise to charge, and they will indict. Does that fill you in, Bro?"

Johnny is astounded with the information dump that has just been dropped on him like a skid of bricks off the side of a telescopic handler crane. Eric is still standing just a few feet away from him awaiting a response to his explanation and question with an intensifying look of unmistakable disappointment across his face.

"Well? Please respond, Bro. Like for real, Man," Eric says.

"No. That actually makes a lot of sense. I was just a mechanic. We would only speculate and talk shit about that upper echelon activity. That makes perfect sense. I didn't mean to take so long responding, I just was processing. That was really my first time hearing that shit you just said. Okay. Keeping it off their radar is the priority. I got you. By all means proceed. Carry on with what I interrupted you from doing. I'm good.

"Very well. I was about to start wondering about you, Johnny. I thought you was hip to most of this stuff. It's not an issue. I don't mind showing you. You just have to pardon me. There are a great many moving parts and the accountability of this whole thang resting upon my shoulders.

"I have exacting standards and the appropriate expectations that come along with them. This move culminates the entirety of the last twenty-one years of my life's efforts. I take every bit of this shit serious. So, I have to take a few tics back and remember I am the only one who understands the whole situation. Just as this is by 'MY' design, it is also the reason I need to remind myself, and at times be reminded, I can't just kick folk around because I am wound up in the awareness of what we are doing big picture.

"When this is all said and done, me and a few others will be on the extreme version of on-the-run, and we will be hunted down with every man they can put on the job. They gonna desperately want to find us and fuck us over before putting us on some sham trial with all the propaganda they can conjure up to defame and discredit our entire lives. I'm cautious now so that I don't make that manhunt easy for them by any means while laying some misdirection along the way."

There is a noticeable sound coming from the other side of the house that is quite noisy. As Johnny goes to investigate, he is curious as to after all that Eric just said. He isn't going along with Eric to find out where that noise is coming from and what it is. Johnny creeps gingerly along the walls of the kitchen, peeking around the corner as the noise grows louder then closer. Johnny gets to the kitchen itself. As he turns the corner, the door in the kitchen that leads out to the garage busts open.

"Who the hell are you, Young Blood?" asks one of the men closest to Johnny.

"Who the hell am I? Unless you live here, it's who the hell are you right about now," Johnny responds, dryly.

By this time, three other men have also entered through the door into the kitchen space. The first one to come through then looks back at Johnny, whom he does not know. He smirks as he recognizes that Johnny has not produced any weapon as he spoke so boldly. But the three that are with him already have theirs pulled partly out from under their shirts, just brandishing its presence on their persons.

"Again, Pat-na, I will ask you one. More. Time. Who the fuck are you? Where is Eric?" asks the man.

Suddenly, Eric comes from the other room.

"Now, why did you even mention my name, Gerald? What's up with that? What if he did not know who he was looking for? What if he had no clue? You just gave him my name, Bro," exclaims Eric.

"Man, quit with that shit right now. Your man almost just got blasted. You might need to put his ass on to a few things while you're at it, Bro. Like damn, Man. I get it and all. But, Man…"

"Okay, okay. Do you have what I asked for?" asks Eric.

"What did I do, Eric, besides say your name and almost shoot your guy? What else did I do? You already know we got you. C'mon."

One of the men comes from the rear into the front and tosses a fairly large duffle bag onto the kitchen table. The bag is all black with forest green straps for carrying. The zipper is also forest green. Johnny stands still, eased by Eric and the strange new faces having familiarity. Eric walks over to the table and reaches for the zipper slowly. He unzips the bag, then looks up at the man after its contents are revealed.

"Yeah. This will do nicely. Yeah. Real good," Eric graciously compliments the bag that is teeming full of cash and several sets of credentials wrapped in rubber bands, separating each identity. There are several bundles of cash separated with rubber bands from one denomination to the next.

"I will get this where it needs to go A.S.A.P. I got you. Give me a second."

Eric pulls out a different mobile device and begins to press on its screen as he navigates through its features. After a considerable amount of activity with his fingers and the screen, he looks up and over to the man and speaks again.

"Freddy, check your account. I just sent that over. I sent more than we discussed. We'll be in touch, and thanks again. As always, you do not disappoint. Love is love."

Freddy and the men who enter the home with him each give Eric handshakes and daps, then they go back through the door and out into the garage. As they are leaving, Eric investigates a few areas of the home as he goes to handle what he has left to do while he is still there. Meeting Freddy is his purpose, and now that that has been accomplished successfully, it is time to leave.

He returns to the kitchen, reaches into the bag, and grabs a handful of both money and two sets of credentials out from the other several sets besides them in the bag and goes back upstairs. When he descends back down the stairs, he gestures to Johnny that it is indeed time to get back to the vehicle outside. Johnny does not hesitate to follow Eric as he exits the front door. They both slip into the rear of the car that is still running with the driver ready.

They pull off and depart the cul de sac back towards the airport. Eric steps out of the vehicle and walks to the other side of the hanger where the plane is being checked for pre-flight approval. The duffle bag, although large, is draped over his back as he holds onto both straps with the hand opposite of the right shoulder it is draped over. Eric boards the plane and stows his duffle bag in the seat across from where he has set himself up to settle into for the trip. Johnny follows suit and sits in the section across the aisle from where Eric sits. The men relax for a moment.

The flight attendant arrives into the outer cabin from the pilot's area and meets a courier at the doorway of the plane. The courier delivers a medium sized bag. The aroma from that bag reveals that whatever that is in its contents is food. The insignia on the brown bag reads "Dobies Steakhouse". The flight attendant grabs a few larger brown bags from the courier after accepting the first one and then takes the items into their preparation area once their exchanges are complete.

The door is then sealed to the plane and the polite announcement comes over the intercom that they are about to be departing the hanger and off towards the taxi runway. As the plane prepares for take-off shortly afterwards, the flight attendants emerge from the partition with the silverware, napkins, and beverage options for both Eric and Johnny to choose from.

"Better soak all this in. Once this shit gets set off, there won't be much of this at all going down. I won't be with you, and you may need to lay real low as a precaution. I'd get used to some cold cuts and tuna fish sandwiches when that time arrives. The more recluse the better. Trust me.

"No need to be foolish and bring any unnecessary attention or scrutiny to yourself and those connected to your name. The individuals who will be looking for breadcrumbs are not the kind you even want to know you exist, Man. Trust me on this one," Eric states, as he takes the napkin set in front of him and releases it from its clasp before he drapes it over his chest and tucks it into the front of his shirt.

"I kinda figured that was what I was signing up for. I plan on sealing myself off in my bunker and staying there out of the reach of infrared scans and the like or unwelcomed guests looking to poke around. My people know the drill," Johnny responds.

A second attendant comes from behind the partition with their plates. Once served, the attendants return to their area to eat what they can of the meals provided for them as well.

Their two-and-a-half-hour flight is close to its end, and they descend upon the city of Dallas, Texas. When they land, the plane does what is does each trip: taxi along the runway into the designated hanger for their service provider. The plane makes its full stop. The door opens, and from the view from where Johnny is sitting, he watches as a strange man exits a vehicle that is parked in the hanger. The plane pulls into the hanger, and the strange man begins to make his way to the recently opened staircase to the cabin of the plane. Instead of getting off the plane, they receive a visitor. The man stands about five foot four, and is of medium slender, toned physique.

"This is nice," mentions the stranger as he steps onboard.

"Nice that you approve. Did you bring me those items?" Eric asks, as he raises up from his seat to walk towards the doorway to greet the man.

The men shake hands. The man hands Eric a small, brown leather attaché case. Eric receives it, and places it down on a seat. He then returns to his seat, opens the large duffle bag, and grabs from within its contents a small pouch from the bag that had many of them inside of the duffle bag. He places an assortment of currencies and a set of credentials into the pouch and stands back erect, walks back to the man, and hands those items over to him. The man peeks into the pouch and nods in approval before shaking his hand yet again and departing the plane.

The flight attendant reseals the door, and the second attendant exits the pilot's area. Within a faint earshot, it can be heard at a low volume the pilot communicating with the flight tower the clearance to get in line to taxi down the runway for takeoff. Within thirty minutes, they are back in the air without needing to refuel.

Johnny watches the landscape transition from rural to urban and then suburban as they travel through the sky. After about an hour, they begin to sink down through the thick, white, puffy clouds. They reach the city of Houston. Once they touch down, their plane does not even go into the hangar.

They pull of the runway in front of the hangar, and there is a vehicle parked out in the general area of where the staircase opens down to when the attendant activates the automated staircase to unfold. This time, instead of a man, there are two women who step from the rear of a late model SUV. Both women are dressed modestly, but obviously not seeking attention.

They enter the plane and greet Eric. Eric does not introduce Johnny. The women nod and acknowledge his presence all the same. Eric takes a bag from them and then hands them each a bag similar in content to what he gave Freddy. Then they leave as well.

"I will be in touch. Inspect your areas, Ladies. The time is not far from now," Eric mentions as he watches them descend back down the staircase and back into their vehicles.

The flight attendants grab a package from the ground crew and take that manila envelope into the cockpit to the pilot. The door is left ajar. It can be heard from the conversation that the pilot is initiating with air flight control that they are discussing the flight plan for the next trip. Johnny can overhear flight control staff confirming with the pilots that the weather forecast for the afternoon is clear and sunny. The door to the pilot's cabin closes, and Johnny can feel the plane begin to move once again.

"Can I bring either of you gentlemen something to drink?"

"Yes, bring me two cold bottles of water please," requests Eric for himself.

"I will take a coffee: milk and three sugars. Then also a cold bottle of water, please. Thank you," Johnny answers to the attendant.

The plane is in line waiting for clearance to enter the taxi runway for takeoff. Eric swaps out the phones again that he and Johnny were using. When he finishes that task, he immediately starts to text. Johnny puts phone his back in his pocket.

The pilot apparently receives the word to initiate his taxi onto the runway. Once they are airborne, after reaching their heights above the atmosphere, Eric is still texting with his device.

Johnny, we are headed to New Orleans. How far from the airport are your guys? How long would it take for them to get there? Eric texts.

…I don't think very far. Like a half an hour. The better question is where are they right now and what they are doing. They knew I would be around just not when. So, I'd say about an hour and some change. I'll give them the heads up now. Do you want them to meet us at the hangar?

That's exactly what we are gonna need. I have a special job for them. I have a guy coming to connect with them for just that purpose.

There isn't much discussion between the two of them after that. However, there isn't any tension, either. Eric is preoccupied with what he is accomplishing with each text, and after seeing so much to this point, Johnny does not seek to deter or distract Eric from whatever he has planned. It is quite obvious that Eric operates in a mindset and a related process that is beyond his familiarity. He is just grateful to have played a role at all at this point.

Johnny sits in his seat, amazed at how correct his long-time friend was about his older brother being uniquely awesome and never without a surprise to his methods and thoughts on things. Eric's understanding of life and what things mean is also intriguing to him as he watches the clouds move around them and observes Eric handle business to come.

Johnny just started to reach out to the guys he intended on meeting with while he was in town. Unfortunately, having some authentic New Orleans cuisine is not going to happen, which he finds slightly disappointing. He was anticipating at least one stop. He thought that even if Eric had something delivered in again, it would be different than traversing the French Quarters for it.

As Johnny takes the time to appreciate his view of the world from above, it becomes noticeable in both his view and his spatial awareness that the plane is again descending back to the ground. He is now able to see the initial viewing of where he is from the buildings and overall layout of the area's iconic landmarks. They are indeed entering the city of New Orleans.

Johnny receives a series of welcomed texts that his people will be in place as requested. Johnny does not wish to disappoint Eric in the field of the punctuality of his associates. Not to stain the respect they all share for Dontre in addition the respect he wants Eric to have for himself as well.

The plane, again, pulls in front of the hangar. The doorway is unsealed, and the staircase extends.

Eric stands up and gestures to Johnny.

"Come join him outside, Johnny."

Johnny stands up at that moment and follows Eric to the exit of the cabin. As they step beyond the threshold, the sky is still bearing sunshine, and the glare forces them both to don sunglasses to their faces as they step into its light. At the moment of their disembarking, Johnny's people are parked nearby inside of the hangar. As they are given the notification of Johnny's arrival, Eric points out to Johnny a town car that has just pulled into the hangar area.

"That's for us."

The town car pulls up, and from within it a tall light-skinned gentleman steps out. He bears a large smile. An obvious emotional moment of enjoyment exists there between them both, Johnny realizes.

After Eric walks up to the gentleman and they embrace with laughter and fulfilment, Eric turns to Johnny. "Johnny. This is my younger cousin Michael."

Johnny approaches Michael and shakes his hand.

"Good to meet you, Johnny. Dontre has told me many good things about you through the years. I am glad to see you now. I am glad to see that Eric has you with him. I know it isn't an easy task riding with this drill sergeant. Not at all," Michael says with humor in his overall tone. "I brought a few friends of my own."

Michael waves at the deep-tinted town car with the waving of his hand in a single, slow motion. Then two other men step out from within the vehicle. There is also a second SUV riding behind the town car with two other men inside. Those men remain in the vehicle.

"From this point, Michael will be with us. After our next stop, he will travel with you for a stop, then you will have a few spots to hit on your own, Johnny. You got it, though," Eric says, confidently. "Where are your peoples? Have them come through."

Johnny pulls his phone from his pocket and starts to text. Sometime later, his associates emerge from within the hangar. Once they arrive in the close proximity of Eric, Michael, his two guys, and himself, he begins to introduce them to Eric and Michael.

"Hey, Eric. This is Tyreef, and this is Conrad. We served with one another on more than a few moves."

The men shake each other's hands at the mass introduction. Michael then introduces the men he brought with him.

"Well, here is Ralph, and there is Henry. In the SUV behind them is Bricks and Frankie."

"Do Bricks have those containers for me, Mike?" Eric turns and asks.

"Yes, he does. Yes, he does."

"Excellent! Johnny, can you have Tyreef or Conrad dip over into the hangar so they can move those containers from their SUV into theirs?"

"Not a problem. Ty, go handle that, Bro," Johnny says.

Ty walks over to the doorway of the hangar as Bricks turns the truck around and drives through its widened opening. As the SUV drives into the hangar and beyond sight, Michael and Eric continue to speak with one another as Johnny and Conrad walk up to them both.

"Hey, Young Brother, I have Bricks unloading several containers in the truck you're in. Those containers will need to be brought to the locations listed in the interior of each container. You and your guy will travel with Bricks. When you hit the designated locations and deal with the people I have in place, you guys will just deliver each container. There are eight," Eric states.

"Johnny, me, you, and Michael will bounce up to New York now. You will head back out to Los Angeles with Michael. He won't continue past L.A. You will then hit San Diego, and then off to Oakland, then Portland. I will have explained where and who you will be seeing in addition to the people you have in those parts. After that trip, the pilot knows to take you back to the A. Then you're done." Eric gives a strong dap to Johnny before he embraces him before the group. "You've been essential. Know that."

A final round of embraces and daps are shared amongst the men before they each go in their separate designated ways per Eric's instructions. Michael is the first to ascend into the staircase leading back into the plane's passenger cabin. He is followed by Eric and lastly Johnny. He takes a moment to send off Conrad with additional motivation.

"Handle your business, Brother. This shit is about to get real. Don't make any calls. Grab some SIM cards from Joe who does the burners in the seventh ward. Grab like twelve batteries, too. Swap them out after every drop. And change out the SIM cards with a new one. Take the old ones, put them in an old chip bag with aluminum coating, and get rid of them. Too much is at stake. Stay low key and keep being off the radar at the center of each move y'all make. Trust me on this."

"Not a problem. I will handle that and stick to the script," Conrad replies.

Once they finish speaking, Johnny turns and starts to make his way up the staircase as well. The three men sit and enjoy a few alcoholic beverages while the Jet is being refueled. It is a much needed series of moments of warm comradery.

As the effects of their few drinks fade from their bodies, they are disturbed by a message over the intercom. "Sir, there is an individual that seems to be a delivery person seeking to gain entrance to the cabin. Should I have security vet them first?" asks a male voice over the intercom.

"Most definitely. Can you put that interaction on my screen from the feed, please?" Eric asks the voice.

As the feed becomes visible, all three of the men become interested in who their visitors are.

Johnny looks in with focus. He is hoping that Eric has ordered some food anyways. He notices that the person at least claims to be a delivery person because the large brown bags he is carrying has a distinctive brand image on their sides.

"That's the Cochon! That's wassup! Eric, you stay on point. This is about to be really good," Johnny exclaims.

"I agree," states Michael. "Now, once Eric is satisfied that they are not posing as our delivery people is the true matter that everyone is awaiting the conclusive evidence to be presented." As they all observe the video feed closely, Michael continues to jest with his cousin. "Nope, no guns… Credentials seemed to match up. I think your guys are on top of this."

Eric smiles as he sees the diligence exuded by the security staff in place. The flight attendant crew comes from the front partition area, unseals the exit door, and meets the delivery person at the foot of the staircase. Once having done so, they reverse the process by contracting the staircase and re-sealing the door of the plane. There is some time that takes place as the pilots are communicating with air traffic control in regard to their flight plans and flight lanes to reach New York that have availabilities for them to reserve usage of during the next available slots of time.

The ground crew takes the time to conduct diagnostics on the jet since it has seen several quick flights in the last twenty-four-hour time span. This process takes some time as well. The flight attendants in recognition of this brings out the food that has been re-heated for their convenience. The men are provided the essential cutlery and place settings to begin the consumption of the food brought out to them.

Eric orders an assortment of entrees and sides. He also has them bring in a few gallons of their house flavored beverages which is something they typically do not do. Eric is just very persuasive and gratuitous.

They laugh some more and drink slightly as they complete the food set before them family style. They all agree the restaurant is very satisfactory. The flight attendants return and discard the debris left from the meal.

Moments later, the male voice returns to the intercom airways. "Gentlemen. We have been given our approval for the submitted flight plan from air traffic control. We are being sent into line for entering the runway. We should be up in the air within fifteen minutes at the maximum. Please take this time to secure all belongings and secure those safety belts located to the right of your hips in your seat. Thank you again. It has been a pleasure serving you. Thank you, Mr. Castille, for that amazing meal. For all of them!" the voice remarks, then disappears.

As the jet begins to taxi and take to the air, the three men sit. Michael and Eric carry on, and Johnny sits quietly in between the insertion into a conversation by both Michael and Eric on occasion.

Their flight is about two and a half hours in the jet. The image of the Statue of Liberty is to their right as they cross over the Hudson en route to their destination of JFK International Airport. They can also see the other iconic landmarks of the most famous city on earth, New York City. The jet finally reaches the tarmac, then into its designated hangar.

Upon their arrival, there is a SUV that has awaited them. They exit the jet and onto the surface of the buffed concrete flooring of the staircase to inside the SUV. The SUV is a Cadillac Sky Captain; there is enough room for all three of them to be seated comfortably in its rear cabin.

Eric steps inside first and chooses the seat equipped with all the computer access and controls for the other devices in its arm rest station. He brings the duffle bag with him and has it sat down in front of him. Johnny enters next as Michael lets him in before himself. Once Michael chooses his seat of the two remaining, the door is closed for him. Moments later, the driver is back in his seat, and the vehicle starts its journey first out of the general airport area. Their first stop is off the Van Wyck Expressway, visiting South Side Queens.

"I want to check in with Ezell's brother Dante," Eric mentions. "Then we will be off, headed uptown."

The driver takes the Linden Boulevard exit, and they make haste until they reach New York Boulevard, also referred to as Guy R. Boulevard. It is at this intersection they pass the light and make the slight left onto O'Donnell Road. When they reach the end of the block, Eric instructs the driver to stop and pull into the home he identifies over the phone with visual cues.

"Stop by the one in front of the fire hydrant."

Eric then reaches into his pocket and begins to text. Shortly after he begins texting, a man emerges from the front door and walks briskly to the rear of the vehicle. The man opens the door and climbs into the vehicle sitting in the lone remaining seat that is unoccupied and closes the door behind him.

"Eric! Good to see you. Ezell told me to expect you sooner than later. So, here we are. We are actually moving forward on this, huh?" Dante asks Eric, as he looks upon the occupants of the vehicle.

"No. We've already begun. We are almost at a launch point," Eric responds stoically, but without disdain. "Things on all levels are being secured in their respective places as we speak. So, with that being said, you know what time it is, and you know what I need from you. What we need from you."

"Yeah. I remember that conversation real well," Dante responds.

Dante pauses in silence a brief moment as he looks into Eric's eyes. Eric looks right back at him, and they both are equally silent. Johnny seems to feel that even though nothing is being said that there apparently is something still being communicated. He desperately watches with curious anticipation for any remnant of communication between the two. He discovers nothing he can readily identify as any sort of exchange. The silence ends almost as quickly as it started unfortunately.

"I will make the call. No, I will make that trip and deliver that message in person," Dante says, with one eye fully open while the other is squinted, close to being shut. "You know he is going to be excited. He was ready when we first discussed the possibility of this move becoming a real thing back before you were certain how you were going to get here exactly. Here we are. Here…"

"Here is exactly where we are, Unc. You already know what it is. Don't get cold feet on me now. Where is that cold steel at that used to course through them veins, Unc?"

Again, both men look at one another in a shorter moment of silence. Dante nods his head towards Eric in agreement. Then Dante reaches for the door, tells everyone else stay on point, and "God bless." He then pulls the handle on the door, opens it wide enough for him to slip through that opening, and jots back into the house.

The vehicle spins around the cul de sac and sprints down the block back to Linden where they turn right heading westbound. Once back on the Van Wyck, they skate through traffic, changing lanes with a moderate purpose as they move through the expressway. After merging onto Grand Central parkway, they move quickly to the next merger. After that, they take the westbound exit onto the Long Island Expressway, taking them in the direction of the 59th Street Bridge.

Johnny, being the one who is not a New York Native, just watches the areas of the city he can see from his window seat. He thinks to himself that for a city at the epicenter of the world's activity, there just doesn't seem to be much brightness. Despite the sunlight, there is just an aura looming over the city— as far as he can see— that definitely encourages him to remain mindful at all times. Even the children playing on the street sidewalks seem to be more than just merely children. There is just something different in their eyes from where he is sitting that strikes him different.

It is quite some time before he is in the city to properly draw a reference as to how he felt the last time he had been through these parts.

Even the 59th Street Bridge just doesn't seem vivid at all. It's as if they found the most unreal, unimaginative variant of a color to paint the entire bridge with. All Johnny can think of is Gotham City from those movies. Just dreary.

Once across the bridge, they whisk through the city, staying on 59th Street. Johnny is even more alert. He thinks the more residential area seems cold. The city itself is beyond what he's ever known to be described as busy. This is truly what they must have meant when the word bustling was created. It is unreal to him all over again, dwarfing whatever memory he may have had previously.

Michael and Eric just stare with a sense of mysticism as they watch the images they all are passing by with hints of nostalgic reverence. They really aren't even paying much attention to him and what he is experiencing as they are mutually captivated in their own ways. Johnny continues to ponder how there are so many people moving along the streets that there isn't enough room to see the ground beneath them, it appears. Still, they each are moving briskly in their strides as if they each are walking along, and by themselves. It is weird to see.

They arrive at Columbus Circle and take the round-a-bout onto Broadway headed north. Johnny continues to marvel at the architecture of the city that seems to have no reason to sleep, or opportunity for the most part, with the degree of foot traffic and vehicular congestion. The driver makes the left on 79th Street at the light, and within a few seconds, they are on the West Side Highway— now renamed Joe DiMaggio Highway. They all watch the piers as the driver makes quick work of navigating their way to the 125th Street exit.

Eventually they arrive where the driver parks the vehicle on the north end of Convent Avenue. The men exit the Cadillac and enter the park where they walk about fifty yards to the landmark remembrance rock. Here, Dontre has already been waiting on them. Johnny and Dontre shake hands, dap it up, and embrace one another. Eric and Michael dap up Dontre. Not too long after, Ezell and Gregory are walking up from the gate to the park off St. Nicholas Terrace towards them. They all exchange minimal greetings, keeping things simple and not over doing it. With all the men standing there along the decorative rough face block wall, Eric moves to the center of their line.

"So, this is where we currently stand. Most of Phase One has been accomplished. That's good. Yet, obviously not near enough. We still need another situation addressed for this to go to plan, Fellas. I got that covered. Well, my homie does," Eric states, ominously. A next person strolls upon them as they stand by the wall as discreetly as they know to. She nods her head accordingly towards Eric. "There is nothing worse than a woman scorned. Am I right?"

"Quite right," replies the mysterious woman.

"This is Shymeika. She is going to cover that part. Her and her network of disgruntled formerly employed crew."

The men look on in curiosity.

Chapter 10

"Final Requisitions"

With the group collected, Eric remains in the center as for his physical position. "We have done a great deal of this without many actual resources allocated to keep things moving and our people effectively motivated. I will need each of you to direct your ball park financial needs to Michael when you get your turn. Just give him the number, and break that number down as to what it's for. Keep it straight forward. The bonus payout for your current troubles and those that lay ahead will be dealt with another time."

Eric walks over to Shymeika, and they begin to converse with her in private.

"Okay. All your people are in place and ready to patch my people in? This can't be screwed up. One-hundred-percent completion or it's a no go," Eric states.

"C'mon, Eric? Why would you do me like that? You know full well I play no games whatsoever. You taught me this too long ago to act brand new now. My people ready. I won't even try you and ask if your people is ready."

Shymeika stands in a defensive posture as she challenges Eric with her body language rather than with her words.

Michael is listening to Ezell and Gregory outline how many different crews they are accounting for and what they will need. Michael is storing the information into a digital device. When they finish giving that information to Michael, the two of them walk off from the group, back towards St. Nicholas Terrace.

"We gonna be sitting by the park on one-two-nine," Ezell says, as they depart from the group.

Johnny approaches Michael next and gives him his information. "I have twelve active units spread out. Each team consists of five main leaders. They each have crews at least ten strong. These guys are gonna need gas masks, zip ties, discrete Taser devices, light armor tactical gear for mobility. I also have a guy who will start creating social media histories for false positive leads to give us all about a month lead when this shit goes to hell. I have a list here that goes into more specific details." Johnny gives Michael a thumb drive. He leans into Michael's ear and whispers, "Password for the encrypted file is 0234231897DGY37."

Johnny walks over to Dontre. They dap each other up, laugh, and walk back along the same path Ezell and Gregory went down towards St. Nicholas Terrace. Eric, Michael, and Shymeika remain left behind. From behind Johnny, Dontre, Ezell, and Gregory on the Convent Ave side comes Dante. He is walking up the path with a slender male at his side. When he arrives at the wall, he approaches Eric.

"Here is my guy. The guy who had been working with the schematic you gave him. He has a working apparatus. Due to the nature of its purpose, its testing has been significantly limited to avoid the obvious detection from any authorities monitoring such activities. This man needs to get paid. And he will need to know how many of these you will be needing and where you will want them to be delivered to," Dante says.

"Excellent. Most excellent. I was waiting to hear back from you. Unfortunately, following up on something like that was not a usual endeavor, but I am satisfied that this is what has become of those plans. This makes these plans extremely reliable. Great news! We will need twelve," Eric responds to Dante. He looks at the gentleman with Dante and repeats, "Twenty-four units."

Michael makes a notation into his device. Then he looks onto the men talking for what he is sure to come next.

"That will be one-point-three million. Plus, the two-hundred-thousand for research, development, and prototype services. A total of one-point-five-million-dollars," continues the gentleman.

Shymeika's eyes grow extra wide when she hears that figure spoken. Michael continues his notation after getting the amount as he is anticipating what is to follow.

"Mike?" Eric calls out.

"Yeah?"

"We will need to include a discretionary spending account for each of the twelve teams. This should cover training, meals, and aftermath preparations," Eric answers.

"That makes sense. Even with that, we are under the expected budget by this stage," Michael states.

"I will get the fund to cut some green point cards and load them under shell corps that go nowhere. Well within the rights of any company to strive for anomality."

Dante and the gentleman seem to be in the need of making their exit. The gentleman doesn't seem very comfortable. Dante daps up Eric and Michael. Eric Whispers into Dante's ear, "I have some people in DC who would really love to meet you and compensate you for some of these same services in a consistent major way. Stay safe and When this blow over reach out to my Guy." Eric then placed a card into Dante's pocket as he released from the hug. Then Dante takes the gentleman back with him towards Convent Ave. With that business concluded, Shymeika takes the walk with them as they now head the three of them out towards the exit of the park onto St. Nicholas Terrace. Shymeika clicks the key fob on her keychain and the lights illuminate on a late-model foreign SUV. She then hits the remote start so it can be ready when she gets inside instead of having to wait.

Eric states, "Mike, I got a follow-up team that will need a card like those you described, but twice the amount. They will be backtracking our movement and ensure that each team has the proper understanding and training to make these moves. He will be connecting the activities between our military vets and our community leaders. This small tactical group will also be ensuring that each team has the supplies and resources they will need to move forward discretely, as I nor any of us will be back in contact with any of them moving forward.

"From here on out, once we get things confirmed and solidified, we will be waiting for the go ahead from me, then you as the legal teams get prepared to do what needs to be done independently from what I will have the groups engaging in. For this we will need to get 'Go-Bags' established and dispensed to all high echelon teams. I already spread phase one of that assistance program. Phase two will be coming in the form that you dispense through my team from the investment group. Cryptocurrency to cash format that will be complicatedly difficult to untraceable," Eric elaborates, as they all stand on the sidewalk.

Shymeika just listens, not surprised by what she has heard. Eric played a major role in raising her up to strive in these New York streets. She turns to Eric and Michael and speaks out to them. "Send over a clean million to us. That's a small fee for what we will be doing in the big picture of the whole matter."

Eric looks at Michael and he shrugs his shoulders.

"We are still considerably under budget at this point. That is definitely doable," Michael answers.

"Then double it," Eric responds to Michael.

"The successful completion of their involvement is irreplaceable."

When it is clear that Eric and Michael need to make their way down to one-two-nine, she takes the cue. She gives each of the men daps and start to walk over her to lush ride. Before she is able to hop into the opened door, Eric shouts to her, "Shymeika! You got it. Deliver your role to the 'T', and I will double the rate for you and your team!"

"Say no more!" Shymeika responds.

She turns back to her opened door, hops in, and turns the stereo up quite loud. It blasts a deep, heavy, bass rhythm tune as she pulls out of her parking spot and zips from out of her tight parking spot and down the block.

Eric and Michael walk and talk on their way to the benches by the park where the rest of the group has been headed to, waiting for them.

"So, what you have planned next, Cousin?" Michael asks Eric, as they briskly bop down the street along the sidewalk. "We need to tighten up the screws on this boat, Bro. I get the feeling we need to speed things up to get ready. The next event isn't far off. I can feel it all over my being."

"Shymeika is going to get us access so Cleveland, Dante, and my contact can have their work come in hand while Bricks is going to roll with Johnny's people to get all those interdiction devices in place. Ezell and Gregory have the streets with us. Johnny and I got them the tactical support. We just need to get them those resources and we should be straight.

"The only thing left is to bullet proof the exit strategy. Just a little bit more. I know what to do in these situations, so I'm straight. However, you should be good as well because you have zero to no actual knowledge of what is going to happen on the record, and what you're doing falls within the scope of the law. You're seeking opportunities to fight the legal system and get cases to change precedent while also fighting to influence legislative action.

"You're straight. Johnny will need help, Gregory, and possibly Ezell. From what I understand, and we can square this away right now, that Ezell and Gregz should be good, too. We can just cover the basics. If what Cleveland has developed works to scope, then Shymeika and her team should be untraceable. We can always insulate their direct involvement with a back-up alibi for their whereabouts for when that event takes place. We won't know what will work until that moment has come. We will just know that is one of the on-the-move decisions we will have to weave into things.

"Sounds tight if you ask me, Family. They won't see you coming, and by the time they do, you will be four to five steps ahead of them. When they follow the bread crumbs you've left for them, you will get that info as it becomes a thing and can easily adapt and maintain four to five steps lead. That's what it looks like from where I see things," Michael comments.

"This sounds true, but you already know I need several contingencies in motion simultaneously. This was then with this thing now. That's even more of an intensified need. I know a guy who also knows a guy that has some real interesting tech in the field of mixing silicone and electronics. It's some trippy stuff, Bro. How much room in this budget do we have? That just might be what separates some of us that seem more exposed than I prefer to include my own needs for those things,", Eric elaborates.

"We are far below the red line figure. The investment team will be pleased. You did that well as well. As long as these silicone devices don't cost north of the tens of millions, we should be very far from having those issues," Michael answers.

"Nah. I doubt they would even go up as high as three-hundred-thousand," Eric says, after he cocks his head sideways as he imagines the calculations of those expenses quickly. "Matter-of-fact, let me hit him up. I think he is home now," Eric mumbles to himself, but loud enough to be heard.

Michael recognizes that for what it is and doesn't bother to respond or ask for any clarification on the statement.

They can both see the crew sitting by the benches in their typical fashion. Old heads at the top and the young bucks on the bottom. They both show that they enjoy seeing this.

"That takes me back in so many ways— that sight. We spent a lot of days and nights right here, Cousin. Sure did," Michael shares.

"Yeah, we did have more than a dozen awesome memories right here alone. There are quite a few spots out here we can say the same for. Reminiscing on all of that we can continue to do almost without end. We definitely have a massive amount of memories between us all that we could laugh all day. Those them moments that keep me focused and remind me what we doing here to keep it a buck. We lost some, too. We lost some that didn't have to go the way they did. Bip comes to mind first on that list, Bro."

"Damn right! Rest easy, Brother!" Michael says, as he looks first at Eric in astonishment; he then looks towards the sky as he kisses his index and middle finger and raises them both towards the sky without raising his elbow on his right arm.

in the process. The crew can see them by this time.

Eric is like, "Nah. Let's dip into the store and get us a drink real quick. For us and the fellas. I'll go into the store, and you just wait out here so they can see you and don't trip as to why we dipped off real quick.," Eric says, as he calls the quick audible to the plan.

Moments later, he comes out with a plastic bag filled with six individually wrapped up bottles of something in paper bags, all tightly nestled in that triple plastic bag he is carrying by the straps.

"That was freakin' fast, E," Michael comments, with amazement.

They cross back over to the other side of the street and continue to move along the sidewalk getting closer to the crew. When they finally arrive at the benches, they dap it up once more briefly. Eric gives out the bottles in their tightly wrapped paper bags.

"These are for reaching half-time, Fellas.

When I called this shit all them years ago at this mutherfuckin' bench no less y'all didn't flinch or falter to ridicule me for saying what was said. Y'all just listened to me rant on and let me have my peace. Now we are here, right now, on the verge of making some legendary, epic shit go down!

"We been brothers already for many, many other certifying reasons more than a few decades deep at this point. This is to the fruits of realness! This is to what support produces through the years. Family bonds that just get stronger and stronger, creating opportunities for us all to be there when we need one another! Drop some for the lost and then let's raise 'em for what it is!" Eric announces, as the men raise their opened bottles, and in random order, each taking swigs on their beverages.

The bottles are not very big. Sixteen ounces at best. Everyone takes to their own individual pace at finishing their beverages as they occupy the benches.

Eric pulls out his phone and sends out a text. Moments later, the Cadillac SUV they had arrives in and pulls up to the curb in front of the benches. Eric reaches into the vehicle with one foot stepped into its cabin. He pulls the duffle bag closer to the doorway. He unzips the bag, and then sits on the doorway facing the benches. One by one, he tosses several pouches in the direction of each of them. As they catch their three pouches, he moves on to focusing on the next one.

When they all have three pouches, Eric continues, "What you each should have— and by all means, check the contents of each pouch so we on the same page here— you should have two pouches with about three-hundred-thousand in each pouch. That should be a total of thirty, ten-thousand-dollar wrapped bundles of USD currency. That holds more weight and can more easily traded in for whatever other currency that would be needed on the move than another currency. So, you each should have six-hundred-thousand-dollars apiece.

"The third pouch has three sets of identification credentials. These documents can get you time all by themselves. The first move once we leave from here is get off these streets and stash them in the safest place you have for the immediate moment until you further develop your safe locations and get these credentials stowed away deep into those cervices of those locations. Get caught with these things and it's game over. Hands down. When the smoke clears I have people in place for the final bags. Much larger amounts."

After they each check their allotments, they turn with enthusiasm towards Eric and are grateful.

"So, each of you need to seriously consider three locations to use as hideouts as this process takes its course. We will each respectively be on the run for the foreseeable next five years at a minimum. If things go to plan, you guys will fall from their interests. If what I just thought about becomes implemented, I will be able to say we may be able to skate altogether. That's a long shot. So, what are your three locations?"

Eric tosses them a note pad and continues, "Write your name, and next to it, three of your top locations. I have a miniature atlas here. Use it if need be. Even if your choice is in the States."

Eric tosses the atlas to Dontre who starts to look through it as Johnny has the notepad first.

Johnny puts his hometown because he thinks his bunker qualifies as one of the three under his logic. Strangely enough, they each picked three different locations apiece without duplications.

"I see we can skip the issue I thought may have been a discussion point in any of you guys selecting the same location as a hideout site. What we do need to discuss is how to live on the run and how to utilize a recluse lifestyle to extend and prolong that on-the-run status until the time arrives where it is beyond the statute of limitations dependent on what they sought to charge in the first place beyond conspiracy.

"You want to live off the grid and shop online. I have people just about everywhere that are already in position to bear the brunt of your needs and assist in any way they will be able to insulate your inconspicuous needs. This includes porch cameras and online accounts under the aliases provided through your new identities.

"I am expecting a friend of mine who we fortunately caught while he was home. He is normally constantly on the move, but he just so happens to be home for a break in-between his constant continued movements of keeping his numerous hustles afloat and prosperous. He has gotten his hands on a product that will revitalize our needs in the area of identity concealment. Until he gets here, we will just finish the business we need to address elsewhere across the game plan.

"We will utilize a three-stage communication authentication process. One or more of us may become compromised, even captured. In any case they may not capture any of us, but may still find a way to piggy back into our channels of communication with one another or through our affiliate contacts as we exchange information pertaining to what we see and any would be close encounters we may witness or those enclosing our whereabouts may witness or experience.

"I will outline this process for each of you. I have developed a master language. Alpha numeric in foundation. Since there are twenty-six letters in the English alphabet, we will take that twenty-six and divide it by two. Since it can be easily divided, we will invert this to our advantage for the first degree of the language.

"A 'one' will equal a 'Z', and a 'one-alpha' will equal an 'A'. That means that one through thirteen will be like reciting the alphabet backwards to the letter 'N'. A number along that one to thirteen line with a hyphenated character will count forward on the alphabet chain. It will mirror the hyphenated symbol. Whatever that message describes or outlines will then be taken to the next degree. A daily newspaper. There are five of us here who will be involved with this chain of communication. We will draw straws shortly. Whatever your number is will be the order in which our calendar will revolve around.

"We will draw for a newspaper as well. So, on day one if Ezell is one, his paper is the paper we utilize to decipher the message of that day. The next day will be who draws second and so forth. Same with the paper associated with the day and person. Only we know who has what paper. We will choose a page correspondent to our existing numbers drawn as to what page of the paper the message will be deciphered through. We have some time I expect to get with it," Eric concludes.

A foreign luxury sedan pulls behind the SUV Eric is sitting in. Eric sees the facial reaction of the crew and a glimpse of the vehicle's lights as it pulls up.

"Daren! Good to see you, and it's good that you had the time to come see me on such short notice," Eric exclaims.

"Not even a question, E. You never cease to amaze me how you stay into something next level. I told you about them joints, and you found a way to apparently utilize them, I figure. You got that bag, though?" Daren asks.

"Why, yes, I do," Eric says in response, as he goes back to the opened door of the SUV and reaches into the duffle bag and grabs a pouch from within it. "Here you are."

Eric waves the pouch until Daren produces what he wants. Daren walks to his trunk and grabs from within the trunk a short duffle bag of his own and tosses it to Eric. Eric walks up to him and tosses the pouch through the passenger window of his sedan discreetly. Eric then unzips the bag and pulls out a plastic bag. Within that plastic bag, he pulls out one of the silicone masks he had just mentioned to Michael on the walk over. Eric moves out of Daren's way and allows Daren to provide a brief display and demonstration of the capabilities of the masks he brought for Eric.

"See, they require a one-hour charge and can be used for two continuous hours off the charger. I have one already charged. You can plug the device through a USB connection like this," Daren says and completes actionable instructions.

Daren continues, "Once the phone is connected, you can select through the small app. I can give you the URL to download from and credentials to do so. You can select any facial image you desire that is in your phone and processed through the app for specs and deliver that facial data to the silicone mask itself, and the electronic technology within the mask activates the nanites to form the features of that face and pigment. These are generation one of the latest models out on an exclusive market right now. Once the process of alteration is complete, like a complete ten minutes tops, you can pull the mask over your face, and there you go."

As Daren walks them through it, he also demonstrates how he found a face to mimic and program the mask with. They wait for a total of seven minutes in silence as they each are in awe of the technology they are witnessing. Once Daren sees the transfer is complete, he turns away from them, faces the inside of the open SUV cabin, pulls the mask over his face, and makes a few adjustments for fitting along its edges. He then turns around to them.

"A new person," Daren says, as each of them are stuck in bewilderment.

Quickly after doing so, he snatches it off his face and throws it back into its bag along with the awkward looking USB cable that came along with it.

"That's what I wanted. Just what we needed, Daren. You got all of them   in   here?"   Eric   asks.

"Most definitely. I don't have to ask about my bag, right?"

"You already know, Dawg," Eric responds.

Eric reaches into his duffle bag. He pulls out five all-black book bags and starts to open them up by unzipping one at a time and placing two of the masks into each one before sealing them back up. One-by-one, he tosses those bags to each of the five who gets the pouches. Daren daps Eric up and slips off into the streets as if he wasn't even noticed. He and Eric exchange a respectful set of head nods as he does so.

"Put all that shit in the bags, and let's get up out of here. We've been here entirely too long at this point. You know what it is. We will drop Greg and Ezell back to their vehicle. Johnny and Mike, you guys already know what is next. Dontre, you sit up front with the driver. C'mon, let's roll, Fellas," Eric instructs with motivational prowess.

Chapter 11

"The Imminent Occurrence"

It is a sunny afternoon, and Eric is sitting in one of his more frequented locations: the barbershop. He is not necessarily waiting in line to receive a cut; moreover, he is hosting court in the rear office. He utilizes the space often since his childhood friend Ramone owns the shop. He is known to use the space to sit and think in between calls and usage of his laptop.

He hears some commotion, even from way back in the office. There is definitely some heated reaction to something up front. Eric gets up and ventures out towards the shop down the hall, curious to see what is exactly the situation. Moving cautiously slow down the hall until he is able to get a glimpse of exactly what the big deal is, he becomes more alert the closer to the door leading to the shop. When he peeks through the door, he can see it is just some of the barbers lamenting over something to do with the televisions. With this, he becomes much less concerned for the countless more serious things they could have been so loud over. He steps out into the shop to see what is on the television to bring such colorful and vibrant reactions of anger and disapproval to the guys in the shop.

"They got another one," one barber named Paul shouts towards the direction of Eric.

"Word. They did another nigga grimy," responds Sean, another barber.

Eric is now very interested in hearing the details of whatever was to have taken place.

"Turn that shit up, yo?" Eric asks, loudly.

One of the other barbers grabs the remote near them and points it at the television Eric is closest to. As he does so, the volume grows louder, and the reporter can be much more easily heard.

"A black male, identified as Rudolph Stevens, was shot and killed by four Tennessee police officers late last night. Body-camera footage is not yet available for the incident. What we do know from field reporters on site is that Mr. Stevens was reportedly approached after he was seen to have made an illegal street crossing, or otherwise referred to as 'J-Walking'. The Memphis police officers who were on the scene describe Mr. Stevens as belligerent and combative.

"In their attempts to peacefully discuss the gravity of the infraction to Mr. Stevens, it was then that they all agreed that it appeared that Mr. Stevens attempted to reach within his jacket for a weapon as he was not willing to comply with becoming civil and accepting the citation. It was at this point sources revealed that Mr. Stevens aggressed the officers one final time in an attempt to pull whatever weapon he was attempting to unsheathe from within his coat pocket upon them. This is the moment where both officers fired several shots at Mr. Stevens.

"When emergency medical services arrived, Mr. Stevens was pronounced dead at the scene. He left behind a wife of fifteen years and four children— three girls and one boy. His wife, Sheila Stevens, has not yet made herself available for a statement. A spokesperson for the family only stated that they are still in a state of deep disbelief," comments the reporter on the television.

"They did that man wrong!" yells a customer in the barber chair closest to the television.

"You and I all know that he didn't brandish no gun. You noticed there was no mention of a weapon found at the scene. They got another one. I know his family hurt right now. He had four children. What about them? For J-walking?" asks the barber who is cutting the hair of the person who said he was done wrong.

Eric stands, watching the news correspondent speak, and thinks strongly about the particulars mentioned in the case. He isn't sure if this is going to be the one that will serve his interests. He looks around the barbershop, shakes his head from the unpleasantness of the matter, and begins to walk back to the rear of the business, back to the offices. Eric does not reach out to anyone after this. He does not want to initiate anything prematurely. He isn't even certain that this situation will create a large enough stir. He returns to what he was doing. Then he receives a telephone call on his basic phone. He stares at the device with focus, waiting for the caller identification information to appear across the screen. *Teresa Goodman*

He sighs briefly as he recognizes the name. He then answers the phone, "Hey, what's the word?"

"Have you seen the news?"

"Yes. I saw the story about the guy shot for J-walking while Black, right?"

"Yes. You're definitely not going to believe this one. That story is just a big fat lie! The news media don't even know, yet, or they wouldn't have even run that story on the incident," Teresa carries on.

"What? So, what are you getting at, Teresa?"

"There was a young girl who was up at the window in her room above the intersection of the incident. She not only saw the whole thing, but she recorded it. None of what those officers reported as to what happened took place. They beat him, ganged up on him, and slowly killed him. She was just recording the street with the new camera she got for her birthday. She was already recording when she saw the police approach that man and saw it felt wrong the way they seemed to look at him, so she continued recording out of curiosity."

"Oh, shit! Who else knows about this? How did you get this information? Where is this little girl now? Where is that footage?" Eric rattles off.

"Slow down, Eric. It's contained for now. Lucky for you, I have family down there. Her neighbor, who bought her the camera, was the first person she called. Both of her parents worked nights. Her uncle is my first cousin. They know I have media contacts, and he called me. I have her put up in a hotel out of the city. Come over and we can discuss the rest."

"I'm headed over now. I will get the jet ready, too. We got to make quick moves."

"I will see you shortly, then,", Teresa responds, and hangs up the line.

Eric gathers his things and calmly walks back down the hallway, out into the barber shop. He says his goodbyes to the men of the shop as he hits the door in stride. He slips on his dark grey sunshades as the light outside is bright. He walks around the corner from where the shop is and pulls a key fob from out of his pocket. He clicks its button, the disarming alarm sound activates, and can be loudly heard. He steps inside his vehicle and closes the door.

Once he is off on his way down 124th Street, he whisks his way down until he gets to Lennox Ave, better known to be called Malcolm X Boulevard. He turns and takes that north until he makes the left on 125th Street, also referred to as Doctor Martin Luther King Junior Boulevard. He feels some ominous instructions being transmitted to him oddly as he crosses between the two streets named after the two men who culminated the plight of the civil rights fight of their time and arguably still to this day. He drives its historic path, and continues to think about the significance of what he is doing and what would either men have to say regarding its elements or outcome?

Then he changes his focus and wonders if what he is about to get the scoop on will be what they have been waiting for. For both what he is needing in addition to what he has Michael waiting for. This can be that two-for-one moment in the timeline. A true catalyst event all-around.

He hops onto the Westside Highway as he knew it to be called but is now titled the Henry Hudson Parkway. He takes the parkway down to

Canal Street. When he reaches Sixth Avenue, he takes the left and then takes the right onto Grand Street. He quickly takes the right and searches for a parking spot on Thompson Street. He exits his vehicle and cuts through Grand Canal Court, alongside the basketball court to Sixth Avenue. From here, he slips up the slender staircase and into the building. Once inside, he ventures forward to the residence where Teresa lives.

After traversing the lobby and mounting its elevator, he proceeds to the twenty-fourth floor. He steps off the elevator with his thoughts now concentrated on fully examining the details he is about to hear. He stops himself in his tracks, realizing he forgot to reach his travel sponsor. He pulls a mobile device from his pocket and sends out a text.

Get the jet ready, I may need to move as quickly as imaginable to Memphis, Tennessee. Keep me posted.

He arrives at her door, and he proceeds to knock lightly, but with firm contact for each knock. The door opens, and he moves inside without haste.

"Good morning, again. Sit over here. I am going to get this tea I just made in the kitchen. Can I get you a bottle of water? I just picked up some alkaline stuff from my friend with that new machine," Teresa says.

"Sure. Is it very cold or just kind of cold?" Eric asks back.

"Very cold. I like them that way, too," Teresa replies.

Eric leans into the cushion on the couch he is sitting on, crosses his legs slowly, then turns his gaze to her with his full focus as she begins to fill him in.

"Okay. Sit back, have a seat, and listen to this shit. It is going to blow your fucking mind, E. You're good on getting there. Not a true need to rush because she is definitely not talking to no one about it. Neither are her parents or neighbor.

"In fact, they may need you to put some inconspicuous people in her area for the whack jobs who, once this is all made known, may try to threaten her or her family for the explosiveness her story most definitely has. I know you got real people who can handle all of that and more just about everywhere. I am not even going to question that because I know what it is," Teresa goes on to tell him.

Eric sits, in stoic anticipation. He nods his head slightly with confidence as he prepares to respond. "Not even an issue. I will have people out there in place before I get out there myself, T. Carry on."

"So, let's start from the little lady. Her name is Sophia Thomas. Her neighbor— my cousin— Donald. He was the first person she ran to after the incident occurred before her eyes, a few stories up in the tenements over the intersection."

Eric tilts his head very modestly as he locks in the two names as she continues to speak.

"Okay. This what she saw, Eric. She was experimenting with the camera she just was given for her twelfth birthday a few days prior to that evening. She finished all her chores and completed every other task that her parents placed before her as they mutually agreed before she was to start playing with the DSLR camera. She started filming the street corner, experimenting with its focus and other features. Then she saw the man she described and confirmed to be the same man from the news broadcast as the late Mr. Rudolph Stevens walking down the street. He looked both ways as he began to cut across the street before the crosswalk lines just before the intersection of Madison Avenue and 2nd Street on the northern side of the intersection in Downtown Memphis, Tennessee.

"Before he managed to get even halfway across 2nd, there came a police vehicle rather quickly eastbound down the one-way path of Madison Avenue. They were moving quickly enough to where when they apparently noticed Mr. Stevens, they stopped abruptly and jolted the vehicle as they did so. Then, they sped to him with their vehicle in the middle of the double-yellow-line as they parked, and then exited the vehicle."

Eric eyes slightly widen as she continues to progress through her report.

"She then said that Mr. Stevens, at the sight of this and recognizing what it meant from his behavior, tried first to get out of their way and finish crossing the street to the west side of the street onto its sidewalk path. This visibly did not deter the two police officers from converging on his position. Flanking him with obvious aggression in the manner in which they drew closer to him."

"She told my cousin that she was unable to hear anything that had been said. She also was not interested in opening the window to be able to hear anything because she was very concerned not to create any noise that would give away her position at the window. She felt very strongly about avoiding any such attention be established."

"She then saw Mr. Stevens attempt to run behind a van that was parked along the sidewalk, not seeing that the second officer was already at the other side of that van waiting for him in advance as they had successfully flanked him. My interpretation, not her words. I understood that what she described was flanking."

Teresa looks at Eric with an exaggerated expression due to the plain obviousness in her need to clarify that it was unlikely for young Sophia to describe their behavior as "flanking".

Teresa continues, "When Mr. Stevens had ran past the front of the van, with his head facing his rear in obvious fear, the second officer clotheslined him, as he thrusted both arms together over the front of his chest to his right as Mr. Stevens cleared the front of the van. It did not appear to her that he ever saw it coming. Mr. Stevens fell immediately and began to crawl towards the cement flower bed at the base of the visible street sign labeled 'Left Lane Must Turn Left'."

"He attempted to pull himself up on its frame as the two officers congratulated themselves as they walked up behind him. It was visible that things were being said to the man on the ground from the two officers, but again, she was unable to capture it within her live recording. She continued to record.

"By now, she grew scared and concerned for her own safety, and she managed to stretch out and grab her tri-pod as she strenuously reached out for it successfully. She applied the camera to the tri-pod's frame without disrupting the quality of the ongoing recording at the time. Once she accomplished those things, she turned the light in the room off in the somewhat increasingly frantic hopes that the lights going out in the room would not have generated any unwanted suspicion from either officer at the time of her doing so.

"Then one of the officers put his foot on the back of Mr. Stevens's neck, pressing it against the corner of the cement flower bed where it met the steel pole that supported the signage about four feet above it. Then a second squad car pulled up, and its occupants ran from out of it and joined the two other cops already there. Nobody stopped the one cop from what he was doing, but they were visibly enjoying the scene without denial."

"Mr. Stevens's left arm stretched out to the other officers in a blatant request for assistance as he was losing his ability to breathe, or as that seemed to be what she felt from where she was watching above. They did nothing for him. As the one officer continued to press his boot to the rear of his neck against the flowerbed, another of the newly arrived officers walked with some haste to the rear of Mr. Stevens and grabbed both of his feet and seemed to pull him away as the officer with the boot on his neck appeared to press harder.

"Seconds later, they all stopped and let him very slowly attempt to stand up on his own. When this appeared to take too long, the other two officers, without compassion, assisted Mr. Stevens to his feet. Once he maintained his upright posture weakly, the four officers stood across his frontside, and one gestured his hand out towards him. At this, Mr. Stevens then attempted to put both of his hands out to the group of officers and express a 'wait, wait' expression with his hands as his arms were fully extended and waving without coordination, no doubt from what he just experienced at their hands. He did not seem coherent at all at that point she noted.

"Then with his left hand still extended and waving about, he attempted with his right to reach into his pocket and grab something for them. This is where all four of the officers, one then another, began reaching for their holstered weapons and initiate firing shots into his body. From the way Mr. Stevens's body reacted to the shots fired, it was painfully obvious that there were several shots matching the horrific sounds of gunfire that could be heard and clearly recognized for they were.

"At this point, Sophia ducked behind the table on the other side of the room and abandoned her new camera and tri-pod. Then she waited for about ten minutes, crawled back to the window, checked to see if the camera had still been in recording mode, then peeked over the windowsill to see what was taking place outside. There were more squad vehicles present at this time. She didn't see them looking up in her direction.

"She pulled the camera away from the window. She then ran with her camera to her computer in her room and uploaded the video to her cloud service. Then she ran to her neighbor's unit and told him what had happened. Ain't that some fucking shit!!!??!"

"That's extraordinary. I wonder what footage will surface from their body cams?" Eric ponders aloud.

"Yeah. That's the other side that this video will make a strong demand to have it brought forward and released to the public," Teresa responds. "There you have it. I know that you have to get going, I am sure. Give my regards to Donald, will you?"

Eric stands up at the same moment as she. They embrace briefly, and the Eric is on his way to the door again with his mobile device pulled out, sending texts.

Hey Mike, how long will it take you to meet me in Memphis? Eric sends to Mike.

4-5e—--13m-1a-2--2b--1a-3c-7-9i-5-5e Eric sends off in a group text followed by, 2, also in a group text response to the initial message.

Once he hits the street on 6th, he maneuvers back to his vehicle, and drives around 6th to Grand, and from there to West Broadway to a parking garage near the end of the block. Before he exits the vehicle, he pops its trunk. He exits the vehicle, walks to its rear, and opens the trunk that is ajar. He thoughtfully rummages through its contents until he pulls out a silver bag. He then opens the bag and pulls from it a vehicle cover. He then applies the cove and the strapping device underneath its undercarriage.

Once he is done, he walks back outside to the street. He sends out a text and waits patiently. Before long, a SUV pulls alongside him, he opens its rear passenger door, and steps inside.

"Take me to JFK, please, to the Sheltair Aviation Offices," Eric requests to the driver.

They travel from the island of Manhattan, over the East River, into the borough of Brooklyn, making their way along several roadways to the airport south of Jamaica, Queens. During this time, Eric receives several responses to his cryptic group text message. He never responds to them; he only reads them.

The vehicle enters the airfield and draws closer to the hangar belonging to Sheltair Aviation. He moves without hesitation as the vehicle stops. He steps out in stride as he redirects his footsteps to that of the base of the staircase for the plane. He was given the directions of the one he'd be flying in.

"Do we have everything prepared for takeoff?" Eric asked the pilots.

A man arrives in a different vehicle, hops out the vehicle, reaches from within, grabs a medium sized book bag, and walks it over to Eric who seems to have expected it. Eric grabs it from the man and carries it alongside his leg. The man then returns to the driver's seat of the vehicle he arrived in and slowly pulls off. He leaves no remarks behind as he does so.

Eric boards the plane and sits comfortably in one of the seats, leaning back, folding his legs casually as he contemplates things. A courier arrives with food for the flight. There is enough for himself and that of the flight crew. Eric sits as there is much movement taking place on his behalf around him from both attendants and the ground crew outside, who he also had food brought in for and beverages.

He runs through his thoughts of how through the past several months he's received reports through the designated code of how each of his five associates had grown more proficient and formidable with the details of their different roles on the run processes. He also reminisces at how each of them had been reporting how the silicone masks had been dispensed and that each member who had them assigned were increasingly improving beyond acceptable threshold as how to utilize them effectively. Knowing that for at least a full month all twelve of his target locations are up to speed and prepared for enactment when the time comes. They are continuously perfecting the response plans with each additional day before they are to be called into action with the utmost discretion in their executions of their trainings and overall preparations.

He smirks as he thinks about the few updates he got from Shymeika during this time, thinking, why in the hell did he tell her about that incentive rate— to double it up when they covered all their bases and delivered an optimal performance. She went out of her way to ensure him he will need those additional bags with regularity.

Eric then double checks his own memories and counts his imaginary checkmarks regarding his contingency plans for what is to potentially come if his original set of contingency plans fall through for full preparation. He is also aware that within the span of the five months since they were last together there were several other small to medium sized cases that did not meet the threshold of a major situation to incite complete public outrage, for litigation in addition to social unrest. He knows, and he knows that Mike will recognize that this is the whale they've only hoped about.

With his thoughts on these matters providing him some slight degree of comfort in having them covered, he begins to center his thoughts on what made this all even more of a powder keg moment. They are in the final year of the current America's presidential term of office. There is a ginormous election campaign taking place all around them.

Everything that reaches the airwaves turn political. Current president Brad Ace is facing the challenger Oscar Gabriel— the tech giant from Colorado. Everyone figures that Ace is on his way out. He was pronounced a one-term president due to his highly inflammatory gestures and incendiary remarks on just about any and everything from race, to women, women's rights, children with disabilities, war veterans, pro athletes, musicians, and the list literally just goes on and on.

Realizing that many of the nation's people share the sentiment that they have had a collective fill of his style of leadership, Ace began challenging the sanctity of the democratic election process. He stated on several occasions that he felt the other political party would steal the election from him. What Eric contemplates as making Brad Ace most dangerous is how President Ace's followers couldn't care less about whatever President Ace does. They don't respond negatively to anything he says, either.

Tensions amass as Election Day draws nearer. His staunch supporters will surely not readily accept any election results that do not hoist him over them at another rally victorious. Eric continues to think over all these pertinent issues as he slowly eats his meal on his three-hour flight to Memphis.

When the plane arrives, Eric grabs the book bag and departs the aircraft. He hops into a vehicle, with the bag still in tow, that is waiting for him. The vehicle pulls from its parked position.

"The Peabody Memphis, please," Eric instructs the driver.

"Not a problem, Sir,", responds the driver, politely.

When the vehicle pulls to the front of Peabody, Eric opens his door by himself at his insistence. He steps out and looks upon the herringbone paving as he stares around, taking in his environment. He then handles the business of securing his reservation for his room. When he finishes with the desk clerk attendant, he turns around, and there is his cousin Michael waiting for Eric to recognize him.

"You know I am going to give your name hell next time I speak with Dontre. The illustrious Eric Castille…caught…slipping… Classic!" Michael gloats into his ear.

"Whatever, yeah, yeah, yeah, Cuz. You legitimately got me this time. I won't even trip if you and Tre go all in on that one. I just checked into my room. I assume since you have time to play you've done the same for yourself?"

"Sore lose much, huh? You know it. Where do you have the witness?" Michael asks next.

Eric answers, "I have the family on a different floor from us. They are already here, getting settled in. I will keep them here for the duration of this ordeal. From what I have been informed, the little one is just traumatized by what she witnessed. I have four teams here spread out and on task to ensure we have a team watching, a team following whoever gets tagged as suspicious, and a next team waiting to ensure they remain safe.

"We will meet in their suite this evening for dinner so she can tell us what she knows. And she can show us the original footage as it played out, even though I personally already have the general play-by-play.

"Okay. Until then, what do you want me to do? We have a couple hours until it's that time of day. You asked me to meet you here about this time?" Michael asks.

"You're an attorney. I have a lead for you to investigate. I've heard from my sources that the Memphis Police Department have indeed recovered their body camera footage from the evening in question. The source has continued to report that the footage is so damning that they are seeking to attempt to just skip any formal hearings or discipline processes and just fire the officers involved and claim that they do not condone or tolerate such behavior versus have this footage be made public for scrutiny due to its highly inflammatory content. We need a copy of that footage before they do, Mike."

"This is what we need investigated. I have my people, and I trust that you have yours. Together, we can attack the matter if inquiry from different angles discreetly and hopefully find some success in our search. Getting that footage in its raw form is without a need to mention going to take your end of this darn near the finish line before you guys get to nipping at its bones," Eric comments to Michael.

Michael cannot find anything in what Eric said to him to disagree with. With that silence, he shrugs his shoulders to gesture he has nothing to say in response. He frowns his face to duplicate the same sentiment and walks away, nodding his head in acknowledgement.

Eric, at the sight of Michael's departure, reaches into his pocket and pulls out a mobile device. He begins to type into its screen as he finds his way to the elevator, headed to his accommodations himself. Once he is settled in, he has a knock to his door. He peeps through the hole and is able to recognize the face on the other side. He opens the door for the gentleman on its other side and allows him to enter the suite.

"Thanks, Hue. I appreciate you grabbing me some things last minute's notice," Eric says to the man.

"Never a problem, My Brother. I know your in-between moves like usual, but before you dip out this time, hopefully, you can swing through the crib. My peoples and the gang would love to see you. It has been a good minute since you've been by," Hue responds.

"You know I don't be the one to say shit and disappoint, Hue. But this time I may come through. I might not be able to for a real long time after all this," Eric replies.

"Understood. I appreciate the consideration, Homie," Hue says back to Eric as he daps him up and departs the room smoothly, closing the door behind him.

The bag is full of clothing, sneakers, and shoes. There are several pairs of socks and underwear. There is also a clothing bag inside of the medium sized duffle bag brought in by Hue. Eric goes through what is there, selects an outfit, and puts the rest neatly back into the bag. Then he showers.

It is drawing near time to meet the Thomases for dinner and discuss the matters at hand. Eric heads that way, meeting Michael in the hallway. The two of them make their way to the staircase and take the stairs down a few flights to the floor the Thomases are staying on. They exit the staircase together and go to the door to the suite the family is in.

Eric knocks. The door opens, and the men go inside once greeted and welcomed in.

Chapter 12

"MEDIA FRENZY"

Michael has been working with the Thomas and Stevens families. He is in a league with Na'Quan Bishop, Sandra Sterling, and Tanisha Kager. They, along with their respective firms, see to the legalities of the pending case with the state attorney regarding the death of Mr. Stevens.

Now, the footage has been leaked in its raw format from all four of the officers on the scene that infamous evening. The coverage was so far reaching that it travelled all over the globe. There is almost no one who is not aware of the situation or the name Rudolph Stevens. Even the officers' names are synonymous with the case and the name Rudolph Stevens. Their families share in their shame as well.

Those videos of the officers' body cam footage corroborated the initial partially edited video released by the family of Sophia Thomas. It was without question a media nightmare for the MPD. The mayor and governor were both seeking refuge from the initial outrage created by these news media disasters plaguing their political existences. The coverage was un-ending and relentless. There was no resting to their coverage of the incident. The mainstream media markets all the way down to the local media outlets of extremely small towns had their representatives swarming the city of Memphis.

Every day, there were media briefings at the Memphis Police Headquarters. Every day, there were more questions regarding the fate of the four officers involved. Some days, the question was asked if the police chief herself was intending to resign, and if there was any pressure from the mayor's office for her to do so. On other days, there were questions asking if the governor had any involvement in seeking both the mayor and the police chief's employment to be terminated.

Still, all that was said was that Rudolph Stevens had been reported mistaken for a drunken homeless man violating loitering laws and pedestrian crossing ordinances. Some of the initial reportings even described Stevens as an addict who was combative and aggressive towards law enforcement officers. This rendition of the facts was obliterated when the Thomas girl's partially edited video was released.

The nation is in outrage as a whole. There is a large cry for action to be taken quickly against the officers. There is much angst surmounting in the city of Memphis. Even neighboring cities like St. Louis, Atlanta, and even as far as Dallas, there are the murmurings of unrest.

President Ace is not helping matters whatsoever. He is desperately clutching for any shred of political advantage. He knows that his legion of obsessed and loyal followers will follow his call to action.

President Ace held a rally the next day once Sophia's video was released. He took to the podium when it was his time to address the hordes of people who made sure they were in attendance to each and just about every rally thrown by him. Its purpose was to support those officers who were recorded in his well-advertised and publicized opinion as "out of context and illegally performed".

"The vagrancy issues plaguing the downtown area of the greater city of Memphis, Tennessee, in that particular sector of the city are well documented! Well known to its very own citizens for the vagrancy that overran its streets. Overran its peaceful expectation of peace and tranquility!

"How long was this to be allowed to just be the expectation of normal? How many patriots are here today? No. I mean real patriots? Well, how many of you have just sat by waiting for any of your law enforcement officials to take a stand for this blight against your liberties and the expectation of peace?" President Ace rambled at his rally.

"Now that a few brave and courageous officers grew a pair and took their precinct back, they are being villainized as unpatriotic, criminalized for doing their jobs. Rest in peace to the poor man who had to lose his life as a result of good policing... but good policing all the same," President Ace continued.

"They say that I am going to lose this election. Have any of you guys heard this rumor?" President Ace touted, provoking the mass crowd before him. "I was like, 'Where do they get this stuff?' I am the patriot's president. This is the land of a great, many patriots. Am I right?"

The crowd roared to an extremely loud decibel level. President Ace stood facing his far right of the stage and the crowd in that direction and waved on more yelling, more roaring. He repeated the action until he had made a full one-hundred-and-eighty-degree rotation from one end of the stage to the other.

He stepped near the microphone again.

"Well, don't allow the deviants to take over the great city of Memphis. Don't let 'em do it!"

This speech was broadcasted over a majority of the airwaves across the nation. Eric was watching it where he was still in the city of Memphis. Eric was still staying at the Peabody. He wanted to embrace the true pulse of the city and its reactions to all of this attention and the city's longstanding experience of police brutality and power abuse of the law enforcement community that hadn't seen an issue with their negative policing trends towards a segment of the city.

There has been about a week from the time the complete story had broken until now for Eric. He gave the decree to be alert and ready for implementation to the team, but he has yet to initiate any action. He feels strongly that this is that watershed moment in the operation. It just is unclear to him at what point the appropriate action to be taken is to let loose the reigns. He recognizes that far too much has been done in the pursuit of making this plan something close to being actualized. He also can't not escape the grim reality that once the bell has been rung to get his move started, it cannot be un-rung.

Eric has the team, who's been spread out strategically, awaiting the call to gauge their cities. In order for this to work, it requires a combined effort. All has to be done simultaneously, or it will not succeed.

He deliberates further as to how to grasp what is transpiring into his mind to painstakingly craft it into a mechanism. It has to produce from itself the ideation that is needed to bring it all together for the purpose of what he needs to take place to make all the time and effort worthwhile.

He changes the channel on the television from the coverage of the president's press rally. He turns to a news station that has not been covering it.

While still stewing in his thoughts, he watches a series of news correspondents who give their negative and oppositional opinions of the president and his presidency at large. It is obvious that for whatever the reason, there is a great deal of divide and indifference emerging from society.

The president stoked a huge flame. He thought that in order to harness such a hailstorm that he obviously had some skill. To deny this would make him foolish, and being foolish almost certainly translated as weak. To have the narrative of what was to come to trump the potential narrative of whatever brilliant attempt to spin it back to the narrative the President and his team of lethal publicists could counteract was the key for him during that moment.

Eric is forced to accept that the quagmire of President Ace's brash behavior is that he spoke to the sentiment of the people's long burning frustration with their collective mistrust of public officials and the business they attend to on the people's so-called behalf versus that of their own financially motivation to gain.

When Eric has his full of all the voiced reactions and criticisms of everything President Ace, he leaves from his hotel and walks the streets of Memphis near the downtown area. At first, he ventures out to clear his head and find focus as to how to lead the crew of people ten toes down on a mission that could lead them all to federal time in the hockey jersey number variety. He is partly interrupted from this undivided thought process to find himself gauging the emotional climate in the streets surrounding him amongst the pedestrians without speaking to anyone at all. Just picking up conversational tid-bits in passing of what is being collectively discussed.

The people he passes by nonchalantly, and inconspicuous to his eavesdropping purposes, are giving him what he needs to hear. He realizes that there is much being discussed right out in the open amongst the pedestrian traffic beyond his lodgings. The subject: President Ace, overly consumed with the pending election day looming around the corner. Literally in a matter of weeks. A true creature of habit, the consensus is that he cannot resist speaking to the people concerning the larger story of alleged police brutality in the face of the lessor attention harnessing subject matter of his re-election campaign.

Many support opinions of disdain for the president's penchant to identify and move along the pulse of what many are thinking, especially those of his constituency. Eric realizes that President Ace is a modern marvel of intuitiveness. If you can get past the social miscues, mishaps, and braggadocios arrogance.

He gathers from the consensus of the people he overheard during his walk that these traits will actually be found as a highly commendable personality trait for an accepted motivational speaker. President Ace is unfortunately not that accepted by many. He had his moments for sure. Eric thinks, even his most staunch hater had to admit, that President

Ace's problem is he is too much of a creature of habit and less of a student of history.

Eric walks through the vicinity of downtown. He thinks that the personality traits that make President Ace so popular and reflective are the criteria of what he needs to better evaluate. This is in the hopes to understand how to manage the message of what he has planned as he introspectively contemplates the entire operation. He cannot escape his recognition of the initial blowback of his operations given their successful completion. What he is doing is not as important as how these actions are perceived.

Eric texts his cousin through the coded language, We need to retain several publicists. For the aftermath and to steer the conversation towards the bigger picture. And steer it back when the opposition successfully deters the attention from the purpose.

If Eric does not choose to actively seek how to merge the potential outcomes of how this move could play out, in conjunction to what needs to be its outcome, their collective efforts could easily be an exercise in futility. An absolute potential for disaster if not thoroughly thought through for the slightest contingency. Putting the action behind his thoughts to get a publicist or set of them to actuate the furtherance of his intentions in their professional workspace is a welcomed act of his self-prized ingenuity.

Election Day is looming around the corner. The power of the president's overwhelming influence of his base constituency is believing that either he will earn a second term, or the election is rigged to deprive him illegally of having that option.

Eric cannot help but wonder that regardless of what happens in Memphis that he would be wise to consider that whatever he plans to do, it needs to be after the election, after the dust clears from that situation. If his assessment is to pan out for what it is, he can easily have all that time and efforts thwarted by the noise of the election. Snapping the public into attention after the noise levels out is even more to his favor. Overall, efficacy and political leverage for what Michael and Mr. Bishop will no doubt be needed for their initiatives to have better footing. Which is the real point, when Eric is forced to be honest with himself.

Eric then pulls his phone back out of his pocket and sends the coded message, Stand by. After the election is over.

Then Eric texts to a different number, We need to connect as soon as you have the availability.

The message is responded to with, Sure. I am actually in Memphis covering the latest incident.

Eric responds, I am here as well. Staying at the Peabody. Can you meet in the morning?

Sure can. Let's try for nine am? Is sent back to him.

Eric agrees to that time and puts his phone back into his pocket as he continues to walk the streets for about an hour before he finds his way back to Peabody. During his trip, he finds some food to take out, and he brings it back to the hotel with him to eat in an environment more comfortable to his liking. Once upstairs and inside his suite, he pulls out his belongings and sits them on the desk around its edges as he sets the table for his meal. He pulls out three phones from his pockets, his wallet, and a few advertisements given to him from various people in the streets.

As he sits and prepares to eat his meal, one of the phones laying on the desk begins to ring.

"Yo…," he answers, mysteriously.

"What you got going on? You see what just popped off? What you pushing it back for after the election for? That's like at least two weeks away," someone inquisitively dumps onto him without taking a breath.

"I got all of this, Man. Just fall back and play your part, Dawg. If you understood, you wouldn't be asking. This isn't what we need to be discussing, though. What we need to be discussing is, do I need to come out there? Do you have everything under wraps and ready for my call when I make that call? You seem to be too concerned with the shit I am doing instead of letting me know how you got all your shit squared away. That makes me think I need to send you some fourth quarter help. So, save me the time. Do I need to send in someone off the bench?" Eric scowls.

"Man… Why the fuck would you do all that and come at me with all that, Nephew? Fuck I did to you?" Ezell laughs. "Tell me that," Ezell mockingly retorts.

"I am just fucking with you, Big Unc. I was expecting yo' ornery ass to call me immediately after I sent out the word. Your way too predictable, Unc. You gonna definitely need to do something about that, for real. I had to throw you a curveball. You wouldn't even be right if I had not," Eric laughs.

The both of them share some heartfelt laughter like they are right alongside one another.

"I appreciate you, Unc!" Eric comments.

"I bet you do, Nephew. I appreciate you. I'm also proud of you. Now go the fuck to bed with yo' brainy ass!" Ezell shouts.

Eric laughs to himself as he begins to devour his meal. He grows more certain that whatever circumstances between then and the appropriate moment after the results of the election are the true testing grounds and opportunities for planned refinement. His vigilance towards the successful outcome is beyond resilient. His focus is unbreakable.

He spends the evening sitting in his bed after he showers just continuing to go through permeations of what is to come. Eventually, the weight of his eyelids and their persistence overcome him for the evening.

It is now morning, and the phone to the room chimes aloud.

When he finally breaks from the somber of his sleep, he leans over half cognizant and picks up the phone from its base with a groggy greeting, "Good…morning…Can I… help you?"

"Yes, Sir. It is eight a.m., and this is your scheduled requested wake-up call," says the desk attendant.

Eric hears this and instantly grows more alert realizing that it is time to get himself in order and get ready for the events planned for the day.

"Thank…you…," he responds, and hangs up the phone slowly.

After two to three minutes of exaggerated procrastination, Eric jumps up, forcing himself into alertness and into the shower. He brings his phone into the bathroom and plays his music aloud as he showers and finalizes his morning grooming rituals. When he finishes, he selects a different outfit and footwear from the bag brought to him by Hue and heads downstairs.

He takes a trip down Union where he meets a slender woman wearing a semi-business casual skirt and matching top. She is drinking on a cup of what appears to be a hot beverage; it is emitting steam from its opening. She meets with Eric in front of the AutoZone Stadium.

"Good morning to you, Mrs. Bellomy. I appreciate you granting me access so short notice."

"You've more than proved yourself worthy, Mr. Woodmere. I always appreciate doing what I can to assist any patron of your dedication to the arts," she replies.

Not too long after he arrives and discusses matters with the woman, a next individual walks up. He shakes Eric's hand and introduces himself vaguely to the woman he is standing next to.

"Good morning. Nice to meet you. I am Farrukh," declares the man.

"Okay, Gentleman. Please follow me, and I will start the tour of our facilities," announces the woman.

The three of them walk beyond the front gates and into the stadium area. The woman leads the way. The man who just arrived follows her as Eric trails behind. The woman carries on about the facility as she leads them through the front of the house. Eric gestures to the woman with just a series of facial expressions, then she changes her tune.

"I will have to take a moment, Gentlemen. I will return shortly. Please invite yourselves to look out to the playing field and the general seating area for its splendor until I return. I will not be very long. Gentlemen," she nods her head before she leaves, giving the impression she is needed elsewhere as she departs with her personal assistant.

Another staffer approaches the two men and asks them if there is a beverage that they desire while they wait for the woman who just departed. They both gave their orders to the gentleman asking.

Afterwards, Eric gestures for the gentleman to follow his lead into the stadium. "Perhaps we can take this opportunity to sit and discuss a few things?" Eric asks Farrukh.

Farrukh follows willingly, eager to hear what is to be discussed. They finally arrive at a section where Eric decides is the best location to have their discussion, and they sit down. It isn't long after that that the staffer returns and delivers to them both what they ordered from the barista to drink.

"What do I say is the reason we are here this morning, Mr. Woodmere?" Farrukh asks Eric.

"I know that you operate in the space of civil rights, and you oftentimes find yourself at the center of some of recent history's more polarized protests. Your organization seems to be at the forefront of the controversial space of activism," Eric states.

"I wouldn't take credit for the timing being something we were absolutely certain of to be real with you. But overall, I have no quarrels with your descriptions thus far. What do those descriptions have to do with this meeting? Or were you preparing me for the conversation you'd hope to have getting more to your actual purpose?

"Well, Farrukh, I am a fan, and I am also a student. Your class in still in session. You organize these outings, and you make sure that whenever a mic is set before anyone connected with your movement that they are prepared to stay on message. That is commendable all to itself. Uncanny in today's age to achieve such cohesiveness in such troublesome and erratic times."

"I am thankful for the pleasantries, Mr. Woodmere. But seriously, what is it that you had in mind? Seriously."

"I need you to coordinate with me for your next protest. I have some insights as to how we can make your next one something epic won't step next to. Is that better?" Eric replies,

"I am definitely listening. This is better than flattery. Continue, please," inquires Farrukh.

"Okay. What took place here not too long ago was an egregious assault on what we have far too long experienced at the hand of law enforcement upon our community of melanated peoples. However, far too often, we protest and have little to gain beyond the immediate attention. But the longer standing rebuke of history when there is nothing attributed with those efforts to say had been gained as a direct result to the suffrage of the sacrifice.

"I just seek to change that paradigm in your space. I seek to link something to the timeline that has never been acquired through protesting alone. I just seek coordination. Not involvement. Coordination with efforts that will not stain what you and your organization stand for, but enhance it and amplify its reach and enigmatize the depth of how what you've stood for during all the years of your work in this space to be seen beyond its profoundness, beyond its provocative stances.

"I am proposing a risky joint-venture that will catapult you in the realms far past Ghandi, Dr. King, and any worthy of being mentioned in the same sentence. Paragraph even. You can disavow any affiliation to our actions if things go afoul of the game plan. Complete plausible deniability is what I offer as a fall out contingency for you to enact if indeed we fail to deliver.

"I do not see what we plan to fail, based on the extensive research and time in preparation for this very opportunity; however, to be honest, we will not be able to pull it off without the organization resources of you and your team in designated areas of strategical importance and advantage," Eric states.

"You have piqued my interest, Mr. Woodmere. You have done that much. Without question, I need to hear what this 'plan' of yours is in its entirety. I need to understand how I can insulate my organization more precisely from the potential to fall out. More importantly, for me to consider your proposal on its face, I need to know and be made to understand how what you have intended helps my organization. How does your plan benefit what we stand for? Tell me this, My Friend. This is what I need to hear most and first," Farrukh says, with rising intensity.

"Your business is the business of bringing awareness to causes that you and your organization feel strongly about. You, like many before you, have fought the fight of trying to bring some significance to the ongoing and seemingly unstoppable reign of those in uniform taking their issues out on people of melanation.

"There are larger issues at stake than the protest I am asking you to collaborate with me on. However, the protest I speak of will be synonymous with the larger movement that will follow. A movement that will for the first time in this nation's history lead to the best chance of actual legislation and the enforcement to follow that may just end this reign of terror on many people.

"I would think that that chance being legitimate would be something you'd have to strongly consider from a standpoint of opportunity instead of a reluctance to backlash. I can promise you that you will not get negative responses because you did the wrong things or were affiliated with things that went wrong. Moreover, you will be condemned for playing a chess game that will be discussed for centuries to come. Because you will be directly associated with the next level of what Ghandi and Dr. King started. That's what I think. This is what I offer.

"I just need you to trust me in the genuine nature of my respect for your portfolio of sacrifice to the cause and your movement for the people that I would never tarnish that will any ill-advised agenda or game plan. We can certainly discuss every detail. Once you give me your word either way, this will remain strictly between you and I in perpetuity.

"I've given you your props for being a stand up person. Can you at least stand up to that confidentiality? If you so choose not to be a part of what I deem a necessity. Because what we have here is an opportunity like no other, and this opportunity has been planned for in anticipation of it being made available. Now we are prepared to turn this situation into a victory for us all.

"I can do this without your assistance. It just becomes a sure victory if I can have your coordinated cooperation. Discretely of course. You will have plausible deniability the entire ride. I am prepared to fall on my own sword if things for whatever reason do not go as planned. I will take the rogue actor title immediately.

"I am certain, though that if you cooperate and coordinate with me, none of that will be remotely necessary whatsoever. So, what will it be? We discuss the details, or you bail before we even go that far?" Eric finishes his pitch, awaiting a response from Farrukh as they both sit, surrounded by the stadium seating.

"We have known one another for a while now. We have very strong mutual friends who have already given you high regard. I see you yourself are committed to a successful outcome. Even if this outcome needs to come at your loss alone. A willingness to take whatever is to come for the sake of your mission. You know that my movement is a nonviolent movement. So I can take that leap of faith with you and trust you enough with my movement due to all these things in listening to your proposition with an open mind and heart.

"The courage to propose such a thing in the face of denial really confirms for me what was described to me long ago of your character and the integrity that has earned you the reputation amongst many circles. Some, you are obviously aware of, and potentially many others you may not be. So talk to me, My Friend. Free from concern and paranoia of who is with you. I am with you. Tell me how we can help.

Tell me what it is that you need from me, and what I make happen. This, I am quite eager to hear. I imagine I am silently even more eager to be an active role player in," Farrukh states.

"This is great to hear. We plan to give the police a demonstration of nonviolent aggression. For each instance of social unrest and civil disobedience in the name of protest, they have been the ultimate victor. Even when their actions were shunned upon in the past and later reflected upon as being despicable upon the reflections of the world weighing in, they have always won the battle.

"I seek to change that dynamic. We intend to issue them their first loss. A loss so bad that its very delivery is an additional loss of unmeasurable magnitude. Their ability to conduct their business as usual afterwards will forever change. May change for the worst as a result. There is a strong possibility to this. The other components to this strategy are already in place to capitalize on the horrific events that transpired here just a few days ago. The reason why you are here gauging your plan of approach to the inevitable reaction you and your team and similarly along with several others striving to establish a well-recognized voice through protest like your own are here. This event is so inevitable you can smell it with your eyes closed in every breath drawn.

"We want to coordinate with you. I definitely see how our causes here as aligned here. That's pretty much the skinny of it all. Once we get some things squared away, we can hash out all the details. Like I said, and I am sure you can agree, the time is drawing close. We may have a day in actuality before things set themselves into motion here."

"Okay. Tell me the specifics," responds Farrukh.

Eric leans in closer, and they discuss his needs. "We need very little from any of the protests here, but we will need to get very in-depth with a simultaneous string of protests to follow that will serve as a visual gesture of solidarity to the one that will shortly occur here. All organic, but primarily set as diversions, with strategic intent to create tactical vulnerabilities and the exploitation of them to produce opportunities for me and my group of teams in each of these cities to render the same exacting outcome in each locale.

"When the smoke clears, I will be target number one. You may have some suspicion placed upon you just as many of my team may have applied to them, but the cover story for each of you has already been professionally— in regards to the works of seasoned publicists— and more importantly, legally drafted statements that will match your alibis for the evening in question, social media histories, and so forth.

"I will be the prime suspect for the coordination of all these events. I will be the one accused of using your protests to facilitate my agenda alone. Just me and maybe a few of my top people. Meanwhile, the actual facts of Mr. Stevens's brutal and fatally disastrous encounter with the four officers of the law will be what haunts the entire law enforcement community to the degree where their quest to find me amidst the bales of hay will produce fruitless results for years to come. If things go accordingly to the plan."

The executive assistant is coming along the walkway through the concessions area approaching where they are amidst the stadium seating. Both of them can hear her distinctive voice through the echoes of the emptiness of the arena unmistakably.

"I get the idea. Shoot me the list of the cities you have intentions to move on. We can discuss our dates and movements for the crowds. If you need anything else in that regard, do not hesitate to reach out. I imagine you have a method of contact that you are reserving for this line of discussion. Yes?" Farrukh asks.

"I do. Here," Eric responds, as he hands Farrukh a burner phone device along with a small plastic Ziploc bag with several packaged SIM cards and several batteries.

The batteries are wrapped in several rubber bands and the same with the packaging encasing the SIM cards. Very neat is their overall presentation. Orderly.

"Thank you."

"No problem. It is I who thanks you now for your leap of faith, and it is I who seek to see you again soon to hash out some additional details. We have appeared to run out of our time here for the moment. My number is programmed into the phone under a new name. It will be the only name programmed into the device. When you discard of each SIM card and a battery, place them in aluminum foil bags like the kind that are packaged around some chip bags of junk food and then discard of them thoroughly," Eric instructs, before he stands tall and offers his hand to be shaken by Farrukh, symbolizing that their discussion has come to its end before the stadium executive fully returns to their location.

"It was a pleasure getting to discuss these matters with you, Mr. Woodmere. My office will be in contact regarding your proposal. Good day."

Farrukh leaves in time to exchange a similarly salutation to the woman rounding the corner in an attempt to reunite with them both.

"I hope things went well, Mr. Woodmere?"

"As a matter of fact, it may very well have potential to, indeed. I must say this arena looks more inspiring each time I step foot inside and soak it all in. I attribute the positivity of that meeting to the ambiance of this establishment. Thank you for allowing the usage of this space," Eric remarks, as he slips the woman a small cashiers envelope before he shakes her hand and begins to follow her lead back to the entrance gate.

They conduct some small pleasantries and basic run-of-the- mill conversation along their way.

Chapter 13

"Duck & Rows"

Tensions grow in and around the downtown area of Memphis, Tennessee in the days leading up to the controversial presidential election. Knowing that time is becoming scarcer with each passing hour, Eric reaches out to Ezell, Gregory, and Johnny.

"Johnny?" Eric asks through the phone, attempting to be sure that he is being heard on the other end.

"I can hear you, Big Dawg. What's the word? I got your message, so I imagine it's getting really close to go time? What do you want me to handle?" Johnny asks Eric, eagerly.

"We are literally moments out. I need you to retrace our steps. Hit up the entire network appropriately and go check on them. Have them in- person walk you through the game plan. I have just brokered a partnership that will provide us cover in the form of a protest everywhere we are going to move. I have to update your details before you do.

"Okay. Whatever you say. I am right here waiting on the word. I will get on the move now. What about travel? You gonna connect me to the flights we were taking? Or will I have to bust open an identification and fly coach?" Johnny asks.

"I will arrange to have your movements accommodated for you. The service provider is extremely discreet and a longtime friend. He has more than a few jets to spare. You will be given a name to travel under," Eric responds.

"Check your thread. I just sent over the agent's contact information. Hit him up, and then use the code I'm sending now to arrange for the car service," Eric continues.

"Got it, thanks. I'm headed out now."

Eric gets a response back from a text he sent to Ezell. What's the word?

After some activity with the phone's on-screen keyboard, Eric checks the position of the ear bud lodged in his right ear as he attempts to call Ezell. Ezell is connected to the call after a few rings, and they get right to it.

"I've been paying close attention to what's happening in Memphis. I imagine you must be near to there by now. From my people, it sounds like those pipes can bust any moment now. Then you hit me. Talk to me, Nephew. What is it that we need to get done?" Ezell asks.

"As usual, you're right on it. I'm sending you some information. I'm wanting for you and Gregz to split the load and retrace your steps. Get everyone in line and make sure they ready. Like you said, we are moments, if not a day or so, from this exploding onto us. Can't afford for it to happen without us being ready to strike," Eric responds.

"Main thing we need is to ensure that the team know what to do and who will be making use of the tool Bricks dropped off to everyone. Shymeika is going to need to collaborate with that person hands on per the encryption method. Her or one of her groups for the area will work hand in hand. That's the focus. That's the priority. That's what's left. We have everything else ready to go from last we spoke.

"Oh yeah, I know I need some sleep, Man. I do. I really do, and it's starting to show.

"We have a new partnership formed with an activist that will establish protest marches in every city we plan to strike in. Their efforts will facilitate the necessary diversion in coordination with our needs. I have to put Shymeika's people in those cities in touch with the team as well. This wasn't necessary until not, but expected. The rest is still what it is," Eric states.

"Either way, you go through the proper channels and run point, making sure you Johnny and Gregz are where y'all need be as soon as possible. Because like you already stated, we can be in position to launch any moment. So, we on borrowed time to get all these ducks in a row here. We didn't come all this way to fall short on the one-yard-line did we, Unc?" Eric asks.

"Hell mother-fuckin-no!" Ezell reacts with enthusiasm.

Eric disconnects the line with Ezell and reaches out to Bricks on a separate phone he grabs out of a pocket along the side of his pants.

"What's the word, Dawg? Where we at with the deliveries?"

"We good, Big Bro. I dropped off the last one last week, and we almost back up top. I just dropped off your man at his place a day back. Been taking the long route back. Everything is good. Done deal," Bricks reports.

"That's what I like to hear. That's what we need to hear right about now, Man. Go up top and see Chupo, and he gonna get you right for that. Bless up," Eric tells Bricks before he disconnects from the conversation.

Eric's phone receives a text message. It is from his brother Dontre. I am coming through. I brought the brothers we spoke on with me. I think we will get there right on time. I'm sure of it. I will hit you when I am downstairs.

Eric sits in a bar downtown and enjoys the comfort of a few drinks as he prepares himself for what is expected to be a pivotal evening by many. While he sits at the bar furthest away from the entrance, he watches the television on display. Someone who is also sitting at the bar asks the bartender to change the channel on the T.V. from the game that is on to the news for a brief moment so they can check to see if their numbers have hit. The bartender complies with the man's request.

While the news is on, before the broadcast reaches the segment where the numbers are to be revealed, the anchor discusses the current situation surrounding the situation with Rudolph Stevens. "With the day drawing closer to evening, and the tension throughout the city at this point, reported throughout the city as 'teeming with angst and frustration', the mayor had yet to made a statement from his office since the incident. This also goes for the police chief who also had yet to make any statements, either regarding the pending discipline of the officers involved in the death of Rudolph Stevens just a few weeks ago.

"The Memphis Police department's spokesperson released a short, straight forward notification through their official website this morning that the four officers have been placed on paid administrative leave until further investigation. Until these investigations have reached their completion, no determination of any disciplinary direction will be made. We are striving to complete a thorough and comprehensive investigation as we continue to serve the community and its valued citizenry of the great City of Memphis. Thank you."

The statement does not bode well amongst the patrons at the bar during this moment. There are people who feel that yet again, the value of life is clearly being discounted and blatantly ignored in the inaction of the city's municipal leadership. There are also others who begin to groan about the process is just and to be expected. Not agreeing with the lamenting of disdain due to the expressed perception of inequality in how the justice system polices itself or the appearance of the lack thereof.

Just within the five minutes from the reading of the statement from the spokesperson's office, the tension grows exponentially in the bar. Eric sees this and realizes that it is very likely to erupt into something violent quickly. He does not intervene. The patron's argument grows intense.

Before a fight breaks out, the bartender intervenes and calms the house down with a few choice words about respecting his bar. He soothes most aggression in a few selective drinks on-the-house. This is followed by changing the channel and the replenishment of yet a second round for all on-the-house. That seems to quell the issue and erase its content from the forefront of the aggravated minds previously at one another's throats.

Eric is still intrigued by what he has witnessed. This is certainly a sign to him that the city's people are at their tipping point. He gorges down his initial drink that he ordered and consumes the drink supplied by the house back-to-back. He grabs his belongings and swiftly heads towards the exit. Once he reaches the sidewalk, he immediately checks his surroundings, recollects his bearings of where he is in relation to where he needs to be headed, and then hastily begins to walk in that direction.

When he arrives back at the Peabody, he makes his way through the lobby with no stagnation. He opens the door to his suite. Eric commences to get showered up and re-dressed. He prepares for what he suspects is going to be the evening he is anticipating; an evening that will provide that catalyst moment he's been preparing for a time almost too long to consider in measurements.

Eric grooms himself before the mirror encased within its contemporary styled L.E.D. frame.

A phone of his begins to alert and make notification chimes. It is his brother Dontre. Hey E. I am downstairs in the lobby. Give me your suite number so the gentlemen I have with me can join you upstairs and have that discussion. It feels like we arrived at the most opportune time for this discussion as it appears to be kicking off around here tonight.

Eric responds 5812, then he returns to putting the final touches of trimming his mustache onto its canvas. He reaches into a small black bag resembling a travel bag and pulls out an assortment of after shave, cologne, and baby powder. Just as smoothly, he lays the contents of the bag he intends to use, uses them, and returns them to their place within the small black bag. He throws that bag back into the larger bag brought to him earlier on during his stay.

He departs the all-white tiled bathroom and ventures out into the adjoining suite. With his hands extended to grab the remote for the television, he presses on a few of its buttons. He turns it on and selects a channel for the news. It plays quietly in the background as he pounces around the living space making sure he is ready to receive guests.

There is a knocking at the door of the adjoined suite. He didn't provide the suite number for where he personally slept and where his personal belongings were, he provided the room where he intended to conduct his meetings. As he approaches the door to respond to the knocking, he first peeps through the door's spyglass. He can easily see through the two-hundred-degree wide-angle concave lens his brother and two semi- business casually dressed men at his side. He opens the door and greets them all as he welcomes them into his room.

"Welcome! Welcome. I have some food on the way. I won't speak for any of you men, but I am slightly on the starving side," Eric announces.

"Eric, these distinguished gentlemen are, to my left, Retired Chicago Police Street Operations Unit Office Administrator Reginald Townes. To my right, also retired, Milwaukee Police Deputy Inspector Wayne Watson. These remarkable young men have some much valued insight into how things are seeming to take off in these tense Memphis Streets tonight. Did I neglect to mention that both of these brothers are former Marines, too! Oorah!" Dontre touts.

Eric greets them both, shaking their hands with friendly, but recognizable, firmness. "First, I want to thank you both for your respective service to the nation. Both with our military and as members of the law enforcement community for large urban municipalities. A place where melanation is much needed amongst its ranks. If I am not mistaken, both of your names bring me to recollect that I have heard my brother discuss matters concerning each of before on separate occasions. Am I correct in this, D?" Eric asks.

"You got it, Bro. For the sake of time, both of these men were essentially forced into retirement by their respective departments for their deemed overindulgence in urban focused objectives that they both felt were beneficial to the reparations of the ongoing disconnect between their individual law enforcement departments and the communities they were serving. Did I nail that one, Fellas?"

Both men smile and agree as they frown up their faces with consideration of what was briefly characterized by Dontre.

"Yeah, from their 'radical' activities, they found themselves on the beach side of their careers. Needless to say, they didn't get any 'Atta boys' or 'team player' accommodations for their tireless endeavors to reunite their departments with the families of their communities and the melanated children feared to potentially not survive their next encounter with any officer of the law," Dontre continues.

"Well, I appreciate what you both no doubt tried your best to be about while you had the platform to risk it all in its execution. Surely wish there was more out there doing the same," Eric commends the men after hearing of what they sacrificed.

Wayne has a burgundy colored cloth bag cradled in his arms. It is covering a bottle of rare and expensive cognac. He presents it to Eric. "Thanks for having us over. I was told that you would like to have our insight on how things are viewed in regards to departmental regulations and protocol in response to protests and riotous activity. I cannot and will not attempt to speak for Reggie, but believe it or not, there is a huge degree of discretion allowed to each officer under normal circumstances in these matters.

"Why it goes south in many cases is due to lack of discipline and an untrained desire to act out one's personal politics behind the protection of their badges. This is 'officially' frowned upon, but we know it happens far too often. The department shies away from properly dealing with—out of honesty— fear."

"Fear that it will upheave the morale amongst the ranks from the inside out. Fear that in doing so and showing any vulnerability or atonement to what has been a longstanding series of litigative liabilities that they would most certainly refrain from any public acceptance or active acknowledgement of their culpability in these ongoing blemishes to the already abysmal public relations issues facing law enforcement as a whole," Wayne explains.

"I completely agree with you. We discuss this far too often. Mainly due to far too many instances where that is exactly the driving circumstances behind what happened in what was expected to be dark remain in the dark, that was drawn out into the light. Setting the stage for the law enforcement community as a whole to once again wear that egg all across our collective faces. Making our jobs more difficult, and by that I do mean more dangerous, as we are walking beats and dealing with the people face to face in the wake of whatever event that happened last type of thing," Reginald responds.

As nightfall echoes over the skies, Eric receives a text message from Farrukh. We mobilizing right now by the stadium on Union. Pray for us all out here, wherever you may be tonight, as we put this work in for the people.

Eric stares at the message from Farrukh on the screen of his phone for a few seconds, lingering to react initially. Realizing what it means overall, he springs up from where he was leaned against the countertop and makes his way to the window that looks over a great portion of Downtown Memphis, including Union Avenue.

"An associate of mine just let me know that there is an active march in its initial formation about to come down Union," Eric informs them all, as now they too begin to approach the large window area with a bird's eye view of the pending action and activities.

Shortly after they are lined up along the window sill, a second knock comes at the door. Dontre looks towards Eric who gives him the understanding through an exchange of facial expressions that he is cool to go and see to whoever is at his door.

It is Michael. He brought Sandra Sterling and the Thomas family along with him. Right behind them is the courier attempting to deliver the large amount of food Eric had the foresight to order. He was expecting a visit from Michael and some guests of his acquaintance. Everyone introduces each other to one another. Soon, they once again, all find themselves back at the window with the spread of food serving as a backdrop to the city as they look down into it.

"Mommy, look down there at all those people. Wow!" Sophia mentions as the first wave of protestors become visible from their initial view of the growing crowd.

"Daddy! What is happening down there?" Sophia continues, looking up towards her father in innocence.

The other men in the room and her mother know exactly what is beginning to take place. Each of them is unable to completely disguise their angst and profound nervousness for what can very well be the outcome of what is developing downstairs into the downtown streets of their beloved city of soul. Wayne and Reginald spare no time in between trips to get an additional morsel of the food provided. They begin to break down from their collective years of exposure and experience in crowd management observing what is transpiring before their eyes down below. And why it is occurring so.

The two men grow more detailed in their crash course of strategic policing as the activities play out beneath them six stories below. The topic is also discussed that it is technically two evenings before Election Day, and the overall state of peace is non-existent as far as they can see from where they are positioned.

The protestors are mostly seen demonstrating for the cause of demanding specific actions from the Memphis Police Department. The protestors desire the police department to address their frustrations of the unnecessary killing of yet another Memphis citizen of African American descent. They demand with their signage for the indictment of the four officers to be brought up on charges for murder and indicted.

The crowd reaches the corner of Union and Second Street. The mass stops moving and remains there as they protest and wave their signs and banners for every activated camera lens to catch vividly. The media has already been unusually over-present in the city since the news of the shooting went viral. The large and increasingly becoming larger crowd amasses at the corner of 2nd and Union Avenue, spilling into each of the four intersections. The crowd is so thick and densely packed at about eight-thirty in the evening that it is indistinguishable as to where the pavement is. There are just that many people present as even more pile in.

After about an hour of them overwhelming the intersection with the horde of people filing into the action, the crowd begins to fill Union Avenue in both directions, east and west. The crowd now spans from Union Avenue and South Front Street all the way east to Union Avenue and B.B. King Boulevard. The crowd is also stretching down 2nd Street towards Monroe Avenue.

They appear to be travelling with a transportable stage system that erects and disassembles when there is a moment where they want to communicate with the people. As the team of protesters speed through their assembly process to erect the makeshift stage, an individual in a three-quarter length trench coat ascends its stairs to be the first individual to speak from their mobile P.A. system.

The individual clears his throat slightly, "Good evening, Fine People. Good evening to all of you who live around the corner, just outside the city, and within the city limits. I understand the frustration with the same problem that prevented our great grand-parents the true ability to experience this illustrious and elusive promise of freedom and the pursuit of happiness. We have collectively had a difficult time realizing these lofty goals in the employment sectors of our lives, the financial sector of our lives in relation to our employment turbulence. However, we cannot even focus on these two obstacles as freely as other Americans because we have never been able to shake the ghost of the past that never left from haunting a significantly hard statistical percentage of that peace. That being the police who haunts us and many generations before now doing the same exact thing."

"It is 2021, and here we are. Thirty years later after Rodney King was recorded being beaten by so-called law enforcement officers who were then as they are now sworn to protect and serve. Rest in peace to Brother King. I will not speak long.

"Brother Farrukh and the Porchlight Foundation has graciously invited me to say a few words this evening to you as we shared an imagination of just how incredibly frustrated potentially each of you are during moments in life such as this. Moments that tie directly to memories of disappointment and anger! I just want you to know that I, Na'Quan Bishop, am here!

"I am not working only for the Stevens family as we seek real justice for the unjustified homicide of Rudolph Stevens! We do not just seek this justice in his name. We seek this justice long overdue for Emmitt Till, Rodney King, and every single person, White, Black, Brown, or Yellow, who has been trounced upon— many times— to their death for the fight against these blatant abuses of power. I fight for Rudolph, I fight for Mr. Floyd, I fight for Ms. Taylor!

"I only request that we remain on the same accord each and every step of the way. We fight an oppressive imperialistic dictatorship when it comes to the subject of equality in this so-called justice system. Remain peaceful tonight. Do not give them any reason to vilify your courage this evening. Please. I fight for Rudolph!" Na'Quan Bishop exalts, as he carefully descends the make shift set of

stairs attached to the not very wide stage system.

When he descends, there are pastors and priests, Imans, and rabbis who quickly take to stage to speak prayers over the crowds before they make any additional movements as a crowd in any direction. When the prayers end, other speakers familiar to these protests take to their bullhorns in the midst of the crowd as they once again start to travel northbound. The stage is de-constructed almost faster than it was erected. The crowd is frustrated and yet seems moderately focused after being prayed over and rationalized with.

"Look, Mommy! Look, Daddy! Is that a crowd full of police officers at the far end of the street over there?" shouts Sophia, while pointing out that there is a crowd amassing at the far end of sight on 2nd Street by what appears to be Adams Avenue located by the Memphis Police headquarters."

"See, I expected this much," comments Reginald.

"For sure. I was expecting the same thing," Wayne retorts.

"They were really waiting to see and not show their hand. There were reports in the news and an overall historical pattern to have this type of protest to have their final destination become the police department where the angst is focused on," Reginald continues.

"Especially in these matters of suspected and 'alleged' police brutality," continues Wayne.

"There isn't nothing 'alleged' about that shit! They fucking murdered that man! In cold motherfucking blood!" rebukes Donte.

"Well, we can see that, Brother. However, when you circumvent a person's constitutional rights to being innocent until proven guilty… especially under extremely extraordinary circumstances like this… An over celebrated sentiment of automatic guilt, despite the existence of irrefutable evidence in the brave and courageous video recorded by the young phenome Sophia Thomas under ridiculous coincidence... this case will be strongly, heavily reliant on public opinions.

"Arrogance is not going to do much but create an opening before trial for an eruption of curiosity towards what is the version of the story from the four officers involved in this disaster. So, pardon me, I've just grown so tired of seeing this play out just that way on the side of law enforcement. All while the side of the victim's, the communities they come from, and future victims most likely to fall to the same clobbering bat being swung viciously against seemingly blindfolded citizenry when it is the justice system that should be visibly blindfolded.

"Time after time, the citizen side of things just don't seem to respond well or adapt their approach to any of these reoccurring patterns. I've watched this despicable process play itself out right around me for twenty frustrating years. Pardon me. I guess that's just me being active in my need to be proactive in the lessening of my stress in these moments," responds Wayne.

"I really wish more people on the civilian side of this far too long-standing systemic failure being so disrespectfully repeated would understand what you just said so painstakingly eloquently. There is a real sad disconnect there. We fight the system, most of us in our own ways every day, but somehow when it comes to these areas of the struggle, we just keep getting beat by the same play, every time," comments Michael.

The adults in the room are silent in response to the gravity of Michael's response. Sophia on the other hand has been overtaken by concern for the thousands of people marching below. The crowd is now heading northbound up South 2nd Street in the opposite direction from which the traffic is designated to flow. By the time the ever-increasing sized crowd reaches Jefferson Avenue, the increased law enforcement presence is attempting to meet them as they now are progressing down 2nd towards them.

What is not easily seen from the ground is that the protest crowds have overgrown so large to where there are additional large and growing crowds also marching northbound up North Main Street in addition to a next branch of that crowd travelling up Maggie S. Isabel Street as well. All seemingly set to converge at Adam Avenue. All while a third branch of that enormous crowd is moving briskly up Highway 14 protesting for the media as they pass the opportunity to turn left back towards the other crowd coming up along Maggie S. Isabel Street. The crowd on Highway 14 seems to be headed up to flank the police at Washington Avenue. It isn't long after this is seen that the helicopter can be seen flying over the crowded area.

Eric and Donte sit back and exchange discreet eye contact with one another periodically as they take observational notes to all the events as they are developing from a rather advantageous angle to had viewed such an assortment of activities from. When the two entities finally come to that geographical impasse, there is an elongated amount of time where the protesters are not challenged, and they are allowed to form their front line ranks and carry on their protests and acts of civil defiance towards the law enforcement community.

Law enforcement works to differentiate between the members of the media deeply entrenched within the crowd. Mostly visible through the bright lights used to better illuminate the subjects of interviews and correspondence regarding the crowds and live audio of what is being said amongst the crowd. Then the police begin to let it be known in a somewhat unsubtle manner of their pending tactical intentions pertaining to their next move regarding the crowd.

By this time, Michael has turned on the television. He then turns through many channels until he finds a station that is airing live coverage of the protest as it is obviously easily assumed to be breaking news. The news correspondent can be heard attempting to announce that they are receiving notification from the spokesperson for the Memphis Police Department that there are to be developments expected to take place shortly. Shortly after, Eric gently gets his hands on the remote and turns the volume up high enough to be heard without straining. The bullhorn squelching however does distract most of the adults in the room as they collectively understand the recognition of its tune to predicate some type of messaging from law enforcement to the crowds.

"MEMBERS OF THE MEDIA! MEMBERS OF THE MEDIA! ANY MEMBERS OF THE MEDIA SEEKING TO AVAIL THEMSELVES OF THE PROTECTIONS OFFERED UNDER CIRCUMSTANCES SUCH

AS CIVIL UNREST NEED TO MOVE TO THE AREA BEING DESIGNATED BY LAW ENFORCEMENT MEMBERS TO MY LEFT, WHICH WOULD BE YOUR RIGHT."

"You know what that means," Reginald says to the room with visible uncertainty and despair.

"All too well, Brother. This may get bad when it didn't even seem like worse was what anyone had wanted. This concerns me dearly, Y'all," Wayne adds.

Sandra speaks up at this moment as she begins to reach for Michael's hand. Holding it firmly, she encourages the room into a moment of silence as she prays over the city and both groups of the crowd preparing for confrontation below.

Sandra prays aloud.

Sophia, being the only child in the room, tries her best to keep her eyes shut, but she's never experienced any of this before or anything like it. The nuance of it all is just too much for her to successfully bear in obedience. She opens her eyes before Sandra is finished reciting her rather lengthy prayer. She looks upon all the adult faces before her in a state of increasing fear and uncertainty about what other bad things she is going to witness before that night comes to its end.

Sandra finishes her prayer over a great many people, situations, and peaceful healings. Sophia manages to successfully shut her eyes as she clutches onto her father's hand moments before everyone else's eyes are reopening again for the first time.

Except for Eric who has been peeking through squinted eyes the entire time. He was initially more focused on his view of what was transporting below than Sophia. However, when he was drawn for whatever odd reason that called upon him to look in her direction, he saw the fear all over her as he squinted quickly to appear as if his eyes were also still closed like the rest of the other adults. Her facial expression was something he is unable to shake from his mind. It is evidently burned into his consciousness in ways he is unable to shake, but it didn't prevent him from focusing on what he was watching.

Some members of the media followed the instructions to move into the designated area across the street. There are a few renegades who chose to stay amongst the protestors, protesting in their own way, touting that their first and ninth amendment rights are being violated by the police and other members of the law enforcement present. Moments later, the front line of officers in formation in front of the church march forward with their tactical gear, gas masks, and shields towards the crowd. Behind them was an additional regiment more prepared to support their position from back on Adams Avenue. Confrontations ensue. Tensions grow thick, and the moment occurs in an instant.

The police start to gas and move in on the protestors who have not made any true aggressive actions towards the police. There was no mentioning of any announced curfew. Some people ran when it was obvious that the police were not being very merciful by any means.

The crowds coming up along North Main Street must have heard wind of what is taking place along 2nd between Jefferson and Adams by the time they are crossing over Adams Avenue, and they rush the police in all their enormity. Many are shot with rubber bullets. Many others are severely gassed with a variant of chemical agents. There is too many still hording in towards where the police have made their stand to properly or effectively compensate for their encroachment of their once secured perimeter.

Now, the center of the crowd travelling up Highway 14 are almost experiencing their own protest and got wind of what was happening along 2nd. Most of the crowd race to their objective along Washington Avenue while a rather large segment of that crowd hurries across Adams to assist the other crowd taking on the police there.

The group in Eric's suite watch in suspense as these events transpire before their eyes. Of all in attendance, Reginald and Wayne grow more and more visibly concerned for what additional measures are sure to be implemented as the crowd is seemingly gaining an advantage over the police near the head quarter building.

More agencies are arriving and even some members of the national guard are beginning to show up as the initial compliment of officers are beginning to be overrun by the crowds converging on them from what seems as all imaginable sides. The footage of these events is mirrored across all networks. In addition to the police helicopter hovering about from point to point. There are four to five additional helicopters circling around as they strive to capture key footage of the commotion below while trying not to collide into one another during their individual pursuits of primetime gold.

As the reinforcements pile into the area, many of the protestors begin running for dear life. Many do not escape the violent and angered clutches of the officers who have had enough of their rambunctious defiance. Many are cornered, sprayed, and brutally beaten before finally finding themselves being apprehended.

As the evening rolls on and the smoke has begun to clear, it is indeed unclear who has been declared as the victor of this confrontation. No vandalism was recorded, or at least not much at all reported. Some have died. No police officer has died, though.

By the time the emergency services vehicles start to roll in and conduct site to site triage on the remaining injured still present, the occupants of Eric's suite are in true dismay after witnessing such a drastically quick negatively ending event. Eric is curious as to where Farrukh is and if he is alright. He then finds himself wondering if a guy like Farrukh is the real deal or is he going to retire after such an unfortunate outing. There were many losses down on the street. Eric experienced a great amount of skepticism regarding the viability of relying on Farrukh for the coordinated events to follow.

Eric watches the news more inventively at this point hoping to catch a segment where he is proving some contextual feedback to any of the many reporters on the scene. He is not successful in that patient observance. Still, he is undeterred as he thanks his guest and consoles others for the horrific events witnessed in his room as they depart the space. At least it is over.

Whatever statement that is to be attached to those events have yet to be declared at this particular point. Added insult to injury to so many amongst those frustrated in the city and in other cities. The message still feels like it missed its mark yet again.

Eric doesn't even take the time to clean up. He turns off the television, closes the drapes, and exits the adjoined suite after shutting off the lights into the room he was using as his personal space.

Chapter 14

"& THE HITS KEEP COMIN'"

Eric and Donte sit in Eric's personal suite eating breakfast as they watch yet another news cast covering the hot bed of agitation and civil unrest around them in Memphis.

Over the television, a newscaster can be heard clearly, "The disastrous toll of the awkwardly out of touch response to the non-violent protest in Memphis has not left the forefront of our media cycle. Each of us fight to extrapolate these recent developments. Just as we approach the opening of the polls before the largely anticipated presidential election. President Ace has been taking a brutal political beating throughout this entire process politically while his loyalists remain undeterred as to who their support remains aligned to, without question.

"The recently obtained polls are as expected: unfavorable towards President Ace. These numbers reveal this trend having a negative impact within his own base after the events of the Memphis protest. President Ace continued to batter the coastal shores of his constituency with convoluted conspiracy theories, declaring the election was in jeopardy of being an unofficial, illegitimate, tainted event."

266

"He urged his supporters while there was still time left for what remained of a free patriot spirit in his beloved nation to spread out— get involved, verify that his supporter's neighborhoods were free from anyone seeking to cast illegal ballots. He spared no rebuke for the federal post office. He challenged the sanctity of absentee ballots. The opposing party has had many a field day amongst their constituents as they mocked his many statements that made their point for them to challenge to the overall efficacy of his hoped campaign for re-election," the reporter carries on in their report.

"Donte, this is going to wind up so freaking huge of a deal that there ain't no way anyone can predict the fallout within any true realm of certainty. Don't get me wrong. There are predictable elements to all of this, but this thang has so many moving parts, it's just unreal," Eric shares with Donte.

"Bro, who you telling? Today is Election Day!" Donte reminds him. "This whole thing is going to heat up exponentially after those results come in. That's not even considering if the election is a close race. I agree. Fall back. You have all the pieces in place to give your game plan solid footing. I'd wait, too and pounce when the moment best suits your purpose overall. The bigger picture preparatory to the long game."

Days after the protest that ended horrifically, many of the people on the street just appeared deflated and out of sorts to the both of them. Eric and Donte took a lap through the path of the protesters to soak it all in firsthand on the ground. There was much consternation regarding the uneasy transition from the events of the last evening to the reality of having the election results being the next news focus later that day that would no doubt have an unmistakable impact on the trajectory of the foreseeable four years to follow. There were several lines of thought that each had its own line of analysis regarding who was going to do what and why they were planning on doing so. Although these were the predominantly more vocalized views overheard from their walks through the downtown community.

"This whole situation is definitely on the verge of imploding. If there was a person who I felt could operate best under such circumstances, it would be you. With that being said, shit… this can easily go a great many ways due to all his extra shit taking place on a real large scale all around this opportunity— moment— however we choose to label it all."

"I've heard most of the plan. Seems genius enough to me. I realize you're a virtuoso of this shit, but damn I know your OCD ass is fucking toiling over managing all this processing up in there," Donte challenges Eric.

"Yeah. There is a lot of serious shit occurring simultaneously. This convergence of random difficulties is not an overall benefit, but not exactly a true detrimental interference all the same. I've taken the time to cultivate from the inception of all this. A batch of extremely vetted contingencies to prepare the viability of my overall goal against any potential interference as it may present itself in any imaginable form."

"I'm not pleased, Bro. Don't get it twisted. I am prepared, though. So much so to where I realize how to turn these sudden developments into fortifying elements to my success in this whole endeavor. Way too deep in now to view the insertion of any event as anything other than an opportunity to utilize whatever into an advantage of any sort, not just some sort," Eric responds.

"One thing we can initially agree on is that the time is here. It may not be completely presented at this precise moment, but make no mistake the time to make that final pivot is a step away at the very least. Today may very well be the last day I get to see you and walk the streets with you so freely. Who knows? My gauge and misdirected breadcrumbs may never lead them to me. Maybe not?

"What I do know is that the time is now, and here we are. I'm going to soak up the blessing of having you here right now. Before all this madness we've prepared for all these years, mums from the drawing board into fruition. Let's just chill and enjoy us for this day. Before this election madness becomes all that remains of the day," Eric speaks, with reflection.

Donte agrees, but internally is unable to resist the feeling that his older brother is being more evasive than he's ever been to his recollection. He fights that discernment stirring within him by trying to identify with the strong potential that he is becoming more aware of the outcome of his long-standing plans and what they will matriculate into for not only himself, but everyone he's spent time with on record for the last five or so years. That with already knowing that his older brother is already historically an intense personality all of his own.

He just slows his brain down from all his speculative thoughts and agreed with his brother to enjoy their time with one another in that moment and the moments they are both obviously grateful to have in the full extent of however long it is to last. Again, realizing his brother is several steps ahead of him as he's always been coming up. He smiles before he finally responds to Eric.

"Word. Let's grab some food, and keep kicking it. I'm with you, Big Bro," Donte replies.

They grab some barbecue from over on B.B. King Boulevard because it feels fitting and head back to Eric's suite. Once they're back in the suite, Michael stops by.

"Hey, Cuz? I am headed back to New Orleans. Then from there I will be off the DC with Bishop. I'll be back to check on the family downstairs periodically. I know you got your team here on that. Other than that, I'm in that wind, Bro," Michael chants, as he walks through the door once Eric lets him in.

When Michael realizes Donte is still there, he addresses him cheerfully as well. "What up, Fam? When you breaking out? We both know this man," he uses his hands to refer to Eric, "won't be here too many more days if tomorrow," Michael jokes slightly.

"You already know. We just kickin' it today before the bottom breaks out of this thang. I'm out tonight, actually. I see you about to be out now, though." Donte reaches for him and embraces him strongly to tell him goodbye. "Love you, Cousin. Stay safe and be watchful and mindful. I know you extra smart and shit. I love you, Dawg. I look forward to seeing you as soon as we can link up again."

"Word, Family. Word," Michael responds, slightly taken by surprise.

He's never seen many, if any, moments where Donte spoke in such a nostalgic way. It caught him off guard.

"Yeah. I will definitely think of this moment for quite some time. Got me thinking of all our parents above. Wondering how proud they are of us for finding success in this life and being a part of something so monumental for the same overall cause they fought for during they lives. We definitely made some purpose of all those days being mischievous little hellions. I gotta run to the back real quick. Mike, you don't have to rush off unless you just have to. You and D kick it while I do this real quick. So we can keep kicking it when I come back. If not for just a little while more,", Eric blurts out before he dashes out of sight into the other room.

That too contributes to throwing Michael off as he never heard Eric ever talk in a nostalgic manner as far as his memory allows him to travel back.

"What the hell y'all brothers smoking on in here? For real. I definitely need to know and see this blunt. Got both y'all acting real strange. Like beyond weird. But… a lot of shit is about to happen. I guess I get it. I love both you, too!"

With a new perspective to the odd vibes taking hold, Michael plops himself onto the much sofa and kicks his feet up.

"It smells like B.B. King's up in here anyway. I hope y'all greedy bums haven't eaten it all. Let me get some," Michael jokes.

Donte laughs aloud.

"You a real clown, still! I got more than I was able to even mess with. It's in that kitchenette. In the microwave," Donte instructs.

Michael jumps up quickly, without any sign of hesitation from being completely stretched out seconds before on the sofa and runs into the kitchenette area of the suite. Eric is still off into the other room. After about a couple of minutes— ten, more accurately— Eric returns to the main room. He sees Michael back on the sofa, stretched out again, snacking on the food he knows Donte had bought that he joked about him seeing with his eyes instead of his stomach.

"You greedy as hell still. Let me get some of that sofa, Bro. Dang," Eric jokes, while laughing out loud.

Donte reaches for the remote for the television and turns the device on. After surfing through several channels, he finds an older television show that is on. Ironically, they would spend Saturday mornings watching this show with their other cousins when they were younger. The show captures their attention, and they sit and watch it through its entirety.

As time passes, Michael has since been long gone. The same of Donte. All who remains at this point is Eric. Eric is preparing to sweep both suites, cleaning his presence from both. He remembers his promise to Hubert. He knows that the time available in his itinerary to visit his friend and family has a slender chance of being acted upon; he also knows that not doing so will not bode well in regard to future issues that can be avoided in making the time to take that time today.

Once he is through collecting what he had and exits the suite, he makes his way downstairs. He gives his suite pass to one of the bellhops he'd befriended through conversation, and oh, yes, steady and largely substantial gratuitous tips. Eric prefers not to have his silhouette on display in the lobby. He slips out the rear stairwell and into the parking garage.

He had called Hubert before he left the room, making sure he was indeed available to scoop him up at that time. Fortunately, at the moment he reached out, Hubert was available, and more importantly, willing to come downtown during rush hour to get him. Eric makes his way down Union Avenue to the side of the stadium. While he stands there waiting for Hubert to arrive, he watches the pedestrian foot traffic come and go.

After about twenty or so minutes of waiting along Union, he receives a text message from "Hue", I'm coming off fifty-one now.

Eric is unaware of what vehicle Hue will be arriving in, so he texts him back, What kind of car are you driving?

After a moment, a text comes back, Blue Jaguar. I see you now. I'm about to honk my horn.

Eric hears a horn being honked once. He turns in the direction of where it seems to have come from. The two men lock eyes. Eric wastes no time before he is at the vehicle's passenger's door. He pulls the door, climbs inside, and before he gets the door closed, they are off on their way.

"I'm not gonna lie to you, Bro. I did not think you was going to have the time to come through and see the family. Thanks for whatever sacrifice you took on the chin coming up this way to me. I know you know what I have going on, and I realize you see my situation. It is what it is, though. Thanks all the same, Fam," Hue says to Eric.

"Don't bother to stress about it, Hue. You been my dawg for a shit long time. I remember when you met Kim. I know that you been taking relationship 'Ls' by always coming through when I've really needed you in and out of the area. She hasn't seen me in many years. I understand how that comes across, and the predicament it has you in more times than not coming through for me because we have that kind of history. I need to come through for you, too. Simple as that. This may be one of those moments.

"While yes, I'm definitely pressed for time, I'm still gonna do my best to swing through your crib tonight. I suspect it will take some of that weight up off you in that department. Plus, I'm looking forward to kicking it with my guy and the family you've created. That's a whole different level of the blessing."

"I will have a car come scoop me before too long. I know with the election taking place Kim is gonna be all over that," Eric laughs. "I will try not to aggravate her too much. If I don't aggravate her at all she gonna definitely suspect I'm up to some shit. Then it will be you that be suspected next," Eric jokes with Hue.

"You're laughing while I'm sitting here envisioning everything you just said. You haven't been here for at least three years, and you nailed it. You should tell me in advance who is going to win this election," Hubert mockingly jokes in return towards Eric.

Eric laughs as they pull off the highway.

"I know who I think stands a chance to win. A strong chance at that. However, President Ace is a stubborn son-of-a-gun. Plus, we all know that his supporters don't even play about that guy. He can walk in front of us right here and lick off a whole magazine in our direction, and we can be comatose on the pavement beneath his feet, and his supporters will drum up a story where we shot ourselves as he was trying to help us cross the damn road while we already in a car!

"I'm just saying. That man has a serious following that is just incapable to see the negative in anything he has said while in office or has done while in office. To be honest, I admire the idea of having such devout support. I'd be giddy if I had two people like that, let alone thousands upon thousands of them.

"I won't be voting in person. I sent my absentee ballot out months ago. I'm probably biased because I do want him to lose. Mainly because I fought for this country, too. He just not a good look in a bigger picture. He just couldn't keep his foot out his mouth. Too many moments to go there, Man," Eric continues.

They pull into the yard. There is much sunlight still in the sky. The evening has just begun its shift on the day. When the car stops in the driveway, the children who know the sound of their father's vehicle start to file out of the house and into the yard.

"Daddy! Daddy! Do you really have Uncle Eric with you? Do you?"

Eric turns quickly and discreetly towards Hubert. "You extra wrong for that. How you got me looking like a deadbeat Uncle? Brooo!" Eric quickly chimes in under his breath, as he grabs ahold of Hubert and mutters under his breath as the children attempt to topple him and bring him to the ground from being overwhelmed.

Eric can smell the garlic bread from the front yard.

Kim must be in a real good mood tonight Eric thinks to himself. The both of them know full well that Eric loves garlic bread and spaghetti. Especially the way she makes it. It has been a while.

The evening carries on. Eric, Hubert, Kim, several other family members, as well as the countless children present enjoy one another's company. Everyone who walked through their doors were interrogated on whether or not they had participated in the election by casting their vote. The aggressive inquisition was foreboding the obvious response if anyone was to actually reply with a "NO".

The time draws near to about eight p.m. Eric had already explained in far advance as best that he could that he is going to be departing around this time. Hubert had also been putting that disclaimer out in advance himself.

When Eric's car pulls up to the house, they have eaten, debated, and shared several loud bouts of laughter to where nobody is in their real feelings when the time comes. Just the children. Eric had a plan for this already.

When his car comes, the driver comes to the door with four large shopping bags. He gives them to Hubert.

"There are items in those bags for you, Kim, and all the children. There are a few additional things in there I will let you parse out to everyone else," Eric whispers, as he waves his goodbyes to the people in the household.

He completely exits the home and is in stride to enter the rear of the vehicle that is waiting for him. He gets on his mobile device and begins to clear the way for the preparation of his next flight.

Eric sits in the comfortable seat as he thinks while he has his travel partner awaiting his directions so they can get everything coordinated on his behalf. He hasn't yet decided where he is going to head off to as election night is certainly taking the trajectory of his plan to a heightened, elevated level of imminence. The initial preliminary results that will be reported earlier on from many polling stations will have come in before he is to potentially land back on ground.

The driver's objective remains the same despite Eric's procrastination or indecisiveness in where he needs to be. The truth is he needs to be nowhere. He has everything set up at this point. He is aware that he can make the call from anywhere. He just doesn't want to use a mobile device to do so. He wants to avoid cell towers from having the ability to triangulate him faster. He realizes the best possible location to be.

Set me up to get to Atlanta Eric types into his mobile device.

By the time they arrive at the airport, Eric expects the notification from the flight and ground crew chiefs that he is going to have to wait before being able to take off. Eric then returns to the vehicle that brought him. The driver gets out of the vehicle and pops the trunk open. When he returns to the front side of the vehicle after foraging through the trunk, he resurfaces with a head rest television monitor. He pulls a few connection wires with it from the box he had come from the trunk with. He works at it for a few moments, seeming to look like he had done these very same actions so many times over.

When he is done, the driver looks at Eric with an expression of accomplishment. It took Eric no more than four minutes from start to finish. Before he fully exits the area, he gives Eric the remote that is to be used with the system he just temporarily installed for his comfort and goes on his way.

Curious and watching his clock, Eric first thanks the gentlemen by shaking his hand and looking him in the eyes, "Thank you, Brotha."

He realizes after checking his watch that there should be some version of an initial report on whatever polling station data that would have been reported at this point in the evening, seeing how the polls just closed within minutes of him reaching the hangar. As he expected, the initial readings indicate that Ace is behind from mostly states that were already expected to be going in the direction of voting within their historical party lines. What is astonishing is that in some cities and their respective states, many polling districts are appearing to deviate from their historical party affiliation. These differences in voting behavior are not in favor of President Ace. It is quite early for making any presumptions as to how the overall vote will turn out to reflect as the winner, but Eric thinks that these developments have to be wearing heavy on the mind of President Ace as the night trickles along towards midnight.

Eric flicks through several channels every now and then with his feet up in relax mode as he awaits the administrative team to notify him either in person or via text that he can board the jet literally twenty feet from his current position. He watches the news coverage regarding the election, while periodically returning to one show that piques his interest to another. After two shows have been watched basically back-to-back in increments of half-an-hour-blocks, Eric is interrupted from another round of getting updated on the election by a tap at the window to his left. Eric rolls down the window of the vehicle.

"Sir, your jet will be ready to depart shortly. You can come aboard now. We have already prepared the television system on board so that you shouldn't miss much in the transition," informs the female member of the flight crew.

Unlike during other flights, this time Eric does not order any meals. He is still rather stuffed from his meal with Hubert and his hilarious family. He is also not going to reward him having to wait with being that gratuitous. He boards the plane. As promised, he is able to essentially pick up with the news and not miss much between the walk from the vehicle to the plane. It is closing in on 9:40 p.m. He changes his mind about his decision to be petty.

He summons the flight attendant. "I know that there have been some efforts taken to expedite things on my behalf. I just need a few moments, if possible, to have something brought over. It should not take very long. I was so distracted about the news coverage of the election that it really just slipped my mind completely."

"Let me convey your wishes to the captain, and it will honestly be a decision for him to make," replies the flight attendant.

She darts off into the front area of the plane. It doesn't take much time at all before she returns to the cabin area to inform Eric that the pilot has a response to his request.

"The captain informed me that he will wait for the time you need. He apologizes for having you wait as long as you did. We will just give our place in line up for a few spots in the hopes that the time that creates will be enough to accommodate your needs," reports the flight attendant.

"Please give him my thanks and express my complete appreciation for his entire message."

Eric wastes no time before he grabs a mobile device from his pocket and begins to text into its keys. Before long, about no more than twenty minutes, several bags are brought into the hangar where they all are. There are bags he redirected to go with the flight crew, and there are bags that come aboard. He orders himself something light and simple. Everyone is feeling good, and this discreetly pleases Eric a great deal. He thinks to himself that he is pleased, because even now, on the verge of taking the plunge into the true unknown and test each plan, each potential contingency established, he is about to move childishly.

He is actually embarrassed at his own behavior. None of the ground crew or flight crew have anything to do with the delay in service. It is he who grew too expectant and complacent with being accommodated after arriving or announcing his travel needs last minute. When he finally realizes the path of his actions, he is happy because he is still able to take care of the crew that are working feverishly hard to get him squared away. He finds relief that he is able to atone for his thoughts and actions while still having the time allotted to him to effectively rectify the situation properly.

The crew is ready. Eric is ready as well. They go through the process of announcing all the safety procedures and safety protocol awareness. By this time as they do these things, the jet is beginning to depart its hangar and onto the tarmac headed towards the beginning of the taxi lanes.

Eric's attention is predominately focused on the television along with most of the flight crew. They will continue to go about their duties for the flight itself, but somehow return to the area of the cabin where the television is on as they check the news if not just by earshot for updates of what is developing.

After about forty-five minutes of flight-time, they are approaching the point on their flight plan where they are to initiate their descent back down below the atmosphere onto the tarmac of the Atlanta airstrip. Before the time is upon them all to turn the television off and prepare to deboard the plane, the election results begin to point in a clear direction. Oscar Gabriel is leading the popular vote by ten million votes. Oscar has the electoral college vote by fifty votes, where it is about two-thirty-five, to President Ace's electoral count of one-hundred-eighty-seven.

There's not much of a mathematical chance that President Ace is able to pull this one out. People are beginning to crudely celebrate in the background of the reporters out in public seeking to gauge the reaction of the people.

When Eric steps out of the plane and down its staircase, he quickly finds his way to climb into the vehicle he had arranged waiting for his arrival. He turns the smaller screen on and begins to watch more news now that the election is for the most part mathematically and statistically out of reach for any reversal of trend to occur. He texts Johnny to see if he is in the state. He is not, but Johnny tells Eric that he is more than welcome to hold out in the bunker until he is either ready to make a move or call the shot.

Atlanta is an ideal place to base camp for Eric. One of the most unique collections of communities that exists in the country.

Come the early morning, Eric awakes after taking a decent length sleep once he arrived to the house and got comfortable on the bed in the back room. He stopped paying attention to the news regarding the election updates. He knew if he continued to give it any attention, he would be up all night.

Eric sits on the edge of the bed as he texts into one of the many mobile devices he keeps on his person. Switching out SIM cards, swapping batteries, and hard resetting phones before he uses one has become a swift second nature for him. When he finishes the routine, he sends out some texts and orders enough breakfast for the entire house above. When it comes, the young children take delight to deliver the food to their father's strange and mysterious friend. When they finally depart with the additional assistance in the form of parental motivational tactics such as vail threats, Eric turns the television on. He sees for his own eyes that President Ace did not get re-elected.

The news attached to that development is no surprise. "Good morning, my fellow Americans. The results of last night's election have been completely tabulated and verified. We have a new president, and that person is Oscar Gabriel! The former president wasted no time at all before he started to challenge the validity of his defeat.

"Many sources close to the former president have shared with members of the press that President Ace made several statements to his cabinet members in the hopes to obtain strategies to express his frustrations to the outcome of the election last evening. He is reportedly having a series of abusive rants where he has expressed how he felt the election was rigged. There were additional reports from sources close to White House officials that President Ace even went as far as to reach out to the Secretary of State in each state he came close to losing or flat out lost to Gabriel. These calls have all reportedly taken the same trajectory, according to the bureau of elections chief demanding that they respectively and immediately re-count all districts within their states.

"The sad fact that the evidence illustrates is that he didn't stop there, ladies and gentlemen of the audience. Utilizing his usual forums within social media, he strongly encouraged and challenged his devoted fan base and loyal supporters to become agitated. He continued in the news to motivate these groups to claim back their country from an egregious act of theft from them in depriving them of having their president legitimately re-elected as he would be found if they were to disregard the outcome of the initial election and re-count all the legal and acceptable ballots of the true American patriots," the news broadcaster reads directly from President Ace's social media postings during parts of the broadcast.

The news of ongoing reports from just about every news outlet that President Ace's unconstitutional crusade to reverse the outcome of the election takes a real toll on Eric's cogitative state of mind. He switches to a next station. This station for the duration of Ace's presidency had been his number one supporter. It had one of their pundits address the ongoing dilemma President Ace had been dragging the nation through his inability to accept the fair and legitimate outcome of the election.

The news person begins their report, and Eric draws his focus on the television yet again. "President Ace continues to refuse to discontinue his assertive attempts to plead his case to the American people that the election was indeed by his standards alone… rigged. When he seemingly accepted the notion that the general citizenry was not concerned with his claims that he nor his large interchanging legal team failed at every opportunity to prove with actual evidence, he turned heavily back to inciting his supporters to begin the consideration of the eventuality that in order to save their country they would have to fight and take it back from the hands of those legislators he claimed to be willing to violate the constitution, by certifying its fraudulent results into ratified law. How is he going about accomplishing this might any of you out there ask? Simple. He has gone as far as encouraging violence to be exacted to strike fear into the hearts any legislative member of either the House or the Senate. State level legislators included," the reporters rage on.

Another news anchor takes over. "Make no mistake, Ladies and Gentlemen. We realize the other party has won the election. Won both the House and the Senate. The loss is real and unmistakably devastating in regards to what policies the other side of the aisle will bully through legislation.

"We didn't just get here by happenstance. I may surely get reprimanded for saying so, but we have blame in this here at Eagle Enterprise News Corp. We have a significant fault in all of this. We as a network have supported this president blindly and without ceasing. He will apparently have no adverse feeling about taking this entire network along with our multi-million supporters and viewers into the depths of the sea along with him. Thus, is selfish, short-sighted, and unacceptable. I must stop."

"I will say this last thing. Be mindful. I say this to each and every one of you watching this telecast. Be careful. Do not allow yourselves or that of your children follow this maddened pied piper into that sea to your severe detriment. The way he is leaning, the way he is directing his statements and speeches, he is setting a dangerous table.

"I, along with many of my colleagues who may be fearful to say so, know that it is obvious that if an adult does not take over, we are approaching a most horrible outcome, Ladies and Gentlemen. More horrible than seen to this date. Something worse is coming if we do not act accordingly.

"I'm getting summoned to see my executives." He grasps for the microphone in his lapel. "Don't let it be you that wears the egg on your face for this person! Don't let this happen to you. Don't mistake this president and his undue influence for patriotism! There are more well-advertised ways available to rectify all of this madness," the news anchor speaks, before the camera angle changes awkwardly.

Now the anchor is seen being escorted off the set, live on-air. The telecast goes viral in little to no time, but it has little effect on the already forming mindset of the now former president's supporters.

"…In other news… There was word that there are to be repercussions in the weeks to come. As the weeks have eroded by that led up to the first step in the process of ratifying the election have drawn near, despite the fact that the results were not considered close enough in margin to constitute any recounts or special attention. However, due to the enhanced scrutiny and alertness related to the rhetoric of former President Ace over his unrelenting claims that the election had been rigged, and tampered with," announces the news anchor.

Eric goes about the business of slipping out and meeting with key associates that are integral in his next move. Evading any law enforcement that will seek to follow his intentionally flawed and conspicuous breadcrumb trail, he spends many days in between his arrival in Atlanta and when the final ratification process is to be conducted.

The counting of the Electoral college ballots.

When the House met at the capitol to certify the results of the popular vote, there was a significantly large amount of protestor presence in the nation's capital.

"President Ace's supporters would rally early in the morning and march throughout the day around the capitol building for many hours. Social media was being lit up with an alarming amount of hate speech and violent threats towards many of the legislative members who stood in association with the party opposing that of the former president. The former president has literally done nothing to quell or dial down his devoted followers. Instead, what he has chosen to do is to ingeniously provoke and inspire their delusional ramblings to becoming even more unstable in their argumentative behaviors towards the Capitol and its members of the House and congress."

The reporter pauses and reaches for her earpiece to better hear the transmission coming through to her. "Ladies and Gentlemen, we have a breaking news moment. Reports have just come in that there is an extremely large gathering in front of the White House. We are receiving word from the White House spokesperson that the former president will not only be in attendance, but with planned intentions to speaking to the enormous crowd that had been gathering in record numbers on Pennsylvania Avenue," the reporter carries on.

Eric has just finished a workout in the state-of-the-art exercise space within the underground bunker he'd been utilizing as his temporary residence before he is to initiate the game plan and begin his excursions. He is fully aware of the news coverage of the scheduled certification process taking place to ratify the electoral college ballots. Eric has an awkward feeling that the process is something he needs to pay attention to, and he watches the procedures as they are broadcasted live.

"Today on Capitol Hill, there is set to be a historical moment being set into action. When the electoral college has been completely counted and the election fully certified, the nation will have its newly elected leader at the helm, and the number one job to conduct first is to repair all that President Ace had done during his presidency. With the certification being set to commence and also find conclusion of the official certification process, these same events occurred that occurred the day they ratified the popular vote. This was the final of the two-phase process being undertaken in accordance with the law to certify the newly won presidency of Oscar Gabriel.

"The commotion across the country had continued to boil to an unprecedented degree. There were murmurs of active plans that detailed the intent of several groups sympathetic to the call to action by the president, to avenge democracy, and stop the sanctified process of the election from being adulterated. Increasing in aggression, and their targeted focus of invading the capitol area becoming the subject of scrutiny of military forces and law enforcement in the area of the District of Columbia. The last obstacle to having the results of the election over turned was about to take place today inside the Capitol building."

The reporter continues, "There are several reports coming in that indicate that there is a chance that when President Ace speaks to the massive crowd outside of the White House along Pennsylvania Avenue, he will either use that platform to move forward and accept the loss of the fair election, or continue to spurn the crows consisting of his followers in their crusade in avenging his illegitimate loss. The moment of truth was without coincidence, and beginning the very same moment that Congress opened its session in regards to verifying the electoral college votes.

"The White House communications cabinet and their staff toiled under time constraint in having everything necessary in place, so when the president took to the podium, the scene would be set for it to work in his best light. He gave an electrifying speech that invigorated his base. He told his supporters at one point in his speech, 'Go down to the Capitol with me and let's take this country back'!" The news reporter comments.

Eric watches the news footage that shows how large of a crowd has amassed in front of the White House in response to the call to action issued by the president to come to the nation's Capitol in a final effort as advertised to reclaim what had been taken by the fraudulent election and the sinister plot of the opposing party's agenda to ruin the county that they have been raised for many generations to hold dear.

What Eric watches happen next on the television is unpredictable for many. The crowd, taking direction, ventures south to the Capitol Building. Once the crowds fully amass in front of the Capitol building, the scores of law enforcement units in place grow more and more aware that the officers that were placed throughout the Capitol area are alarmingly out-manned and becoming out-positioned.

The mayor calls in the National Guard in the hopes that they can arrive very quickly enough to prevent more injuries than what the projections already expect. The situation surrounding the Capitol is worsening by the minute. There are only a few protestors now labeled seditionists who have been recorded as to having any substantial injuries. However, there are more than a dozen officers who sustained varying degrees of injuries.

When the melee ends and the dust has time to clear, the so-called seditionists retreat their momentary positions in and around the Capitol building not very long after former President Ace asked his supporters to discontinue their assault. This request for such action came from an increasingly strong call to do so by many of the leadership members of their political party. Initially, there was outrage in the very act of storming the hallowed Capitol Building all by itself. Soon after, that outrage sentiment had its moment in the media. There are continuous additions of videos that are being released from the many participants on the ground, highlighting and making it quite clear from their content that it is a collection of different groups with different organizational backgrounds that found unification in their disdain for how the election resulted. Their videos turn a bright light onto the unifying connections between their seeking to challenge, and more importantly, overturn the outcome of the election he lost.

All of them feel and express a devout spirit of allegiance and support for the former president in his ongoing call to action in these matters as he continues to speak out and send messages throughout social media platforms to his disapproval. As this angst marinates and increases its potency amongst these groups, still a new outrage is coming to the forefront of the overall story.

Just weeks before that event at the Capitol, there was the publicly witnessed protest turned violent and deadly that occurred in Memphis, Tennessee. There is a disparaging contrast between how those overall peaceful and non-violent protestors were treated and responded to as they remained in the streets and marched without violence or destruction to or the defacing of any property. Neither any personal or commercial property had produced any reports saying otherwise. Yet, that crowd was treated differently in every visible way. When the crowd at the Capitol was aggressively violent, they injured officers. They also demonstrated the intent and motives to injure any officer of the law who stood in their unlawful way or path beyond where they were allowed in the Capitol.

This outrage is what piqued the interest of Eric for the impact it was to obviously have on his pending decision to move and when. Since the events in Memphis, Eric has reconnected with Farrukh. Farrukh is all the way in on his desire to assist Eric in his move due to the outcome of the Memphis protest. Farrukh's group of movement supporters were so viciously dealt with in Memphis at the hands of their local police department. And more specifically, the police have had deliberate dragging of their feet in making any disciplinary decisions transparent.

The country is torn and disparaged. The next days continue to deepen the bleak sentiment. It becomes more surrounded on either side of the perspective on the emerging voices of outrage growing more vivid with each new video of the attempted sedition at the Capitol. Adding to that are the continuously loud and louder voices speaking on more and more televised forums about the racially charged subject of law enforcement oversight; the continuously loud and louder voices speaking on the transparent accountability that was agreed upon throughout those speaking is over eighty years past due.

Eric and Farrukh plans onward.

Chapter 15

"OUTRAGE FOR OUTRAGE"

"Being the face of the legal team in regards to the nature of this high-spectacle and controversial case, Na'Quan Bishop was getting ready to speak to the world live from the lobby of the Peabody Hotel located in the heart of Memphis, Tennessee's downtown district," says a news anchor on the television.

Eric is still in Atlanta where he is finalizing his moves in preparation for the commencement of putting his long-awaited plan into action. He still nurtures significantly stronger ties with more than a few dozen individuals in the area to maintain his proverbial ear to the street.

He flicks and surfs through a dozen channels as he chows down on the breakfast brought to him by the children upstairs. Alongside taking advantage of having access to the well curated home gym setup in the bunker along with him, he also tunes in to the news to stay somewhat aware of what story is being told. He finds a different network for the news and stops surfing. He goes back to nibbling on the corners of what is left of the breakfast he was given. He switches from an occasional bite to the next set of repetitions of the exercise regimen he is progressing through for today. As he finds the channel he intends to listen to during the next stretch, he catches a news anchor beginning to speak.

"...Yes, we are being told by sources close to the legal team that have pledged to fight and bring justice back to the family that Mr. Bishop, the lead counsel, will be addressing the members of the media present in just a short while. This announcement comes on the public response from Shelby County's District attorney's office where there seems to be somewhat of a standout between their office and that of the family's legal team. There was a legitimate tremor felt across the legal industry when the initially startling clips from the video had been released from a third-party witness to the events that led to the untimely death of Mr. Rudolph Stevens. There were only still images that represented that there was in fact an alternate recording of the details at this point were only being shared and described by the officers involved in the incident. Still, with the damaging imagery, the Memphis Police department continued to double down on their stance of supporting their officers until the matter was completely investigated," the reporter finishes.

"The district attorney's office and the Chief of Police continued to push for a thoroughly and lengthy trial process where they can most likely elongate the proceedings with their records and less about the actual events that led to the questionable death of Rudolph Stevens. They continued to use their claims of anything outside of that would be to interrupt the delivery of the officers' rights to their constitutional rights of having access to due process under the law. We were unsuccessful in getting any direct response to the contradicting story being told and shared at an increasing rate regarding the images released anonymously from the person or entity of the video that the photos were snapped from.

The officers have not been indicted, yet, and are all still on the administrative leave, receiving full pay since the day after the incident occurred. That alone has angered many and is a constant source of tension between the varying sides of perspectives regarding this subject matter of police brutality and the unfortunate many similar incidents before this recent one," responds the co-anchor.

Eric is in between reps as these developments play out across his screen.

"Ladies and Gentlemen. We are being told that Mr. Na'Quan Bishop has come from the back area of the hotel and has stepped to the podium and its microphone. Stand by as we ensure the audio feed from the P.A. system," interrupts another reporter as the screen transitions to where she is at the scene in the lobby of the Peabody.

Mr. Bishop is already at the podium, reaching for the microphone and adjusting it to his preference before he starts to speak to the group of representatives from various media outlets local, national, and international in his presence. Moments following, he finishes his tweaking to the positioning of the microphone. All the people present lean in with their full attention, notepads, and camera with boom mics and some just with digital recorders at the ready as it is apparent Bishop is just about to speak.

"Welcome and good morning to each of you. I will be brief. Just a month ago we witnessed yet another fact manifest before us as a nation yet again. Members of the African American community still need to be fearful of the so-called community of law enforcement agencies paid by taxes from all Americans when law enforcement apparently only seeks to serve and protect one segment of society. The governor, the Memphis mayor, and this police chief have chosen to be complicit as the district attorney for the county facilitates perjury. They all continue to share a version of the events that led the sad and unfortunate, preventable, and untimely death of the late Mr. Rudolph Stevens who has left behind a wife and two children that will never get to see or embrace their loved one again in this lifetime.

"I am certain that may sound simple enough to overlook and disregard. I am still sure that each of you have a family, a significant other, even a cat or a dog waiting on your return from work each day. Just imagine that one day they are left with the unbreakable grief when you do not make it home and never are to return home ever again. And why? Because of people that you yourself contribute to their collective salaries to ensure they have what they need to serve and protect in regards to resources and salaries.

"This is once again nothing new. No nuance to any of this. The police have had many from within their ranks that have been abusing and brutalizing men, women, and even their children of the African American community. Many good-hearted, mentally sound and stable, rational, and procedure-minded members of the overall law enforcement have a deep stain on their name as well as profession. Why should anyone brave enough, courageous enough to step into the shoes of a hero's profession have to ever be scorned with such a negative stereotype of this sort. Because they love to recite and repeat to us this kind of garbage during times that follow incidents such as this? 'Do not allow a bad apple become what labels the whole batch'? The answer is ironically simple and hidden apparently from preventing their collective cognitive dissonance from solving its riddle: 'Then why have y'all?'

"How long while from working side-by-side, up close, and personal with individuals who demonstrate a depraved mind towards the precinct that you have a sworn duty, a sworn-duty to serve, and not be compelled to do something about it? Do something to take that criminal out of a uniform and off of the streets because you seek out criminality but fail to root it out when you're visibly and hopefully spiritually in close proximity. It should be the simplest investigative effort you as an officer of the law could encounter.

"But enough about that. Regretfully, we can extrapolate an endless number of issues and identify countless reasons to just continuously discuss that and identify much that would need addressing. This is not the main purpose of my conference today. That is normally my purpose. That is normally the focus of my drive every day and for the last ten years as a litigator. Fighting that system for the same damn crime, time after time. Just against one beautiful, melanated face after another.

"In this case, a man, a husband, a father was coming home after having a few drinks at a bar. Chose to walk home instead of drive while having a few drinks. Not even enough to be considered as intoxicated by law, but enough to where he refused to even take the chance of hurting anyone, let alone himself.

"During that walk, he was aggressed by these four officers for J-Walking. At three in the morning when a simple citation would have sufficed, if that. The police department has lied to the general at every turn thus far. They lied about the events of the incident. Then they lied about the autopsy report and its true results of the body of the deceased Mr. Stevens. They have done nothing but spew one stereotypical lie after another.

"We plan to eviscerate these lies and expose these people and their failure to conduct themselves in an ethical manner to the public. Starting with this— the video of the actual details to the events of that evening and the incident of confrontation between Mr. Stevens and those four officers the entire city and state law enforcement officials have been supporting and not conducting any such investigation whatsoever! This will also be made clear.

"What you all are about to witness should cripple your sensibilities as members of the most touted nation in the world for decency. This video should rock your very core as to what this self-proclaimed decency actually is in reality. What else do you not know with certainty about the people these departments hire to serve and so called protect each of you?

"I want you to forget about his one to two drinks. Forget about that. Notice his actions only. Then weigh them against the actions of the first two officers on the scene in addition to what transpired when the other two arrived and inserted themselves into the situation instead of being what the badge requires them to be in such situations."

Mr. Bishop steps away from the podium. One of the hotel staff and an assistant of his attend to the rolling out of a rather large television mounted onto a sturdy cart into the area next to the podium in front of the press core. Under the direction of Mr. Bishop, the television is turned on. Moments later, the lighting around that area of the hotel lobby is turned down as the video begins to play. The video is shown in its entirety.

It shows Mr. Stevens casually walking down 2nd Street, not visibly drunk whatsoever. Mr. Stevens appears to make the sudden decision to cross the street when there was no traffic coming. The first squad vehicle must have seen him at the precise moment they were crossing on Madison. They intercepted Mr. Stevens, provoked him to run, and then sneak attacked him with aggressive physical force, knocking him immediately and violently to the concrete after being viciously clotheslined like in a caged wrestling match.

Once he was down and barely coherent, the officer continued to aggress him while he was visibly struggling to regain his full consciousness as he crawled to the cement flowerbed to use it to assist him in possibly getting back on his feet. This is where the other officers arrived on the scene.

Once they exited their vehicles, they walked over to the scene where Mr. Stevens was still laying on the ground crawling. The officer then trapped Mr. Stevens's neck and throat between the cement flowerbed and the pole supporting the street sign in front of it. This was done as one of the other officers who just arrived on the scene re-positioned himself to the feet of Mr. Stevens and grabbed his feet, pulling him away from the flowerbed.

This maneuver produced a situation where Mr. Stevens's neck and throat were being brutally pressed against the corner where the sign pole and the flowerbed met. The officer at his feet was pulling his body in the opposite direction, choking him, strangling him. Before he lost consciousness again, they let him go.

There is no audio, so all that can be seen is the four officers facing him as he attempted to get on his feet. Seemingly at their directions to do so. Next, the video shows the officers gesturing towards an incoherent Mr. Stevens, just barely able to maintain his standing posture without wobbling about. Mr. Stevens attempted to reach for his rear pocket slowly as he struggled to do so. It also appears that he struggled to maintain balance and stand at the same time. As he reached for his back pocket, the four officers seemed to start shouting at him. Then they fired several rounds into him in a barrage of gunfire. Mr. Stevens viciously took those shots and then fell lifeless to the ground beneath him.

The officers then called into their radio units. Moments later, a lone EMT truck arrived. Instead of checking for vitals, the EMT tech conversed with the officers as they occasionally pointed in the direction of the lifeless body of Mr. Stevens; his body lied on the ground, becoming surrounded by an increasingly larger pool of his blood slowly growing out from him onto the concrete around him as they spoke feet away. Moments after this, other emergency units arrived to the scene, and the video stopped.

The television is turned off, and the lights are returned to their original brightness. Mr. Bishop returns to the podium.

"Now that you all have seen the full video of about fifteen minutes of terrorizing horrors, I assume you have some questions?" Mr. Bishop asks.

"Who recorded this video, and where were they during the incident to have such a good view while not alerting the officers to their presence?" asked one reporter.

"That information I cannot reveal for concern of that individual's personal safety and that of those connected to them and their safety as well," Mr. Bishop replies.

"What about the timing? Can you explain how they were in position to record Mr. Stevens, and what was it about those moments that proceeded the incident that drew their attention to record him in the first place?" asks another reporter.

"The question you asked will be answered during official court proceedings that are certain to come when this documentation will become admitted into evidence for such proceedings. Now we have answered enough questions. What you need to do is go back to your networks, re-hash these images, and allow your hearts and minds to re-evaluate what was shown here. Cross-reference that information against what you have been told thus far. Go back and replay my opening statement this morning. Then we can readdress the matter in discussion at a later date. Hopefully by then we will have the results back from the independent autopsy and a no-doubt revised statement for the people. Thank you, Ladies and Gentlemen. Have productive days," announces Mr. Bishop before departing from behind the microphone and podium back into the rear areas of the Peabody Hotel.

"Ooohhh, shit!" exclaims Eric, as he hears what is said after seeing the full video again, this time on live television.

This is an eventuality to be expected, and it is an explosive one. After Bishop's press conference, the television news stations go insane. There are reporters upon reporters descending upon the police station near Downtown Memphis, the mayor's office, and even the governor's office. There is mention of this from the press core's questioning of the White House press secretary during a rare morning briefing being held moments after the Memphis press conference of Mr. Na'Quan Bishop. All are attempting to obtain the next soundbite in response to the horrific violence that was on display for about ten minutes for the world to see. They are all being asked to make statements on the matter. Starting with the police chief of the Memphis Police department, statements are released in the initial aftermath of the video's airing.

"The Memphis Police Department is disappointed in Mr. Bishop's ongoing attempt to besmirch yet another law enforcement agency in his quest for relevance and fame. To discredit the validity of the existing autopsy report defaming the credibility of members of the local law enforcement community is reproachable at the very least. We stand by the diligence of our service members in the fulfillment of their duties for this city, day in, day out," a reporter reads aloud for the viewers.

The mayor's office releases a similar statement of support for its police department. The governor's office also releases a statement in support of one of its prized municipalities mayor's office and their leadership in dealing with Mr. Bishop's press conference. The White House press secretary also, when asked, responds by merely stating that, "The president stands with the governor of Tennessee in the matter, and when the case moves along through its judicial process through the justice system if deemed warranted to go through those measures, then democracy will be carried out, and the American way preserved."

Later in the day, after all these official statements have been made, each respective spokesperson presiding over the communications responsibilities involved have had their ample allotment of time to get the story straight.

While Eric is discreetly getting his haircut at a local barbershop, he recalls his cousin Michael informing him that his pervasive investigative reach uncovered a willing ally within the Memphis police department that would be willing to assist him in obtaining information considered to be "public information". Just as he did so, there was a news flash of "Breaking news deemed to be just coming in" from a seemingly distraught reporter.

"Ladies and Gentlemen, what we have for you this afternoon is truly a groundbreaking exclusive! We vetted the video and verified its authenticity in advance to this airing. We have the body cam footage directly from MPD of the four officers involved in the brutal death of Rudolph Stevens. This footage was leaked. Leaked in the pursuit of justice by the courageous bravery of an anonymous whistle blower risking their career to stand for truth, justice, and the real American way.

"Just as it was shown in the video to the entire world earlier this morning from the legal team of that of Mr. Na'Quan Bishop, these videos confirm the authenticity of the story previously captured in the video revealed earlier today. Be advised: not only is the video consistent with the terrifying footage from this morning, this footage has audio," the reporter adds, before requesting her engineer to transition to the video itself.

The video plays in full audio the same details from earlier that day, with the only difference being angle of the recording and the audio of what was being said. When the footage of all four officers' body cams end, the reporter comes back into view and stands speechless to the camera recording her. After realizing she is back live, she speaks to her audience.

"My apologies, Ladies and Gentlemen. I saw the footage as we got it in initially, and even now as I watch it again, it takes my complete breath away hearing what these officers were saying as they carried out these despicable acts of evil," the reporter states, before she turns from the frame of the camera; the camera is then placed upon a next anchor at the dais table.

This event causes an even more enormous run of the press to obtain statements once more. Now there are other municipalities weighing in. States and their leadership similar to that of Tennessee are also weighing in. Some are not making any harsh stance as to where they stand against the evidence given to the people via the free press; others condemn the video and the damning audio for what they seen it as. This carries on for several hours into the mid-evening where finally there is a statement released. This time it comes from the Tennessee governor's office.

"In light of the MPD having information not approved for public release as it pertained to a pending open investigation of state official business, we are directing this matter to the office of the Inspector General for further evaluation at this point. Until that time, we shall not make any additional statements on the matter of Mr. Stevens and the officers involved in his untimely death. Thank You."

As the news reporter shares the statement with its viewers and they discuss the meaning of its message amongst themselves, Eric is now back in the basement getting things together in his head. He can smell his moment arriving at any given time on any of the next foreseeable days of this week into the following week at its longest out.

Moments later on the same broadcast, there is a next statement released. This time it is from the MPD Headquarters. "In accordance to the message released by our governor's office, we will not be administering any discipline onto the careers of the four officers involved. They remain on staff pending the full and complete investigation by that of the independent Inspector General's office. This decision will remain in place until at a later time designated by the Inspector General for it to be rescinded or amended. Thank you."

Shortly after those announcements, more breaking news are being announced.

"More public outrage ensued into the night as people took to the streets and began small rioting. Other cities experienced larger crowds that resulted in higher degree of riotous activity across the nation," the news anchor shares.

After a few hours of footage being taken across the nation regarding these "mini riots", the anchor later reports that the activity is short lived. People participated for a few hours then returned to their homes after several activists, entertainers, and athletes urged strongly for them to do so across their platforms of influence.

"…However, law enforcement across the nation are interpreting these actions as precursors of what was to still to come," the anchor continues.

After a day of silence, and brewing tension over the issue, news pundits deliberate over the matters that have been taking place for the past few days, weeks, and months leading to the focus of the day.

"There are even more discussions taking place around D.C. as to what will the defeated president do in reaction to these developments before he leaves office in a few weeks. Will he do anything?" asks one reporter to another, as they sit in round-table fashion discussing these subjects.

Eric continues to gauge things as he goes about his day. There are several conversations with Farrukh regarding some small coordinative planning. Eric met with Farrukh in Atlanta on more than one occasion before now. They are scheduled to meet in a few days.

There is a next announcement regarding a second press conference by Na'Quan Bishop. It is to start in an hour. Eric goes here and there throughout the city, being driven from that place to this place. He winds up at a bar watching the news on one of its hoisted televisions as he eats some wings and a burger.

"Mr. Bishop's press conference is about to take place," the bartender says.

Eric repositions himself to face the screen as the press conference is about to begin. Mr. Bishop can be seen on screen behind the podium. He clears his throat before he addresses the members of the press in attendance.

"Ladies and gentlemen of the press and the multitude of people watching this abroad out and about at work or in the comfort of your own homes...Today I address you all in continuance to our last press conference. The family, as I have shared previously, have sought after an independent entity to perform an unencumbered autopsy on the late Rudolph Stevens. The results of such endeavor have been completed, and I have them here for you now. As expected, the blood alcohol of the late Mr. Stevens at the time of death was at a point zero, zero two. This shows that he was hardly intoxicated in contrast to what the MPD, the mayor, and sadly, the governor would have you to believe.

"Next, the cause of death. The independent autopsy concludes that Mr. Stevens was brought to near margins to death from mechanical asphyxia. This is when a choking, strangling action is forced upon a person utilizing a hard surface to force restriction to one's breathing. But make no mistake. The cause of death came from over forty-five bullets from several angles of entry by the four officers. Officers who were not near any remote perceived sense of danger to any of them. Either directly or indirectly.

"I conclude. This was a cold-blooded murder! We plan to address it as such. We have the resources to see this case into the next millennium if deemed necessary. These matters have been shared with the general public. If our elected and appointed official continue to refuse to triple-down and not accept the reality of what has been laid before them and do what is right, there is no telling the damage that their failure will create for the entire justice system, yet alone the tension brewing around us all over the long-stemmed systematic failure to provide and ensure justice for all. This blue-wall of indifference must be torn down. Good day. Don't ask me the question. Go ask them," speaks Mr. Bishop.

When Eric meets with Farrukh days later, they continue to plan the strategic elements of where they will implement their plan. Doing so at the precise moment and being ready for that moment consumes the subject matter of their discussion. The uncertainty of more riots planned by other activists pose great danger to their goals. The unpredictable response from law enforcement only complicates these discussions. Determined to see it through, more contingencies are established.

Chapter 16

"There You have it"

More protests took place during the days after the breaking news that the MPD were planning to delay any potential discipline against the four officers. The nights afterwards were beginning to go from moderate rioting to what was expected during the upcoming evenings. Worse demonstrations of civil unrest in the form of riotous activity are expected to follow. Eric remains patient and sticks to his plan. Despite the increasingly agitated rhetoric coming from the defeated and soon to be unseated President Brad Ace.

"Earlier this morning, Former President Brad Ace spoke to a large gathering at a rally he was holding in Tucson, Arizona. We have some footage of his speech."

The image on the screen transitions to the footage from the rally.

"My fellow Americans, unlike ever before, we are facing unprecedented times in civil disobedience. These criminals must be stopped in advance before they strike again in your communities and sectors of commerce! They must be prevented from disturbing the peace at all costs!"

The news reporter returns to the view of the camera facing the reporter, then the reporter begins to speak to the audience once again on the subject of what was just shown on the video feed.

"Former President Ace hammered away with his consistently expressed desire to utilize the National Guard troops against American citizens. His argument has been that in order to restore order and deter additional demonstrations of unrest, it was a necessary action to prevent future attempts at disrupting the peace of any community where they see the need to occupy its streets and seize the peace from the people. He called himself addressing, and I quote, 'The real Americans like you and like me!'

Ace told this to his supporters at an early morning rally in Arizona regarding the state of tension across the country amidst the recent events concerning Rudolph Stevens.

"With less than a few weeks remaining before the transition between administrations was to occur, the former president continued to label all participants of the riots as bad actors, while he has been questionably silent on having any characterization of the members of the several groups who stormed the Capitol Building under the flags that represent his administration, campaign, and slogans. Something he has received non-stop criticism from— not just the opposing party, but his own. His silence on those events, yet boisterous vitriol, for the protestors who initially were non-violent until law enforcement approached them with indifference and physical aggression.

"The disparity between the two approaches to two visibly different crowds in regards to their obvious demographic differences of composition was tearing the country apart at its seams. I for one, Scott, cannot understand how our leaders do not see this for what it is and have done very close to nothing to eliminate the sentiment of partiality," the anchor expresses to her colleague, as they discuss the matter for their viewers.

"That's a solid question, Pamela. I and many annoyed Americans out there would probably want an answer to that as well. What I can say is that it appears to me to be a watershed moment for the topic and discussion of racial inequality and absence of any tangible evidence of accountability for the subject matter. The systemic plague to what the nation stands for on a global perspective. The kind of things that lends to the question being asked at many of these non-violent protests of 'What is the value of a Black life to this country?'

"Sadly, I see implosions and additional explosions being expected as the eventual certainty. How long will the leaders of these states, cities, police departments, in addition to our leaders on the federal level continue to sweep the importance of the contributing factors under the rug? I have never felt this degree of tension in all my years. Not like it's a blatant wall, a membrane that smack runs into me every day, regardless of where I travel. It is a despicable thing to feel and see.

"Pamela, I guess to conclude and respond directly to your question, I just don't know what to say at this point. I can only pray that things do not go nuclear out there in the community," Reporter Scott finishes.

As Eric is finishing the lunch he has before him, he reaches for his mobile device and sends out a group text through the established encrypted language for the team spread out across their designated cities.

The translation for that message once finally decoded by his team reads, Tomorrow, EST, mid, PST, eight, timed. Simultaneous… GOD Speed to you all.

It is go-time. He is to meet with Farrukh one last time to hand deliver the very same message. They had already discussed the time and date as the most viable opportunity before things grew too much out of hand around them with other activists and organizers working to do their own things in the same cities that are not a part of the coordinated activity they had established to this point. Eric and Farrukh realize that they are inserting themselves into the mix as a result of the increasingly louder public outcry for defiance and demands for justice for Rudolph Stevens and a countless many more before his name was added to that dreadful and disrespectful list of names who met similar fates.

Eric showers, gets himself dressed, and takes actions to leave the residence supplied to him by his brother's friend for the final time after residing there and being the recipient of the other occupants' hospitality for the last three weeks. He says to the adults and children upstairs his goodbyes and thank yous before he departs with a lone bag. He jumps into a blacked-out SUV into its rear cabin. The vehicle drives off and Eric looks through its rear window slit as the house and neighborhood grow smaller and smaller. Eventually completely out of sight.

The driver of the vehicle takes him to the entrance of a downtown Atlanta parking garage. Once there, the driver goes inside and leaves Eric alone in the vehicle parked along the curb outside. In a few minutes, he returns.

"The area is ready, Eric. The camera system has been rendered as malfunctioning. The DVR has been corrupted and thusly disabled until technicians arrive to repair it. Is your colleague nearby?" the driver asks.

"He is. We can remain out here until he arrives. When he does, they will enter first, and we will follow them into the structure," Eric instructs.

The driver acknowledges what was said to him. "Yes, Sir. Waiting on you."

The men sit in the SUV that does not stand out. Before long, a less inconspicuous sedan arrives, and with it, a new text message is received by one of the mobile devices Eric has on his person. I am here. What now?

Pull into the structure, and go to the second level, follow along the path, making two rights then park by the concrete beam, Eric texts back.

When the sedan appears and enters into the structure, Eric's driver follows loosely behind at about a distance of two and a half car lengths. When they depart their parked position, a blacked out SUV takes the spot they left behind with precision.

With both vehicles finally parked in proximity to one another, Eric sends a next text to Farrukh, Leave your vehicle and come to the rear passenger door of mine. Then open the door and come inside.

When the door is pulled open moments later, Eric's driver then departs the vehicle. The two men have privacy, and they immediately begin to exchange communication.

"Good morning," says Farrukh, quickly

"Indeed. A great morning it is," responds Eric.

"So…the plan? Right? Okay… I have teams like we discussed in New York City, north Philly, southeast Washington D.C., and here in Atlanta for the move at midnight in this time zone. Whereas at the same exact time I have teams established and ready to move also in Memphis, southside Chicago, sunnyside-southeast Houston, and Central City, New Orleans.

"Due to the time zone differences, they will jump off at eleven at night, precisely timed with the rest of us out here. Finally, the cities on the west coast in the pacific standard time zone. That will be Los Angles near that of Compton, Oakland, and Portland. These events will seem to be at the earliest. They will be in synchronous activity with the rest of us. It will just be earlier in their evening, more visible, which is why we have additional measures in place there to compensate for that strategically weakening of the plan overall. They will jump off at nine at night," Eric concludes.

Farrukh is inventively attentive the entire time Eric has been speaking. Before he responds, he was catching up with the notes he was taking in shorthand. As he was writing, he was stopping and thinking about what he was writing. Eric, used to this behavior pattern of Farrukh when he is focused and working, sat still and just watched him in slight marvel as he was doing what he did that produced the outcomes he was known for in the space of civil disobedience of the non-violent variety. Finally, when he comes to a point along his process where he can catch a moment to breathe, he picks his head up from where it has been focused on his writings to look at Eric and speak.

"I have all of that, and we are ready, too. This should not take long once we jump it off. By the time all of your people have got it done, we will remain in place looking surprised and in various states of shock, then amusement. Then we will un-restrain the officers by the time the cameras arrive. Brilliant," Farrukh replies.

They both extend their arms, shake hands, and Farrukh rushes from inside of the SUV back to the vehicle he arrived in. They not too long after are gone. In the wind.

Eric's driver returns to the driver's seat and they depart. Eric is going to get things situated in Atlanta before he is to get into the wind and start his journey of avoiding law enforcement in advance. He takes the remainder of the day getting his side of things situated as he briefly converses with Ezell, Johnny, Gregory, Dontre, and Shymeika, tightening the bolts on the plan through the language they developed and the system required to decipher it.

He gets with Bricks, and they discuss the technical specifics of the equipment in place. There is an understood and expressed window of activation. Then the efficient evacuation of those equipments out of the active zone and back on the road inconspicuously is of high importance. Shymeika and Eric also need to nail down a few areas of clarification and confirmation regarding what systems she and members of her respective team would seek to target.

Once Eric spends the time to make the rounds and gets everyone squared away, he goes to grab some food. There is a place he really likes northwest of the city by a college. He sends his driver in to pick up their meals. Eric eats and continues to get his mind together in anticipation for the expected as well as the endless stream of potentially unexpected outcomes and the responses they will require of him to keep things moving forward and unencumbered.

Having left Johnny's residence with no intention of returning, he finds a next location to sleep for the night. He utilizes the rear office inside of an associate's vehicle dealership. He was given complete facility access to include the security features allocated over the building. He remotely accessed the facility before his arrival and disengaged the entire security system, starting with all camera feeds.

When he arrives, he bypasses the security with its code for the door he approaches. Once inside, he turns the security system back on for the front showroom area. He keeps it off for the offices located in the innermost rear section beyond the showroom. The area is normally utilized for the accounting department.

Eric has a few of his people outside watching the perimeter of the lot where the facility stands. While inside, Eric actually gets himself ready to get the best sleep he's had in a while and potentially his last for quite some time to come at the same time. He sees variables in outcome where this will end in his favor. He applied resources, effort, and implementation tactics to make that highly desired outcome to be the result. But in order for that to become reality, he still needs to disappear as pieces fall into place and other agents on his behalf complete several other acts to make it so.

He showers in the executive offices, cleans up, eats well, then he retires to sleep for the evening. His last task is to effectively fight the high-speed traffic on the highway of his racing mind long enough to catch those deeply desired "Z's". After about forty-five minutes, he is fast asleep. His people outside remain vigilant in their duties watching every little actionable opportunity to tag movement and any perceived abnormality as they know Eric is inside resting.

When the morning of Thursday January fifteenth arrives, Eric finds himself looking at the clock as it reads 6:00 a.m. He knows he has a short amount of time to wipe his tracks and depart the building as the cleaning crew is scheduled to arrive around 7:00 a.m. He is gone by 6:40 a.m. He restores the facility to its original status in all systems as he departs with his team. They grab breakfast together.

"Hey, Fox, monitor these news networks for me," Eric says, as he gives him a tablet device and points to a list of hyperlinks on a spreadsheet. "I can't focus on both today. If something relevant develops, put me on. Okay?"

Fox acknowledges his instructions, "Got you, E," and commences to take the tablet delicately from his grasp.

It appears that Eric is about to take to the stage of an enormous concert event. He is now currently backstage preparing. All who come in contact with him just watch in awe. They are in close proximity to greatness in the making, in the precursor moments to another demonstration of excellence. They watch over his movements like the rock star he is viewed as.

The early bird protestors across the nation got their start on the east coast as planned. As the day grows into itself from east to west, the pace of the day is predictably normal. Normal for the recent sequence of events after the killing of Rudolph Stevens.

Most police departments do not interfere with the activities of the daytime protestors. This is due to the significantly high visibility in just having an unmeasurable number of witnesses to their peaceful demeanors and cheerful determination to bring awareness to a horrible pattern of events.

The night before, however, a miracle that may be considered one of the most integral to the overall plan's success was accomplished. Farrukh was able to convince many of his peers in the space of organizers of these protests to call the evening off for any protests or rioting. Small vigils and light protests at best. There were a few who did as they wished anyway, but overall, it was quiet. That bought them time.

Law enforcement did not have the justification to treat the matter as completely ongoing as a result. At least not without treading upon the precipice of evoking Marshal Law without true cause or need to take such measures. It was agreed upon in advance that if Farrukh were able to accomplish this feat the day before go-time, then it would create the opportunity for the late commencement of action on the east coast without causing any unnecessary interruptions.

As the evening draws close to midnight, most people are retiring for work come Friday. Law enforcement is cautious, but back on their routine activities concerning patrol patterns. They are also about at their typical response times across the board, due to the previous evenings.

From up under the surface of 6th Avenue, between West 3rd and West 4th Streets, around eleven p.m. in the evening, a large crowd of people start to emerge from the subway staircases along both sides of the street. The large and growing crowds begin to fill and constrict movement along West 3rd all the way back to MacDougal Street. Then back around filling West 4th in the same fashion from the intersection of MacDougal and West 4th to the intersection of West 4th and 6th Avenue. When these crowds grow to start to escape the perimeter, slowly, many of them begin to start off to surround and later fill Washington Square Park.

During this time, several members of Shymeika's team have been getting themselves into position. There is one group of the team pulling up to a building along Christopher Street between Hudson and Bleecker Streets. The next group of the team positions themselves on Charles Street, also between Hudson and Bleecker Streets. With 10th Street in between them both, they step inside buildings along their respective streets. Each team takes their separate routes to the rooftops of their buildings. Once there, they carefully approach as close of a viewpoint they can undetected to get a proper angle of view on the police precinct below. The Sixth Precinct to be exact.

Next, her team connects their equipment and prepares for their hacking activities soon to get put into play. As expected, the calls come in and several officers are seen shooting from the precinct house in the direction of Washington Square Park. With more and more officers departing the station house, the less scrutiny there is time for what they are doing. Immediately, the team silences their ability to effectively communicate with other precincts effectively through their normal processes. They are alone for the moment and do not even realize it. All Shymeika did was just exploit current and pre-existing system weaknesses that are historically deemed non-essential to have repaired.

There was no need for real panic initially, but as the reports come in, there is an increased need for operational support from other precincts.

Meanwhile, back on the north side of Washington Square North overlooking the park from above, behind the veil of a construction site, Bricks's crew for New York stands in place above the rooftops of the construction zone awaiting the initiation of their move. When the police arrive, it is about eleven thirty-three in the evening. At first, being taken by surprise by the randomness to the late hour of these sudden developments, the officer present basically observes the crowd and just watches. They are overly peaceful. However, the outer rim of the crowd is made up mostly of people-of-color. So, the law enforcement that is present responds how they historically have when this is to be the case—aggressively.

Law enforcement begin to approach the gathering not knowing that there is a whole legion of non-people-of-color within the inner sanctum of the crowd. Then the crowd makes a swift and quick maneuver, switching the group on the edges and its outer rim with the White members on its interior. This produces an alarming reaction from the police, and they stop in their tracks from their in-process aggression; they retreat back to re-access the situation at hand.

After being so exposed and for all present to see vividly, the crowd cheers and jeers the officers for their hypocrisy. Now publicly embarrassed and even more so challenged, the officers grow angered by the events as they are developing. After about ten minutes, they become revitalized in their forceful intent to control what is not out of control, contained into a park designed for gathering.

The police move in. And when they do, the time of their re-approach towards the crowd is around eleven fifty-five. When the clock hits midnight, those who know understand what is happening across the country in similar ways; therefore, it is understood that it is now or never. They engage with the police present appropriately.

Luring them into the park for them to re-attempt to aggress their numbers, they take several minutes to allow backup to fill in behind the aggressive show of force. Then on the rooftops they engage the EMP device. There is an additional EMP blast where Shymeika and her team are near the precinct. Then those teams pack up in the darkness and immediately get out of the area through the cover of the darkness they had just created. The other teams move in.

They tranquilize the officers under the guidance of night vision goggles and laser scoped weapons that discharges their rounds. Once they can establish that each of the officers are incapacitated, they rush in closer, zip-hog-tie each of them, and move them in groups near one another. Next, they rush to exit the area. Their team didn't encounter any need to utilize their anti-aircraft technology or the hacking activities associated with its implementation fortunately. So all that remains is for the city to regain its power eventually and the local news media to respond. They will see that it was the protestors who reacted to the events and cut the restraints off the officers bound up and restrained atop one another on the ground in clusters. The images of these scenes are certainly going to be applied to their earliest of editions of each local and national newspaper without a single question.

Eric sits in a room without windows as he watches his television screen; he is watching a news telecast. The news anchor is speaking…

"... What was soon discovered, making this story a national incident of mysterious intrigue and a collective embarrassment to law enforcement agencies across the nation. Reports were slamming in to the station, telling tales of these exact events, occurring almost in identical details in incidents all at about the same exact time in cities like: Philadelphia; Pennsylvania; Baltimore, Maryland; Washington, D.C.; and Atlanta, Georgia. There were additional reports that more events with eerily similar details also having taken place in Chicago, Illinois; Houston, Texas; New Orleans, Louisiana; and, yes... Memphis, Tennessee.

"I apologize, Ladies and Gentlemen. We have yet another news bulletin from our west coast affiliate station of more strange events that seemingly were well coordinated and repetitive in tactical strategy across the nation this evening. We are trying to understand exactly what has taken place as we learn of three more events that took place in Los Angeles and Oakland, California, as well as in Portland, Oregon. The likes of such an event, let alone twelve seemingly close, if not identical events, all to occur simultaneously has never been seen before in the world on such a scale. This will no doubt be an evening the world will never be able to forget.

"What is most peculiar regarding these events is that in each case, local and county law enforcement were responding to a last-minute emerging protest with aggression and then everything goes black. When visibility and record-ability was resumed, each member of law enforcement was discovered to be tranquilized, zip-hog-tied, and defenseless, but unharmed all the same. Get this: surrounded by the very groups they planned to aggress. Then the larger irony in these situations... we've been informed that it was indeed the protestors who were the ones setting the officers free and nursing them back into consciousness as they recovered from being tranquilized. I promise you, Ladies and Gentlemen that these are indeed the details of legitimate reports being brought to our attention."

Eric sits and continues to watch inventively as he is satisfied that the initiating city went as planned. He has discarded of every mobile device he previously had.

He now responds to a coded knock on the door to the room he is in. Only a hand pops through the slit created between the door and its frame he provided. A hand gives him two small boxes: a set of black boxes. He returns to his seat and opens the slightly larger box. It is a newer and slightly different shaped box. Along its side is a note attached. The note has a simple inscription: *For a job well done, from a mind best suited to succeed. Signed Uncle D.*

Eric doesn't bother to even look surprised in the gift finding him. He smiles, takes a moment, and then opens up the smaller box. This box contains the prototype voice augmentation device he had earlier requested from Dante's inventive associate. As he looks upon the gadgets, he notices that alongside the phone there is a small insignia that he has no clue as to how to make out its design. He vaguely remembers seeing something similar to it a while ago somewhere during his time working in D.C.

He slowly assembles the phone and resets its power core quickly. When it comes back online, he sends out a message through the usual channels to the team. That message when translated reads, NY, done, status report from everyone else everywhere else.

Almost after about ten gruelingly long minutes, the new device starts to chime non-stop with new messages in response no doubt to the one he sent out. Eric is anxious to learn how his plan was carried out. He pauses briefly, looks around his room, then he says to himself, *Fuck it.*

He flips the device over and begins to scroll through the responses. They translate:

Done – LA, on point, in the mf wind (emoji) dawg

Shit went correctly -H-town

Done, straight – Philly. wind (emoji)

ATL all good, wind (emoji)

DC – wind (emoji)

B-More- Gone Checkmark (emoji), Wind (emoji)

NO – Wind (emoji), Checkmark (emoji)

Done @ the Crib – double Wind (emoji)

OK in the BAY – Wind (emoji)

Port got the fort – Wind (emoji)

Once Eric sees these messages, he simply sends a group response that translates to Check for the bags…. get ghost (emoji), lose a nickel in the wind (emoji)

The media coverage of the string of similar events run all through the evening and into the morning.

"Former President Ace continued to stir things up amongst his base by using the string of incidents as an attempted terroristic event and a collective series of attacks against the security of the nation at large. While the law enforcement is making statements about the desire to thoroughly investigate what took place and possibly ascertain who was involved with what seemed to be agreeably a coordinated series of events. Those comments have been followed up by members of federal law enforcement agencies such as Homeland Security, the FBI, and the CIA. They just released a joint statement regarding the events of last evening across the nation in some of our biggest cities."

The screen transitions to a next screen where a visual copy of the statement is shown. The caption indicator projects the words being read by the anchor as they read them across the middle of the screen, much like a teleprompter would do.

"We jointly see and view these events as incursions against our national security. Anytime where police precincts and station house of local municipalities and their law enforcement entities come under cyber-attack, to include the infrastructure of the city via power grids, water supply, telecommunications, we are obligated to investigate the matter or matters on a level of high priority and of the utmost importance. If any person should have knowledge of anyone potentially capable of being involved with these incidents, please do not hesitate to contact us through the contact information provided for the joint task force being put into action by POTUS to bring this individual or individuals to justice."

The volatility of the story and its coverage mentions of ridiculous rewards are beginning to get out of hand, and it is just Friday afternoon. What the string of incidents did, as well as cause governmental chaos, was highlight how critical systems had been compromised to accomplish what had taken place. There were zero injuries and zero deaths. In fact, the protestors and officers involved were drawn closer together in the mayhem. The entire nation is discussing the events from litany of perspectives.

After a week, it is unclear if whoever coordinated this is going to serve time in Guantanamo Bay or given the Nobel Peace Prize. It is certainly not a clear distinction of what the nation could agree upon. There was a serious meeting that just concluded within the pentagon.

As the attendees are dispersing back about their days and places to be next, there is a group of men waiting in the long, wide ivory marbled hallway. A fully dressed colonel exits the meeting hall and approaches the five men who are waiting patiently in the hallway. They are waiting to receive orders as to their assignment.

"I assume you are Ridnoel, Dean, Francis, Pike, and Manchester?" asks the colonel with two of his next in line flanking his rear, all with severely stoic faces as their colonel speaks.

They are standing at ease, but it feels as if they are at attention all the same from their facial expressions in conjunction with their postures.

"Follow me," the colonel commands, sternly.

They follow him as he walks briskly from the Army "C-Ring" to the lower level into the courtyard. Once they arrive, the colonel turns to an individual who is on a phone, wearing a sleek pair of slacks and a sports coat as he turns upon the arrival of the colonel.

"Good morning, Colonel. How can I be of service to you today?"

"These men are here to fill out your office and initial detail, Mr. Fernsby."

"Very well then. Go follow my assistant who will meet you by the elevator, and they will show you to our office. They will show you to the file where I have set aside instructions for your first ten days. I will not be back in the office for five of those days. When I return, we will have a briefing and will take things from there. By all means…familiarize yourselves with the materials I have provided for you. We will not have much time after my return to get some traction. The scent is disappearing quickly. Good day, and I will see you gentlemen in a few days."

The men walk off, get found by the assistant by the elevator, and follow her to their office suite.

"Mr. Fernsby, huh?" one of the gentlemen recites.

About the Author

My name is Jomo Sekou Henderson. All my life, there was absolutely nothing that I achieved or obtained that did not exact a price. I was raised in a home where self-awareness was the outcome, my inert passion for human behavior was honed into a keen sense. The totality of my life's experiences created a formidable mind and a resilient individual who to this day can only be described by those who actually know my legitimate interaction as relentless, determined, multi-faceted. While still having much to learn in many other areas, I've had no other choice thus far but to figure out a great many of things on my own. This dis-advantage/ vantage point (perspective) merely forged me into an active listener and developing an astute recognition of behavioral patterns many may not pick up at first or second glance. Between working jobs, sometimes in my youth three at a time, mostly talking myself into the front door without taking "No" for an answer. In addition to my initial exploration of independent entrepreneurial endeavors during the same timeframe. Often leaving me without time nor the desire to sleep for days. Much was absorbed. Much had been learned on a myriad of subjects in many varying degrees of interpretation. Countless experience was gained in the process. An ample amount was learned regarding varying ideas of defining employment, the practice of conducting business and what it can mean to actually live one's life.

9 786277 544379